D0996419

THE SOMME STATIONS

by the same author

BILTON
THE BOBBY DAZZLERS

In the 'Jim Stringer, Steam Detective' series:

THE NECROPOLIS RAILWAY
THE BLACKPOOL HIGHFLYER
THE LOST LUGGAGE PORTER
MURDER AT DEVIATION JUNCTION
DEATH ON A BRANCH LINE
THE LAST TRAIN TO SCARBOROUGH

ANDREW MARTIN

The Somme Stations

faber and faber

First published in 2011
by Faber and Faber Ltd
Bloomsbury House
74–77 Great Russell Street
London WC1B 3DA

Typeset by Faber and Faber Limited
Printed in England by CPI Mackays, Chatham

A CIP record for this book
is available from the British Library

ISBN 978-0-571-24960-2

2 4 6 8 10 9 7 5 3 1

Acknowledgements

I am particularly grateful to Richard Callaghan, curator of the Royal Military Police Museum, and to Lieutenant Colonel Parkinson, head of Media and Protocol at Sandhurst. I am also indebted to Bob Gratton and Dale Coton, both of the Ashover Light Railway; to Rupert Lodge of the Leighton Buzzard Railway, and David Negus of the Southwold Railway Trust; to Dr John Bourne, of the Centre for First World War Studies at the University of Birmingham; to Major David James-Roll, and to F. Martin. All embellishment of the historical facts, and all mistakes, are mine and not theirs.

Author's Note

The characters in this novel are completely imaginary, and bear no relation to anyone who might really have lived in York during the First World War, or served on the light railways of the Western Front, or fought with that noble body of men, the 17th Northumberland Fusiliers.

PROLOGUE

Ilkley

Moor View,
The Grove,
Ilkley,
Yorkshire.
October 6th, 1916

Dearest Lillian,

An unseen man's voice gives the shout of 'Right away!' and the little locomotive moves forward on tracks running over what might be hard mud with pools of dark water, or a shining table top. There is darkness in the sky, or in the room, and an orange fire-glow coming from one side. There are small men inside the engine, and riding on the wagons pulled behind, but they are not quite as small as their train, and they stick out from it at peculiar angles. It is an odd accommodation: men who are perhaps toy soldiers riding in what may be a toy train. And some of them are unquestionably leaning far too far over, and seem very likely at any minute to fall, but there is nothing to be done about that. (I forgot to say, or I forgot to notice, Lillian, that the load carried consists of so many bombs.)

The first part of the line is straight and all is well, the train goes smoothly. But it is coming up to a bump where the track has not been flattened down quite enough, and a clock is ticking somewhere that I don't like the sound of. The train is now at the bump, and the engine runs over it well enough, although the first wagon jolts, and tilts . . . The train stays on the track. It has no time to settle down, however, for it is coming up to a bend now, and seems to be coming up far too fast. I tell it to slow down, but I know I cannot be heard, I am too far away. The engine speeds into the bend, leaning. A man riding on the rear wagon falls over backwards, but stays on the wagon, and the train remains upright. Encouraged by this success, the train is racing faster now, and coming up to a place where another line goes off – a complication in the track that will surely spill it if it does not slow. The engine seems to batter its way through the complication, and the first following wagon does likewise, as do the second and the third, but the fourth and last gives a jump. Is it over? Yes, although the little man who had earlier fallen over skitters away by the side of the track, and another curve is coming, and the train is hurtling towards it at full speed. The wheels on the far side are off the ground; the speed increases, and I cry out . . . But the train is over, and the locomotive is on its side. Its wheels still spin, but there is a sudden silence, which makes me realise there had been a great whirring before. There is now only the steady ticking of the clock, and the little men lying about on either side of the wreckage.

'Are they dead?' I ask the voice.

'Of course they are,' the voice replies. 'What did you expect?'

Well, dearest, you must think me quite . . .

'Ardenlea',
Queen's Drive,
Ilkley,
Yorkshire.
October 9th, 1916

Dearest Lillian,

I am writing this in the library of the railwaymen's convalescent home on the edge of Ilkley Moor, where 'Life Passes in A Pleasant Dream' – that is according to the sign over the door. I am supposed to be making the second of my one-hour daily visits with Jim, but he is asleep, so instead I am sitting by an open window in the library, looking at the autumn display in the gardens, the low sun on the Moor beyond, and writing to you at last. (I should say that I started a letter to you three days ago, on my first arriving here. It was an account of a nightmare and I decided, after a turn in the park, that it was altogether too strange to send.)

The shell smashed Jim's right femur (that's a thigh bone to you and me), and when he was brought to Ilkley, it was discovered that the bone had not been set properly by the army doctors, so it was re-set here at the Ilkley hospital by another army doctor, name of Hawks, but I take comfort from the fact that this one is a Colonel. (You can't get much higher than that, can you?)

Hawks let me know through one of his nurses that the re-setting had gone extremely well (but then he'd hardly say he'd fouled it up, would he?) and that Jim's leg ought to mend without difficulty. He does seem very quiet, and very pale, and he talks in his sleep. Just now in his room, he was muttering over and again, 'little and often, little and often' and 'fine style, fine style'. I've no idea what this means, and fear it may mean nothing at all.

But let me tell you a little about this place.

The house was opened last year by a man with the perfectly ridiculous name of Sir Godfrey Glanville Gordon, General Manager of the North Eastern Railway, which is quite appropriate since he founded the North Eastern Railway regiment in the service of which some of the men here were so disastrously wounded. It is built in 'the Renaissance style' (I won't pretend that means anything much to me, dear), is fitted out in expensive mahogany, and is very hushed, or supposedly so, because of the nervous cases. The men wear pale blue uniforms, and are all inveterate smokers. Jim hardly smoked before the war, but now he is 'on', as he told me yesterday while sitting up in bed, a packet a day. His cigarettes are called Virginians Select. They are horribly smelly, and of course they're doing him no good at all.

There is a tower here: fifty stairs to the top of it, where a terrace with a low railing overlooks the River Swale and Ilkley Moor, which as you know is practically a mountain. According to the notices in the lobby, 'the well-wooded hillside of the Moor affords pleasant walks'. There are in addition 'tranquil lanes' for strolling by the river, and walkways among the gardens and grounds; and it is boasted everywhere that we are only ten minutes' walk from the station.

Dear Lillian, half the men here can't walk.

The lying down cases are kept on the second floor (which doesn't seem very logical) and are carried down by the orderlies on long chairs. They are then very often taken directly to the billiard room where they watch or play . . . well not billiards, evidently, but snooker. It is a game that can at a pinch be played by a man on crutches, but they must take care at the beginning. The first thing that happens in the game as played properly is that the player smashes the white ball into all the others. This is called breaking off (I think). Now there are men here – the nervous cases – who can hear the crash of those balls from anywhere in the house and the noise is capable of bringing on a collapse. So the snooker players do not 'break off' but scatter the balls with their hands to get the game going. At all times, the men are careful not to make a commotion. They do not talk to each other very much, but play their snooker and cards, and sit and smoke. They all understand each other perfectly, and without need of conversation. They have all been 'through it', over there in France, even though they were not all in the same places. Those who have not been there cannot possibly be expected to understand.

Well, on that rather gloomy note, I think I will close, dear. I also think I am about to be ejected by the Matron here, a woman called Oldfield, who looks just as you would expect from that name. Give my love to the children. Oh, and tell Harry that Jim has a very sensational tale touching on the copy of 'The Count of Monte Cristo' that Harry gave him. The telling of it quite bucked him up yesterday. (Although I'm not completely sure I believe him.)

But that's for later.

With all my love,
Lydia.

'Ardenlea',
Queen's Drive,
Ilkley,
Yorkshire.
October 12th, 1916

Dear Lillian,

Jim was very pale today, also very sleepy, and very hot. According to the sister, a sweet girl who seems to work all hours, he talked constantly in his sleep during the night. I went immediately to see the Matron, Mrs Oldfield, who is rather more grand than is needful and hardly ever seen about the house at all. I don't care for her, and the feeling is evidently mutual. (I suppose I should never have asked her why she kept all the crippled men upstairs and those with full capacity on the ground floor.) On her desk were two calling cards from undertakers. She saw me looking at them, and made no move to put them away as I said, 'I would like to ask about Jim Stringer.'

She said, 'Do you mean James?'

I said, 'No.'

After an interval of staring at me, she went over to a cabinet to collect a card, and having looked at it, or pretended to, for a while, she said, 'The bones in his leg are meshing satisfactorily,' just as though she'd been looking at those bones there and then – and that was the end of the interview. I must believe her, I suppose. At any rate I must until I can speak to the surgeon, Hawks, who comes here from the Ilkley hospital, usually arriving alone in an ambulance carriage, in which he leaves accompanied by those men he proposes operating upon. Not only is Hawks a surgeon and a colonel, but also a professor into the bargain. As a result, he is incredibly pompous, generally speaking through third parties, and always calling Jim's leg his 'lower extremity'. He is expected later this afternoon, and I mean to wait for him.

I am certain that Jim is far too morose and silent for a man 'on the mend', and he is fearfully distracted. Oh, I know not to ask him questions about the precise goings on, so yesterday I started in on a general discussion of the war, and I asked him when he thought it might end.

'Never!'

. . . And he turned away towards the window.

Something happened there to account for his silence. I mean one death that was worse than the others in some way – a matter of treachery among Jim's own unit of men, the particular gang put to working the trains. The little trains, that is, the ones running at night on tracks laid down in an instant.

Those silly little trains. I have seen photographs of them, and these, together with Jim's own vague accounts of working on the trains, caused the nightmare that I mentioned to you. The driver can hardly fit into the cab. His head pokes out of it, and I cannot help but picture them as pleasure railways, running at night – because they only ever _do_ run them at night – under a sky filled with fireworks. But the fireworks are bombs falling, and the men cannot dodge the falling bombs since they must stay with the train, and the train must stay on the tracks . . . and the train itself _carries_ bombs. For Jim, the danger is not passed. He is fighting his own war within the bigger war, and I believe his own is not done yet, just as the bigger one is not . . . This, I think, is why he has spent so much of his time looking through the window at the grounds and the driveway that approaches the house.

Lillian, I still hope to be back on Friday, but this now

depends on what the surgeon says. Give my love to the children, and tell them their father is well, as I pray that he is, or will be.

With all my love,
Lydia.

Moor View Guest House,
The Grove,
Ilkley.
October 13th, 1916

Dearest Lillian,

This has been about the worst day of my life.

Jim has a sepsis, and has been taken directly to the hospital. This is blood poisoning because of the wound to his leg. I was with him this morning; his leg and hip are fearfully swollen; he had a fever, and kept muttering about an owl. I asked him, 'Was there an owl in the night?' 'No,' he said. 'In the day.' When Hawks came, he said this was 'A very grave matter' and I saw the horrible Oldfield nodding in the background. No apology for saying the 'bone was setting satisfactorily' after I'd told her that Jim was ill. No mention from Hawks that this poisoning comes from his re-setting of the bone. He is going to try 'excision', which is scraping out the poison.

When Jim had been taken from the room, and I was alone with Hawks for a moment, I said, 'What if that doesn't work? You will amputate the leg won't you?' He replied, 'If the position is not already hopeless.' So I thought I had said the worst thing, but evidently not. I insisted on accompanying Jim, and, on being refused – and being told that Jim would be returned to Ardenlea after four hours or so – I walked straight to the Ilkley library, where I read up on sepsis in the bone, which I think is osteomyelitis. From my reading, I dare to hope that the infection was caught in time. I am trusting to the pomposity of Hawks: he would say the worst, because then he will look better when he finds the cure.

I went back to Ardenlea after the four hours, to await Jim's return from the operation. As I walked along the drive, a tall man in a perfectly pressed uniform came towards me. He was making for the gate. He wore riding boots and a red cloth cover over his cap, and carried a valise under his arm. He touched his cap to me as we passed. The Matron, Oldfield, stood in the doorway, watching as he departed and I approached.

'Is my husband back yet?' I asked her.

She shook her head. 'He will not be back until about midnight. I have just told that gentleman the same thing.'

'Has there been some complication?'

'I don't know, I'm sure.'

I contemplated telling her that she was a sadist, plain and simple. Then I thought to ask: 'Who *was* that man?' (We could still hear his brisk retreating footsteps on the gravel of the drive.)

'He's in the Military Mounted Police.'

Being in a kind of daze, I said, 'Well, I didn't see his horse.'

'He came by train.'

'What does he want with Jim?'

And so, Lillian, I gave Oldfield the opportunity of experiencing the most wonderful pleasure, for she said:

'I see no reason why I shouldn't tell you. He means to take your husband in charge.'

'Why? On what charge?'

'On a charge of murder.'

'Well then. There has obviously been a mistake.'

'Sergeant Major Thackeray', she said, nodding towards the opened gate, which the man in the red-covered hat was now walking through, wheeling to the right, as though giving himself marching orders, 'has come all the way from France expressly to bring the charge, so I shouldn't think there's been a mistake. I am to be responsible for making sure that on returning to these premises, your husband does not quit his room before the gentleman returns in the morning.'

I might have fainted at that moment . . . only a light snow was beginning to fall in the gardens of Ardenlea. The snowflakes that touched my face had a reviving effect.

'When Jim returns', I said to Oldfield, 'he will be unconscious.'

She nodded.

'And he can't walk anyway . . .'

She nodded again.

'So I should have thought that keeping him here would be well within your powers.'

I turned on my boot-heel and walked. (Not that I knew where I was going.) It is now nearly midnight, and I will return to Ardenlea in a moment, posting this on the way. Not a word of this to the children, dearest. I don't know how to thank you for all your kindness in looking after them. As you now see, I cannot hope to be there on Friday, but will write again tomorrow.

With all my love, as ever,
Lydia.

PART ONE

Blighty

York: September 1914

In the North Eastern Railway police office, which faced on to platforms four and thirteen at York station, Constable Scholes was telling how he'd lately encountered a man who had been carrying an owl in a Third Class carriage of a train going between Leeds and York. Scholes was talking, as ever, to his best pal, Constable Flower. Being only constables, the two shared a desk, and at that moment Flower was sitting at it and Scholes was sitting *upon* it, by which any man who knew the office would have been able to tell that the Chief wasn't about. I was listening in while assembling the papers for the prosecution on a charge of Indecent Exposure of a man called John Read who'd walked out of the Gentlemen's lavatory on platform eight while in a state of undress.

But the story of the owl man had my attention for the present. He had worn the bird on his wrist, 'like a watch', and when asked what he was about had said the owl was his companion, and went everywhere with him.

'I told him it was against the by-laws,' Scholes was saying, at which Flower, who had the *Police Manual* on his knee, gave chapter and verse: 'It's against company by-law number eleven.'

'Exactly,' said Scholes. 'So the bloke . . . Which number did you say again?'

'Eleven,' said Flower. 'No wait, that's "Entering or Leaving a Train in Motion".' He turned the pages of the book. 'Here we are: by-law fourteen. "Carriage of Animals in . . . a Carriage." Let's see what he would have been liable for.'

'It makes no odds, since I don't have his name and address,' said Scholes.

'Forty shillings maximum for a first offence,' said Flower, ignoring Scholes, 'or five pounds if he's done it before.'

'I never took his name,' Scholes repeated. 'I said to him, "You'll get off at York, and you'll walk quickly out of the station and you'll not come back with that thing." He said, "Will I now?" I said, "Yes, you flipping well will." He said "Well how do you expect the owl to get back to Leeds?"'

'It could fly,' Flower put in. 'It was a bird, after all.'

'It was attached to his wrist by a leather strap.'

'And what happened then?' asked Flower.

'He got off the train and went through the ticket gate.'

The interesting part of their conversation was over, so I looked up from the cards and said, 'Where's the Chief?' at which Scholes climbed off the desk. (The word 'Chief' was enough to make him do it.)

'Old station, I think,' said Flower.

The old station, which was across the way from the new one, had been taken over by the military, and the Chief was very thick with that lot. I looked down at the papers relating to Read. Without paying attention to the detail of the case (he seldom did *that*) the Chief had expressed surprise that I'd arrested a bloke on this charge. 'I've never run a fellow in for indecent exposure,' he'd told me, seeming to take a pride in the fact, and the *Police Manual* did urge that the greatest care be taken in such cases, since 'the charges are sometimes made by nervous or hysterical females on the most slender evidence'.

Where Read had gone wrong was in exposing himself to the wife of an Alderman and the sister of the Chairman of the York Corporation Finance Committee, and there'd been nothing hysterical about that pair. They had testified that Read's member had been clearly displayed but was 'not in a state of tumescence', which was an odd thing to say, as though the two were very experienced as witnesses in these sorts of cases, and usually the members *were* in a state of tumescence. (It was just the right word – I'd looked it up after questioning them.) But then again Read himself, a broken down man in the middle fifties, had had no answer to the charge. He'd left the Gentlemen's, he told me, in 'rather a hurry'. 'Why?' I asked him, and he kept silence for a long time before replying, 'I wanted to go to the Post Office.'

I stuffed the papers back in the pasteboard envelope. Read had exposed himself on the day the war started, and I wondered whether the two events had been related. There'd been some strange behaviour since August 4th, and the numbers of Drunk and Incapables on the station had practically doubled.

I stood up and took off my suit-coat, which was something Scholes and Flower, being uniformed men, were not allowed to do – which perhaps served to remind them why they didn't care for my company. Anyhow they both just then quit the office to go on station patrol. Scholes would take the 'Up' side, Flower the 'Down' (or the other way about), with many meetings for a chat on the footbridge. It was two-thirty on a hot, sleepy afternoon, and I had the place to myself.

I stood in the office doorway with my coat over my shoulder, and watched a London train pull out of the 'Up'. As it moved, it revealed the platform across the way, the main 'Down', which was crowded with sweating excursionists, shortly to depart for points north. In the first fortnight of the war, the station had been full of trippers returning home, breaking off from holidays because of the emergency, but now folk had started going away again, and the ones who'd come back and lost their holidays as a result felt daft. Buffets in brown paper and bottles of lemonade were being passed out among the excursionists – all adults but they looked like a school party, excited at getting their grub. Half of them didn't know which way to face to look for the train. As I watched them, I saw Old Man Wright, the police office clerk, moving at a lick through their ranks, making for the footbridge and looking like he meant business. I knew then that something was up; that somebody would be in bother, for Wright fed on the misfortunes of others.

I turned aside from the door, closed it, retreated back into the office in spite of the heat (I was trying to banish the image of Wright, I suppose). For some reason, I walked over to the office notice-board. A photographic portrait of Constable Scholes had been pinned there. Why? I had no notion. It was not official; he was not in uniform. Perhaps he thought it flattering, and had put it up for swank. Or had someone put it there as a joke? I looked at the face, considering: moustache went down, eyes went down; *hair* went across, but Scholes had a very droopy face all told. Next to it was a detail of a York Temperance Society meeting and that I knew for a surety *was* a joke. Below this was a photograph of the new shooting range at the Railway Institute Sports Ground off Holgate. The targets were marked by signs reading '25 Yards', '50 Yards', '100 Yards'. Next to the hundred yards target, a man was lying down – 'reclining' as they say in photographs. It was as if he'd just scored a row of bullseyes at the hardest target, and had earned himself a good rest. This of course had been posted up by the Chief. He was always trying to get us to take up shooting – and now most of us would be doing just that, whether we liked it or not. A little further down was a card advertising a chamber concert at the Institute: Miss Leila Willoughby would be playing the violin, which took me back to Scholes. This musical notice was his doing; he played the flute. He was 'artistic', hence the droopy face. *Flower* ought to have been the artist, with a name like his, but of the two he was the better man in a scrap, and would bring in the Drunk and Incapables on his own, whereas Scholes would whistle for assistance.

I heard bootsteps from outside; the door banged open, bringing in the noise of a train whistle, traces of a hot black cloud, and Old Man Wright. I distinctly recall thinking: there's a bloody great empty space in the middle of this notice-board, when Wright leant over my shoulder and fixed a notice into that very spot with a single pin. I read:

PROPOSED FORMATION OF A NORTH EASTERN RAILWAY BATTALION

In order to meet the case of those who would prefer to enlist among men whom they know, application has been made to Lord Kitchener for authority to enrol a North Eastern Railway Battalion of his new Army, and if sufficient support is given it is hoped that sanction will be obtained. The Directors feel that many men who might otherwise hesitate to serve among strangers would be prepared to join such a battalion.

All trained men 45 years of age and under and untrained men 19 to 35 years of age should apply to their District Officers for full information.

'Bugger,' I said, and Wright gave out a single bark of laughter. I now did turn about, and he was watching me with a kind of smirk.

'Actually, I'd been *hoping* the Company would form its own unit,' I said.

Wright pulled a face, as if to say: 'Don't come it.'

'You'll be training at Hull,' he said. 'They've commandeered Alexandra Dock.'

I figured the docks at Hull, and could picture nothing but rain.

Wright himself was out of it, of course, being in the middle sixties, as was the Chief. The difference was that the Chief resented the fact. The first Kitchener appeals posted up about York had asked for men aged up to thirty, which had put *me* out of it as well, since I was thirty-two, but the Chief had offered – with no prompting on my part – to write me a special letter of recommendation to get round the difficulty. That would not now be necessary, since the War Office seemed to be raising the upper age limit by the week.

'I must do my duty,' I said to Old Man Wright, 'England's in peril.'

'Too bloody true,' he said, sitting down at his desk and unfolding that day's edition of the *Yorkshire Evening Press*. His head was grey, bald and too small – like a turkey's head, which he now began moving from side to side.

'A hundred and sixty-three killed . . .' he said. Looking up at me, he added, 'Over *four thousand* wounded . . . Peer's son dies of wounds received at Mons,' he was saying as I quit the police office.

According to the *Yorkshire Evening Press*, we kept thrashing the Germans; they kept reaching 'the limit of their effort', and yet our men would keep dying. Something was amiss – the Chief had told me as much himself.

I decided to scout him out, and as I stepped out onto platform four, a train came in and I caught a small shower of condensed steam. Our little girl, Sylvia, had a word for this: a 'train cloud'. Not a rain cloud, but a train cloud. She was clever with words. The fireman, leaning off the footplate, gave me a grin, which might have been by way of apology. I gave him a wave back anyhow. Footplate men were in reserved occupations, so he could afford to smile.

A man sat on a baggage trolley outside the First Class waiting room. His suit told me he wanted to be *in* there but wasn't up to the mark. He too read the *Press*, and I saw: 'The War Will Not Make Any Difference to Dale and Dalby's. They Have Started Their Summer Sale'. The London train was unloading on my right side as I walked. A scruffy porter brought down a tin trunk rather roughly from a First Class carriage, and the man standing in the doorway, topper in hand, called out, 'Be careful with that piece!'

I knew that porter – name of Bernard Dawson – by reputation. He was from down south. He was evidently fond of a glass of wallop, and his face was crumpled in such a way that you could tell he was a cockney just by looking at him. Also his moustache was famous on York station. It was hardly there. It was as if he'd drunk some brown Windsor soup about a week before and not washed since. The Night Station Master, Samuels, had a campaign against it, said it put off the passengers, that Dawson should either shave or let it grow out. But Dawson paid no mind. He was his own man. That said, he didn't take against the man with the topper.

'Sorry, guv,' he said.

Topper hadn't heard him, since he was being pestered by his wife in the carriage doorway: 'But I want a change of magazine', she was saying.

Ahead, and to the left of me, two engines stood alongside each other at the bay platforms, three and two. One of the North Eastern's 4-6-os and one of Lancashire and Yorkshire Railway's of the same wheel arrangement. A lad looked on, comparing them. I'd seen him about; I believed he was a cleaner in the North Shed, an aspirant driver as I'd once been myself. The first engine – ours – was not over-clean, whereas the other gleamed.

I nodded at the kid, saying, 'I reckon the Lanky's shown us up there.'

'That's just what I was thinking,' said the lad, and he coloured up, being a loyal company servant. Beyond him, I saw two gangers or platelayers entering the station from the south end: two blokes who looked like gypsies – dark, and long-haired; they were railwaymen, but dressed anyhow, in old corduroy suits. That was one privilege of the permanent way men; another was that they could enter a station by walking on the tracks. There weren't too many besides those.

I walked through the ticket gate, with hands in pockets. It was something to be able to saunter in and out of the principal traffic centre of the North without needing a ticket; it was something to be a three pound ten a week man set fair for promotion to inspector. It was something, but not enough. I had been growing bored, and the thought of fighting in a war excited as well as scared me. For much of the past few years, I had lived a quiet life under the iron station arches, like Jonah sleeping in the belly of the whale.

I crossed in front of the bookstall. 'A Railway Battalion' I read, on the board advertising that day's *Press*. I walked through the booking hall, with the ticket windows on each side. The glass above was cleaner here, there being no engines, and the light was bright blue. This was the clean side of the station – and filled at all times with the echoing voices of the ticket clerks, who had to shout through the 'pigeon holes' in the window glass.

'First Class return?' I heard a clerk calling out to a man in a dinty bowler. 'That'll be four pounds ten and six!'

Dinty bowler turned his head aside, thinking it over.

'Maybe not, eh?' the ticket clerk yelled through the glass.

Beyond him, in the hot darkness of the booking office, I saw the ticket office deputy superintendent. I saw him in profile. He was not shouting, but smoking a pipe and staring into the middle distance. He was of an age with me but looked older; a little overweight, freckled, with wavy red hair – and quiet natured, evidently something of an intellect. He'd once said something about Homer, the ancient Greek, and so the ticket clerks all called him 'Oamer'. I couldn't recall his right name. Would *he* be going off to fight? He was the wrong shape for a soldier, and that was fact.

I walked on towards the booking hall doors, which were all propped open for ventilation. Beyond lay the rushing trams and cabs and the high, blue sky of York. I made for the middle doors, and there I coincided with the Chief, who was coming in, but before I could speak to him, the station runner came up. The runners were generally just 'The Lad', but the better – or better *liked* – ones would graduate to a name, and this one was William, and was famed for the speed with which he charged about the place. He handed the Chief an envelope, and the Chief hardly looked at it, but asked William, 'You've seen about the battalion?'

'Signed up this morning, sir,' said William, and he was out through the doors. The Chief and William, I recalled, had a special connection, William being in the Riflemen's League, and an enthusiast for military matters generally, as you could tell by his highly polished brass buttons and his keenness on calling blokes 'Sir'.

'Isn't he too young?' I asked the Chief.

'How old *is* he?' asked the Chief, in a sort of daze.

'I believe he's seventeen,' I said.

The Chief now glanced down at the envelope he'd been handed. He seemed miles away, as he frequently did.

'They'll ask William his age,' said Chief, tearing open the envelope. 'If he says he's seventeen . . . they'll ask him again.'

'But what about his height?' I said.

'What about it?'

'He's too small. He's never five foot three.'

'How do you know?' said the Chief, looking over the letter. 'Have you fucking measured him?' he added, looking up. Which question was immediately followed by another: 'Can you ride a horse?'

'Who? Me?' I said.

'Aye,' said the Chief, thoughtful-like, reading again.

What in buggeration was he on about?

'I'm signing up for the new battalion,' I said, although I knew my thunder had been stolen by the news that young William had already done it.

The Chief nodded as he lit a new cigar. In the past month he'd given up his little ones and moved to a bigger size – Marcellas, one and six a go – just as though he was celebrating the coming of the war, the return to a man's normal state of existence. In his own day, the Chief had risen to sergeant major. He'd fought in Africa in the 1880s; chasing the mad Madhi and his still madder dervishes across the Sudan, or being chased by them, it made no bloody difference to the Chief. I figured him in the desert: red headed (he would have had a little more hair in those days), red skinned and red coated, picking off the fuzzy-wuzzies with his Winchester rifle in 122 Fahrenheit.

'If you join the Military Mounted Police,' said the Chief, glancing down at his letter, 'they'll teach you to ride a horse.'

'Is that what the letter's about, sir?'

(I would 'sir' the Chief *occasionally*.)

'All railway police are encouraged to go into the Military Police. I'm to report back on the progress of my recruiting,' the Chief said, tearing the letter clean in two, and folding the pieces into the top pocket of his tunic. I knew that the Chief did not consider the Military Police to be true soldiers.

'You stick with the railway boys,' said the Chief. Then, 'Fancy a pint, lad?' and I knew that was the nearest I'd come to my congratulations.

We walked out of the station, turned right, and climbed Station Road. On the right was the new station, on the left the old, the connecting tracks running beneath. In the sidings around the old station, the remnants of smoke hung in the heat haze. Some big freight had lately pulled out. A couple of rakes of horse wagons stood unattended, and a long line of wagons of a sort I'd never seen before – a special type of low loader – extended from under the station glass. I saw no soldiers just then.

'What's going off there?' I asked the Chief.

'Secret, lad,' said the Chief. But then he added, 'They loaded five tons of Lee Enfield Mark Threes this morning for immediate dispatch to France.'

I looked behind. Oamer, the ticket office number two, was walking up the road in his steady, thoughtful way, with his coat over his shoulder, and puffing on his pipe, like a steam-powered man.

'That's a good sort of rifle, is it?' I asked the Chief. 'The Mark Three?'

'The rifle's all right,' said the Chief. 'It's the bullet that gives the trouble.'

I thought: yes, it generally *is* the bullet that gives the trouble, but the Chief was talking about how rimmed cartridges were thought necessary, when in fact they weren't, and how they would snag somehow. The Germans made do without rimmed cartridges, and consequently their machine guns in particular worked better than ours. I didn't want to think about German machine guns. But the Chief hadn't let up by the time we arrived at the Bootham Hotel, which was where all the railwaymen went for their afternoon pints.

The Chief led the way into the close beer and smoke smell – faint manure smell into the bargain, for it was cattle market day and the place was ram-packed. The Chief was still talking about bloody bullets: the British Army had been buggering about with ammunition since the Boer War, when what was needed was simplicity and consistency. At the bar stood Dawson, the cockney porter. How had he slipped out of the station ahead of me? The Chief broke off to order the pints, and two rounds of fish paste sandwiches. Along from Dawson at the bar was a train guard – his guard's cap was on the bar before him, and I looked at his shining black hair, swept back. I knew him for an ingratiating fellow, the oil on his hair seeming to have leaked into his character, and he had an oily first name to match: Oliver. (I couldn't recall his second.)

'It's bloody criminal when you consider what was brewing up with Germany,' said the Chief.

'But nobody *did* know, did they sir?' as we found two chairs near the dusty fireplace.

'Course they knew,' said the Chief, lighting a cigar, '*I* knew, so I'm bloody sure the War Office did.'

'*How* did you know war was coming?' I enquired, at which the Chief fell silent for a space. He was eyeing Dawson, who was after another pint of John Smith's Best Bitter.

'You've put three away in the last two minutes,' Don Wolstenholmes, who ran the Bootham, was saying to Dawson. 'I think you've had enough.'

'I've had enough of *you,*' said Dawson, and he was loud enough to make the pub go quiet for a moment.

Wolstenholmes did pour another pint for Dawson, and the Chief directed his gaze at the sandwich in his hand. He folded it like a piece of paper and put it into his mouth. Then, while eating, he said, 'I knew from 1910.'

'What happened then?'

The Chief folded another sandwich and put it in.

'The Entente fucking Cordiale, with the fucking French,' he said, with crumbs and fish paste flying. 'We wouldn't be palling up to those buggers if we didn't know a scrap was coming with the Germans.'

The Chief then took a draw on his cigar. He would always smoke while eating, and while doing most other things. Oliver had come over from the bar, and was standing at the Chief's shoulder.

'I don't blame you police chaps for staying out of it,' he said, indicating Dawson. 'He was born drunk, he was. Best thing to do is steer clear.'

The Chief began turning about, with the dazed look on his face, having been rudely diverted, so to speak, from international diplomacy. But Oliver had gone by the time the Chief's manoeuvre was completed, which left him staring directly at the drunken porter, Dawson.

And now the clockwork machine, having been wound up to the fullest, began to work.

'Who the fuck are you?' said Dawson, just as though the Chief's gold-braided tunic and police insignia wouldn't have told him; just as if every man on the Company strength didn't know Chief Inspector Weatherill.

The Chief looked at me, as if expecting me to supply the answer on his behalf, which I did.

'He's the head of police at York railway station, as you know very well.'

'Right enough,' said Dawson, 'and otherwise *what*?'

He was drunker than I thought, and had become meaningless. How had he managed it in that short interval of time since leaving the station?

'This gentleman', I said, 'is second only to the Chief Officer, Fairclough, up at Newcastle, and you would be very well advised –'

I broke off, for I'd noticed that the Chief had put his cigar out even though it was only halfway through. The Chief never put a cigar out when it was only halfway through.

'Fairclough?' Dawson was saying. 'Who's *he* when he's at home?'

'I've just told you who he is.'

The Chief had not only put his cigar out, he was also hitching up the sleeves of his tunic.

'And who are *you*,' Dawson was asking me, as the Chief rose from his chair, 'that you go round sticking up for him?'

'Would you stop asking everybody who they are?' said the Chief, in a voice that didn't sound like him. It sounded like the Chief very far away. 'You're a disgrace to your uniform,' he said, facing Dawson.

The pub was quite silent once again.

'You can talk,' said Dawson, for as well as gold braid there was a quantity of fish paste and cigarette ash on the Chief's tunic. The Chief pushed closer towards him.

'Eh?' said the Chief. 'What do you mean?'

He wanted Dawson to lay a finger on him. Mere abuse did not justify blows. *The Railway Police Manual* said as much.

Dawson raised his hands, and pointed at the smudge on the Chief's chest: 'You're clarted in bloody . . .'

He touched the Chief, who frowned at him – not angry but puzzled rather. I was eyeing Dawson's nose, which was of a good size, and wondering how it would look smashed. Was there a word that might spare it? I barked out 'Apologise', but that was too long a word, and the blow, and the cracking sound, came before I could get it fully out. The Chief was getting on in years, but his punch had some special bonus feature. I'd felt it myself on one occasion, and seen its effect on several station loungers. It was spring-loaded somehow; told by its speed rather than its force. Dawson went down.

'I've a mind to charge you,' the Chief said, at which I made out a voice from the saloon bar throng:

'. . . Only you can't, because this is not company premises.'

It was Oliver, and he was dead right. The Bootham Hotel was not company premises, and that was precisely why it was full of railwaymen, who were not to be seen drinking on railway territory. Dawson could not be charged with assaulting a police officer, because the Chief and I did not count as police officers in that place. We had the ordinary citizen's power of arrest, and nothing more. The Chief peered into the crowd, and just then seemed a very old man indeed. A commotion at the back of the throng signified the departure of Oliver.

The Chief said to Dawson (who had now risen to his feet, and whose nose was still more or less as was, but a good deal bloodied), 'You'll come and see me tomorrow morning in the police office.'

Dawson looked over the Chief's shoulder, over the heads of the pub blokes, and . . . he seemed to be gazing through the clear glass of the public bar window. He then fixed his gaze on the Chief, saying, 'I'm joining the fucking army tomorrow morning.'

That knocked the Chief, at least for a moment.

'You'd better not be spinning me a line,' he said. 'When you sign up, you'll be given the King's Shilling. You'll bring me yours at midday. As proof.'

Dawson, sobered by the punch, quit the Bootham Hotel. The Chief and I took another pint with Don Wolstenholmes, who said he'd had trouble from Dawson before, and would be glad to see the back of him.

At about half past three, I was standing by the high doorstep of the Bootham Hotel, while the Chief took his leave of Wolstenholmes. The heat of the day had hardly abated, and all the pedestrians pushing on down Micklegate looked worn out. Over the road from the Bootham Hotel stood The Lion, a mysterious territory – a pub ignored for some reason by all railwaymen. From above the pub sign – which was a painting of a lion with one paw resting on the York city crest – two Union flags drooped. I looked from them to the window of the Bootham Hotel public bar, tracing the line of Dawson's gaze of a short while earlier. I didn't believe he'd meant to enlist until catching sight of that flag. It had struck him as something to say that might shame the Chief. Well, he was in a fix now, for he would have to go through with it.

The Chief had now finished his talk with Wolstenholmes, and we set off back. I said, 'That was Oliver who spoke out in the pub.'

Silence from the Chief.

'He was right wasn't he? About the Bootham being out of our jurisdiction?'

Still the Chief kept silence.

'I suppose Dawson will bring you his shilling . . .'

The Chief stopped and turned to me.

'You'll bring me yours as well. Then I'll have shot of the bloody pair of you.'

I ought not to have reminded him about the jurisdiction.

Below us on the right hand side, the old station was packed with army again, and all the sidings were taken up with the special low loaders. It was a relief to regain the cool of the booking hall, where the Chief and I parted. My eye then fell on Constable Scholes.

'You haven't seen a bloke with an owl, have you?' he said, coming up to me. 'Funny looking sort of bloke with . . . Well, he's carrying this owl, so you can't really mistake him.'

'The one from before, you mean?'

I watched him realise that I'd overheard his talk with Flower on the subject.

'Aye,' he said.

'I thought he'd cleared off,' I said.

'I know but Flower saw him not ten minutes since. I know he means to bring the bloody thing back onto a train. If he did, it would be in express contradiction of my instructions.'

'It would,' I said, nodding. 'Have you signed up for the battalion?'

'Oh aye,' he said, '. . . did that at dinner time. Went over with Flower.'

'Went over where?'

The recruitment office was evidently in the Railway Institute gymnasium. The office had closed at three, so I'd missed my chance for that day, and would have to go tomorrow. Just then Constable Flower marched into the booking hall, signalling at Scholes.

'The bugger's out here,' he was saying, indicating the taxi rank, and meaning the owl man. 'And I reckon he's stolen that bloody bird.'

'Have you got any evidence?' said Scholes.

'Course not,' said Flower, 'but I've seen him before, in the bloody police court. Come on!'

And they went off together. Flower was leading Scholes towards the confrontation with the Owl Man, and I didn't doubt that he'd dragged him towards the recruiting office as well. Scholes was always led by Flower, but I was impressed by the coolness of the *pair* of them just then. They might just have signed their very lives away, but here they were, fretting about a bloody owl, while I was thinking about German machine guns, and whether I might come up against the troublesome porter, Dawson, in the railway battalion.

Thorpe-on-Ouse

The sun was low and ragged as I opened the garden gate, and walked towards the wife, my work valise under my arm. She was on the 'spare' part of the lawn, where it ran under the three apple trees. Black boots; old blue dress; brown face; hair neither up nor down; trowel in hand. She'd only have been home from her own work at the Women's Co-Operative Guild half an hour since, but was already hard at it. She was no great hand at housework – well, she had no taste for it – but made an effort with the garden. I walked up and kissed her, saying 'Hello kidder' which made her look at me suspiciously.

The wife had a paper bag of bulbs in front of her. She crouched down, took a handful of them – daffodils, we'd bought them in the market the week before – and pitched them under the trees. That was how it was done: you made a 'run' to give a natural effect, but it looked like an act of despair.

She said, 'What's happened, Jim?' and I believe she half knew.

I said, 'Sir Godfrey Glanville Gordon . . .'

'*That* idiot.'

'You don't know who he is.'

'He *sounds* like an idiot.'

'He's the general manager of the North Eastern Railway.' The wife was gathering up the bulbs, not satisfied with the run. 'He's raising a battalion from all the railwaymen, and I mean to sign up tomorrow.'

No reply. She threw the bulbs again – another roll of the dice.

She looked up and said, 'What are you going to do, Jim? Run the Germans over with trains?'

'I should think we'll be a bit like the Royal Engineers.'

'And is this man Gordon joining up? Will he be fighting alongside you all?'

'Well he's got a railway to run. The Chief reckons the commanding officer's going to be a chap called Colonel Aubrey Butterfield.'

'*Audrey*? That's ridiculous.'

'*Aubrey*.'

'Why, Jim?' she said, brushing her skirts and rising to her feet. 'Why are you joining up?'

'Everyone else is.'

'Try again, Jim.'

'All right, to keep the Germans out of wherever it is . . . Belgium.'

'It's a bit late for that.'

'France, then.'

We walked over our lawn, which was too big, and stood before our house, which was likewise, but rather tumbled-down. At first we'd rented it, but the wife had insisted on buying it, which she managed at a knock-down price, her perpetual aim being to keep up with the other socialist ladies, who were all rich.

Without a word, we stepped through the gate, and onto the narrow road that led to Thorpe. To our right, beyond the hedge, lay the flat field that was used for cricket. Two boys had it all to themselves.

'That's the end of the cottage garden,' the wife said at length.

'What is?'

'Your joining up.' I was supposed to be building a cottage garden, whatever that was. In any event, it must be bordered by a wall of expensive brick. 'When will you go off?'

'Oh, not for a couple of weeks, and at first I'll be close by. We're to train at Hull . . . I'll plant the cottage garden next year.'

I kicked a stone.

'You're very sanguine.'

'Yes,' I said. 'What does that mean?'

Well, I knew really, and the fact was that I was not sanguine. The thought of war, even a short one, put me in a considerable state of nerve tension. 'Anyhow,' I said. 'Do you want us to fight them or not? Your lot seem torn on the question.'

By this, I meant all those committees in which the wife was involved by virtue of her part-time job with the Women's Co-Operative Guild: the movements for women's suffrage, Labour Party governance, Christian Socialism and whatnot. The committees were all in favour of brotherly (or sisterly) love but in practice argued constantly about whether feminism went with Christianity, violence, protectionism, and now war. But it wasn't all high principle with the wife. For example, she opposed point blank anything suggested by a certain Mrs Barratt, who was her main rival in York Co-Operation. The wife had several enemies, all women (according to her) of a 'pushing' kind. Many of these, it appeared, had come out strongly for pacifism, which inclined the wife rather in favour of the war.

'After all,' I said, 'there'll be no votes for women, or anyone, if the Germans win.'

By way of reply, she said, 'Where are we going, Jim?'

'I thought we were off to collect Harry and Sylvia.'

'They won't have had their teas yet.'

The children were being looked after – as always on the wife's workdays – by Lillian Backhouse, who was the wife of Peter Backhouse, verger of St Andrew's Church, Thorpe-on-Ouse.

On Thorpe-on-Ouse Main Street, we stood in the middle of the road. All the houses were hidden behind the great hedges. I looked down at the dust on my boots. In the distance, I could hear the rattle of a thresher.

'Fancy a drink?' I said to the wife. She nodded, and we stepped into the darkness of the Bay Horse inn, where I bought a pint for myself, and a lemonade for the wife, before returning once more into the light – the garden, which was overgrown, and quite empty. We set down our drinks on a rough wood table with benches alongside. At the foot of the garden was a half-wrecked railway carriage in the green of the North Eastern livery. It had been meant as a sort of summer house, and it had been wrecked before it was brought into this garden, having been in a smash at Knaresborough station. I had often mentioned this to the wife, but she never took it in.

'It's just engulfing us all,' she said with a sigh as I drank my beer.

I went back inside to buy another pint, and when I came out and sat down, the wife's mood had improved.

'You must be made an officer, Jim. You might be a captain.'

There was a regular army captain in Thorpe: a Captain Briggs, and at church he sat in his own pew, marked with a little tin badge reading 'Captain Briggs'.

'Can't you be made an officer for showing valour in the field?' asked the wife.

'Not if you went to Baytown National School.'

'What's the one below captain?'

'Second lieutenant.'

'What a mouthful.'

I could tell what she was thinking: it wouldn't fit on one of those little plaques.

'I've just thought,' I said, 'Lillian's taking them swimming in the river.' (I meant the children.) 'Have we to go and watch them?'

'No,' said the wife, and she was looking at the old carriage.

'Do you want to go behind that . . . thing?' she said.

And we went behind, where there was a little copse, and no fear of an interruption. There we did what we had done a couple of times before in that spot, although not for years, which is to say that we committed a nuisance or indecency, in the words of the *Police Manual*.

Ten minutes later, we were out in Main Street, and kicking the stones on the dusty road again. I was thinking of myself as an army officer. Why not? They were making men up from the ranks at a great rate, and how many of the new officers had faced down desperate men on lonely station platforms? How many had hunted up murderers? I had done those things – not easily, and not without fear, but I had done them. And I would look well in an officer's uniform. What had that junior coat cutter in Brown's, the best York tailors, said when the wife had forced me to buy a handmade suit? 'It's a pleasure to fit you, sir . . . The greyhound breed.'

But he probably said that to any normal-sized fellow.

Lillian Backhouse was walking towards us with one of her own children in tow, and our two. All the children had wet hair, fiercely brushed in the same way. Harry carried a book, as usual. The wife wanted him at the Grammar school, so that he'd become a good citizen (and rich into the bargain), for which he'd have to be coached up in Latin and Greek, at a longer cost than we could really afford. Lillian smiled at Lydia, who kissed her, saying, 'Hello love', immediately afterwards giving a strange glance back at me. It was all to do with not wanting the children back yet.

Harry and Sylvia came rushing up to us, and the wife – her strange mood continuing – said straightaway, 'Your father's signed up for the army.'

'Not yet,' I said.

'He means to do it tomorrow,' said the wife.

I looked at Lillian Backhouse, and she didn't know what to say. Her husband, Peter, was over forty and worn out from digging graves, so I didn't think he'd be going off. Young Sylvia was looking at me curiously.

'Do you *want* to get killed?'

'I will definitely not get killed,' I said.

Harry sat down on the edge of the road, and opened his book. I walked up, pulled off his cap, and ruffled his hair, to which he made no reply. I looked down at his page: two cowboys, both firing pistols at Indians on horses. One was instructing the other, 'Only shoot to "wing".'

Sylvia walked up, and said to Harry, 'You should use a blade of grass.'

'What for?' he said, for he would speak to *her*.

'To mark the place.'

'I haven't left off reading yet.'

'No, but you will do.'

Harry turned the page, and I saw the same number of cowboys, but many more Indians.

'You're not going to sit there the whole of your life reading, are you?' said Sylvia.

Harry made no reply.

'I think he might very well do,' Sylvia said to me, then: 'Dad, will you be going to France?'

'He must be trained first, idiot,' said Harry, finally looking up from his book.

'He's right,' I said to Sylvia. 'Well, he's not right to call you an idiot, and if he does it again, he'll get a thick ear. But I'm to go first to Hull.'

'Oh dear,' said Sylvia, who suddenly looked near to tears. She was only six, and to my knowledge, she had never been to Hull, nor had any knowledge of it. But it was just the sound of the word that was so disheartening.

Hull: October 1914

Lights-out at had been at ten-fifteen, half an hour since. I looked directly upwards, at the concrete ceiling, feeling like my own son, as I lay worrying, with my three blankets pulled right up about my neck and the book that my own son had sent me, *The Count of Monte Cristo*, under the blankets beside me. On top of my blankets I'd spread out a copy of the *Yorkshire Evening Press* for a bit of extra warmth. The largest of the headings read, 'Allies Continue to Make Steady Progress'. Apparently we'd been making steady progress ever since the show began. By rights we ought to have been in Berlin by now. Only we weren't.

On the floor above, bags of grain were still kept, and the Number One Warehouse at 'C' Wharf of Alexandra Dock, smelt barn-like as a result. On the floor below were drill hall, mess room, reading room, quartermaster's stores and so on. At the end of my cot, and shuddering at intervals in the sea wind, were mighty double doors, barricaded up to a height of four feet by sandbags. If you pulled away the sandbags, opened those doors and stepped through, you'd drop down onto the dockside and be instantly killed. They were meant for connecting, via gangways, with the decks of ships. But there was only one ship in dock at present, and that was the North Eastern company's own steamer, the SS *Rievaulx Abbey*, and it housed the officers of the battalion: the 17th Northumberland Fusiliers; or the Railway Pals.

We'd spent most of the day drilling in squads on the quays and doing Swedish exercises, which was what the army called physical jerks. I ought to have been worn out . . .

There were fifty cots in my row, which housed 'E' Company. I was in E Platoon of 'E' Company, so that was easy to remember. We were mainly York blokes in E Platoon. To my right lay Alfred Tinsley, the engine cleaner I'd seen eyeing the Lanky engine on the day the news about the battalion had been circulated. He'd turned eighteen on our arrival at Hull – so he'd lied about his age on enlisting. He'd latched on to me, having recognised me after that brief exchange of ours, and having heard I'd started my railway life on the footplate before giving it up for some mysterious reason.

He was reading, as best he could in the faint light from the few hurricane lamps that burned low between the cots – the *Railway Magazine*. He was a subscriber, as I was myself, but I knew that Tinsley kept his very carefully, so he could send them home for binding in red cloth with gold lettering. As I looked on, he closed the pages and slid the magazine under his bed, at which a voice called out, rather nastily: 'No time for the railway hobby now, Tinsley.' Well, we might have been called 'The Railway Pals', but that didn't mean we *were*.

I turned the other way and there, separated from me by three snoring porters, was Oliver Butler, head propped on hand, staring my way. He didn't flinch as I faced him, either, but just carried on staring as if it was his perfect right.

Was it all on account of that business in the Bootham Hotel, when he'd reminded the Chief that he was beyond his jurisdiction? It was Dawson, the cockney porter, who'd been rated by the Chief, not Butler himself, so why was he looking daggers at me? In fact, I had a pretty good idea. We were rivals: we were of about an age; both married men; both kept a clean collar at work; both hoping to be promoted, but keeping quiet about the fact. I was a detective sergeant in civilian life, so I was part of the boss class, and could expect to be promoted before him. Secondly, I had previously been a footplate man, and all train guards have a down on footplate men, since they ride at the business end of the trains.

I turned and lay flat, looking up again, listening to the hundreds of snorers, like a band playing out of time. Dawson himself did not seem to be on the battalion strength; at any rate, I had not yet set eyes on him. He must have dodged the Chief somehow.

'*Fusilier*,' whispered Butler. We were called fusiliers, not privates, and he was addressing me.

I faced him again. His white face had the glow of candlewax; his hair had an oily black shine about it. He looked like a man who considered himself handsome.

'You're to go in to see the CO tomorrow,' he said, and something that turned out to be a smile crept over his face.

'How do you know?'

It was the first I'd heard of it.

'It's on the dining hall notice-board – went up just after supper.'

He was ever watchful of that notice-board, keeping an eye out for all promotions.

'Why?' I said.

'Well, they wouldn't keep a good chap like you in the ranks.'

From behind him, a very Yorkshire voice, shaky with held-back laughter, said:

'I'm off now . . . off to sleep.'

Another, similar voice replied, 'Are you 'n' all?'

After an interval, the first one said, 'I'm going now . . . I'm on my way.'

A further pause, then the second one said, 'Have you gone yet?' and I could hear the first bloke laughing under his blankets, so that the word 'Aye' came out with a splutter of laughter.

Oliver Butler held my gaze throughout. The speakers were his two cracked brothers: the identical twins, Andy and Roy, who called each other 'Andy-lad' and 'Roy-boy' and hardly ever spoke to anyone else. They belonged to the ruffian's profession of platelayers or track walkers, which meant they'd spent most of their working days out in the fields. In the Butler family, all the effort seemed to have gone into creating the one wonderful creature: Oliver, the gold-braided train guard. The brothers were made of leftovers. They looked like drawings in the funny papers of very tired men: hollow faces, jaws hanging loose, eyes bulging – and their heads were too small. They were tough blokes though, no question.

For the next little while, I shifted about on my thin straw mattress, but no position answered. Oliver Butler had left off staring at me. Why was I being called in? It *must* be promotion. Every day, you'd see blokes sitting around sewing their new stripes onto their tunics, and trying not to look too chuffed. I would write to the wife as soon as I knew.

At midnight, I heard the distant clocks of central Hull chiming. Shortly after, I heard one bloke a few rows over say to another, very distinctly, 'Will you stop *breathing* like that, mate?' He must have had one of the snorers for a neighbour. The sound of the waves became quite distinct at three or so; at half after four, I heard a hydraulic motor start up in one of the other docks – and, not long after, footsteps on the dormitory floor. It was too much to hope that this was a bloke getting up for a piss, for they were *boot* steps and not stockinged feet. It was the regimental bugler, and I braced myself for the bloody racket.

The first thing I did was check the notice-board in the dining hall. I was due 'on the ship' for my interview with Colonel Aubrey Butterfield, commanding officer of the battalion, directly after dismiss on the square (which was one of the quays of the dock). I would be marched over there by our section commander, Corporal Prendergast, who was in fact Oamer, the easy-going, pipe-smoking number two of the York booking office.

I went to the washrooms for a sluice-down.

All the taps were taken up, mostly with men shaving as best they could under the cold running water. The drill was that you stood behind a man shaving and waited your turn, but the man ahead of me was more boy than man, and so was not shaving but only washing. It was William, the York station runner – surname Harvey, as I had now discovered – and he made Alfred Tinsley, the eighteen-year-old would-be engine driver, look like a veteran. Both were slightly built, and more boys than men, and both had lied about their age when enlisting, but Harvey had lied more, since he'd barely turned seventeen when he walked into the recruitment office. William Harvey looked the part of the young hero as well, with his blue eyes and blond curls, whereas Tinsley was a gawky individual with a face and body he'd not yet grown into. Just then William was talking to his neighbour, who I didn't know.

'The Germans are frightened to death – ' he said, before flattening his curls under the icy water, ' – at the sight of a bloody bullet,' he added, coming up with a gasp. He left off washing, turned to me with a grin, and stepped aside.

'Lovely day for it, eh . . . Mr Stringer?' he said, towelling his hair.

'For what, son?' I said, setting about my chin with a none-too-sharp razor. 'And call me Jim.'

'The big march,' he said.

'I'd forgotten about that.'

The battalion, we had been informed, had secured the use of a very spacious field about four miles off, and we would be marching there for sporting activities. Young William was all in favour of it, red hot with excitement at the thought, he was.

The kid had moved off, and I saw that someone else had come into the position behind me, waiting for the tap . . . and it was that creeping Jesus Oliver Butler himself. When I'd finished shaving, I turned to him, and said, 'It's all yours, mate,' at which Butler shook his head, saying, 'I've already shaved.' 'Then get the fuck out of it,' I wanted to say, but Butler said, 'I think we'd better have a word about my brothers . . . I could see you getting mad at them last night. I bet you'd have liked to come over and lay 'em out.'

'Not a bit of it,' I said.

'Or maybe you didn't fancy your chances? See, Jim, you might think they're a pair of simpletons, but what do you think the real business is going to be for us when we get over there in bloody France? Do you think we're going in with the infantry, Jim? Perhaps you think we're going to be building railways?'

'Could you just get to the point?'

'Right, Jim. Well, the empire is at the crisis of her fate, and she needs some blokes to shovel shit. Have you been down to the QM stores and had a look? There's eleven hundred shovels there, Jim.'

'We're to get rifles as well, you know.'

'Your most important bit of kit is going to be your shovel and the question is: can you use it? Can you dig an earth rampart, Jim? Can you dig a fucking *trench*? You've no taste for danger, I can see that – nor have I, we're both intelligent men – and you'll want to get behind cover in double-quick time. That's where Andy and Roy come in. You might not see the point of them now, Jim, but put those boys in a field with a shovel in their hands when the machine guns are opening up . . . Different matter, Jim, *very different matter*.' He stuck out his hand, saying, 'Now look, I've said my piece . . . Shall we be mates?'

I shook his hand – well, it seemed the quickest way of getting shot of him – and he moved off to his breakfast.

I went through to the hall myself a few minutes later. The place was vast, lines stretching to infinity of men sitting on plain forms at long deal tables. At every place was a white plate with a hunk of bread and bacon on it. Trolleys on which sat giant tea urns were wheeled by squads of orderlies, and I did not like to see their thin white suits, because they put me in mind of hospitals. We ordinary soldiers wore civilian clothes: dark trousers and tunic shirts with braces hanging down. We didn't have uniforms yet, only boots and caps – and there were only two sizes of caps: large and small, whereas most of the blokes, of course, were medium-sized. The officers did have uniforms, and there were plenty of that lot strolling about, for they'd breakfasted earlier, on their boat. I saw our platoon commander, Second Lieutenant Quinn, late of the North Eastern Railway Engineers' Drawing Office at York. 'Unfortunately . . .' he was saying to a fellow officer. He was a good-looking chap, was Quinn, with a square face, sad brown eyes and a mournful way of talking. He'd been to St Peter's School, York: the Eton of the bloody North.

In spite of the officers, the dining hall was in uproar. 'You fellows, you're always bloody grousing!' I heard; and someone near me called out, 'Wang it over, mate!' at which an empty cup went soaring over my head. I saw young William Harvey. He'd already finished his breakfast: 'Set me up just nicely, that has!' he was saying to someone. A few places along from him were constables – now fusiliers – Scholes and Flower. They were talking together, as usual, being about as thick with each other as the weird Butler twins.

I walked further, and saw a place next to Tinsley, the young train watcher. I made to push on, since I knew he'd shoot some railway question at me the moment I sat down. But Tinsley looked up and saw me, and perhaps knew what I was about, so I took the place next to him. He weighed straight in as I set about my bacon and bread: 'Why did you not continue on the footplate, Mr Stringer?'

'Well, there's more money in the police,' I said, 'and you keep a clean collar.'

'But even so,' said Tinsley.

I couldn't bring myself to tell the tale. He evidently felt the high-speed life of the engine man to be in every way superior to that of the plodding copper. Without waiting for my answer, Tinsley started in about an engine driver he knew in the York South Shed, who put up 'the hardest running of any man on the North Eastern Railway'. As he rabbited on, a new bloke sat down over opposite.

It was Dawson, the cockney porter, and he nodded at me, which was a turn-up.

'Going on all right?' I said, a bit guardedly.

'Top hole,' he said. 'All right, son?' he added, nodding at young Tinsley.

I introduced the two of them, but Dawson, being only a porter, hardly existed as far as young Tinsley was concerned. There were all kinds of snobs, and Tinsley was a railway snob.

When not drunk, I realised, Dawson was a different proposition, even looked different. His scrubby little moustache was more of an amusing error rather than anything, and the crumples of his face all added up to good humour. I couldn't believe this was the same man as had been rated by the Chief in the Bootham Hotel.

'The Chief talked you into enlisting then?' I said.

'What?' said Dawson, examining his bacon. He looked up. 'Fact is, I'd been asking myself . . . Am I more use to the country scrounging for tips in York station or getting killed in France?' He took a belt of his tea. 'Crikey,' he said, and all his face crumples became evident. He was squinting down into his cup. 'Talk about stewed,' he said.

'Mine's practically water,' I said.

'That right? . . . Versatile, these army cooks.'

He was looking all around the hall, taking it all in.

Someone called out, 'Silence for the sergeant major!'

A bloke stood on a form at the end of the hall, and announced that, after the after-breakfast parade, there'd be a five-mile route march for the whole company.

'Nice,' said Dawson, grinning at me.

This march, the SM announced, was to be in 'extended order drill'.

'What's that when it's at home?' Alfred Tinsley asked me, and a high voice came from across the table.

'You ought to know.'

It was the other kid, Harvey, and I realised that his had been the voice raised the night before against Tinsley's reading of the *Railway Magazine*.

Evidently, the boy and the other boy did not get on.

Five minutes after emerging from the dock, the 'march at ease' had sounded, at which everyone began walking more or less normally, most of the blokes smoking at the same time. Young William had called it a lovely day. Well, it might have been a lovely day for Hull. It wasn't raining *much*. The town was unfolding in a series of long wide streets, endless tram lines, and hoardings bigger than the houses, many of them advertising B. Cooke and Sons, whoever they were. In the gaps between the hoardings, the grey sea came and went, and I thought back over my interview with Butterfield.

His office was a cabin of the SS *Rievaulx Abbey*, and behind it were two oil paintings: one showing the crest of the North Eastern Railway Company, the other some Northumberland Fusiliers of a different, older battalion. (They looked to be out in India, or somewhere.) Oamer had marched me in, and my heart sank at Butterfield's first words.

'There is at present no vacancy within our *regimental* police . . .'

(I had not asked whether there was.)

'. . . but I would be happy to recommend that you be transferred to the corps of *Military Mounted* Police, who are the elite of the force. You would seem an excellent man for the job. I have good reports of you from both your section and platoon commanders and of course you were a policeman in civilian life.'

Of course I was, I thought . . . but why couldn't everybody leave off about the military police? It wasn't proper soldiering as far as I was concerned. I wondered whether the same pressure had been applied to Scholes and Flower.

I said, 'If it's all the same, I'd rather stick with the battalion, sir' and he'd said, 'It's all the same to *me,* Stringer, but it may not be all the same to you.'

When I came out, I said to Oamer, 'I didn't seem to get any points for loyalty to the battalion.'

'But you may do in time,' he said.

'When?'

'When the penny drops that you *have* been loyal.'

He was perhaps saying that Butterfield was rather dim, which didn't help me at all – and I had an inkling that the path to promotion would now be blocked as long as I said no to the Military Mounted Police.

For a while, the blokes at the back of the troop had been singing 'Another Little Drink Wouldn't Do Us Any Harm'. It was all about the Prime Minister, who liked a drop. Now they switched to 'Watkins of the Railway Gang', and this they kept up manfully as we passed a never-ending cemetery, but when another, still bigger cemetery came into view . . . Well, it seemed to knock the heart out of them, and they gave it up. The only exceptions were those odd boys, the Butler twins, marching a little way ahead of me, who sang to each other a private song: something about 'a mistake's been made' or, as they had it, 'a mistek's bin med', and 'He's got no eyes, cos he's got no head' and 'He's got no feet, cos he's got no legs', and this did tickle them.

Our troop was a quarter mile long. The Hull citizenry could see we were soldiers from our ragged formation and the officers riding alongside but, not having any guns, we didn't command respect, and the looks that came our way . . . they were half amused, as though people were thinking: 'You *mugs*!' After we'd turned a corner in a somewhat disorganised manner, Alfred Tinsley, the railway-nut, was chattering away alongside me, talking shop.

'Would you break up the coal while riding?' he enquired.

'No time for coal trimming on the road,' I said. 'I'd do it beforehand, while my mate's going round with the oil can.'

'But wouldn't you want to supervise your mate as he oiled up?'

'No,' I said, 'I'd trust him.'

'I wouldn't,' said Tinsley. 'It's a job that has to be done right.'

Presently, we came to a closed level crossing gate, and this threw us out of formation. When we were rearranged, I found myself alongside the bulky figure of Oamer, who was puffing away on his pipe. He was a dark horse, Oamer. He was a good shot, and he'd been in the Territorials, but his red hair was surely longer than regulation army length, and the sweat was prickling on his forehead. He was overweight, and not quite in A1 condition. Young William Harvey was on the other side of him, and our supposed 'four' was completed by Scholes. It was odd to see Scholes without his mate, Flower, but Flower was in another 'four' and there was nothing either of them could do about it. Scholes's face looked especially droopy as a result. 'You seen the *North Eastern Railway Journal*?' he asked me. 'The latest number of it, I mean?'

'I have not,' I said.

'They've opened the bloody roll of honour,' he said, 'for all those company blokes who've gone out already, with other regiments.'

He didn't half sound depressed about it.

'You mean for the blokes who've won medals?'

'*Some* of them have won medals,' he said. 'They're *all* bloody dead.'

At this, Oamer took his pipe from his mouth.

'The term roll of honour is used in two senses,' he said, in his slow, thoughtful way that sat so oddly with the two stripes on his arm. (He ought to have been a major on the Staff, ought Oamer.) 'Firstly, as a record of certain notable new recruits, transfers and so on – '

'How are they notable?' I cut in.

'They are notable in the sense that they have come to the attention of the compiler of the roll of honour. Secondly, it is used as a record of men who have – '

' – had their heads blown off in France,' said Scholes.

' – those who have suffered in the cause of liberty in the field.'

I looked sidelong at young William. He had no time for this morbid talk.

'Why are you called Oamer, Corporal Prendergast?' he enquired.

I watched Oamer smoke for a while. Every time he put his pipe in his mouth, his red bushy moustache cleaned the stem. It was a highly convenient arrangement. At length, he answered the kid's question.

'Oamer is a mispronunciation of Homer, who is apparently taken to be a *philosopher* by the men of the York ticket office. They believe – and it's *very* flattering, I must say – that I am on the philosophical side myself. Hence the name.'

'Do you mind it, Corporal?' asked William.

'Not a bit of it. Homer is the greatest name in epic poetry, a figure comparable with Shakespeare. I am, or was, the deputy superintendent of a ticket office.'

'But it's a very *big* ticket office,' said William, and Oamer flashed a grin at me over the kid's head.

We came to the famous field – a recreation ground with a football pitch marked out, and a gang of seagulls parading in the centre circle. As I walked through the gates, I caught sight of our platoon officer, Second Lieutenant Quinn, and he was talking to a fellow officer and uttering, very slowly and deliberately, his favourite word, 'Unfortunately . . . It's not quite big enough.'

The ground was overlooked by hoardings for a shipping company; railway signals and masts lay beyond the boundary fence. An advance party of the battalion, quartered in a bell tent on the touchline, had made the ground ready for us. Among other entertainments was a line of sandbags with a long rope draped over, and a likely-looking sergeant standing by – that would be for tug of war. A track was marked out for the hundred-yard dash; a long sandpit had been dug – for the long jump, of which the army was very fond. But as they split off into their platoons, most of the blokes eyed the gibbet-like arrangement on the far touchline of the football pitch. From this dangled an over-sized scarecrow with a pasteboard disc for a face, and another disc lower down: the heart. Fifty yards in advance of this, neatly aligned on the grass, lay a line of rifles with bayonets fixed.

All the platoon sergeants were shouting (how had the North Eastern Railway thrown up men who could shout like that?) and it seemed we could make for our activity of choice. Whatever you chose, you had twenty minutes at it, and one option was 'rest easy' or some such cushy number. You'd sit and smoke in the drizzling rain and watch the others. I thought: the officers'll look out for who goes there first, then they'll be down on them for the rest of the bloody war.

The red hot types dashed straight over to the shooting range or the bayonet practice. Other tough nuts went for the tug of war. Young Tinsley was heading that way. Dawson walked past me with shoulders hunched. He was lighting a cigarette, trying to keep the rain off it.

'Where you off to?' I called after him.

'Hazard a guess, mate,' he said, turning round and grinning.

I explained my theory to him, and he did a sort of mock-frown, making his face very crumpled.

'Trouble is, mate,' he said, 'I've already lit up, and it's a Woodbine. Lovely smoke, is a Woodbine. Here, help yourself.'

And he held out the packet.

If there was one thing I'd learnt so far from the British Army, it was the value of a Woodbine, so I took one, and as Dawson trooped off to 'Rest Easy' together with every last slope-shouldered slacker of the battalion, I looked across the recreation ground. Most of the blokes criss-crossing the ground were younger than me, as were most of the officers.

I was beginning to think like the wife: in a pushing sort of way. Why shouldn't *I* be sitting up there on a great, grey horse?

I puffed away at the Woodbine for a while, then set off for the shooting range. I was no cracksman, but a decent shot when I had my eye in. As I made off, there came a horrible penetrating scream – a man's scream, which is the worst kind. It sent all the seagulls rising up from the boundary fence, to where they'd retreated upon our arrival, and it came from the direction of the bayonet practice. The instructor, bent practically double with bayonet to the fore, was charging at the straw figure, and every last man had stood still and was watching. The bayonet went right through the cardboard heart . . . and the instructor had no end of a job yanking it out again. There didn't seem to be any established procedure for pulling a bayonet *out* of a man, and there was some laughter at this but not much, because most of the blokes had been put in mind of France all of a sudden.

When he'd recovered his weapon, the instructor steadied the

dummy, and walked back to the line of blokes waiting their turn. First in line was the smallest and youngest man in the battalion, hardly a man at all: William. What kind of scream would he produce? He was handed his rifle, and I watched as he readied himself for his rush at the swinging scarecrow. But William had seen something amiss in the way the bayonet was fixed. With a crowd of blokes holding rifles behind him, and agitating at him to get on with it, he tried to shove the thing more firmly into its housing, which he did by directly grasping the blade. A sort of dismayed groan came from the blokes behind him; the man running the show dashed over to him, and the shout went up for medical orderlies. The kid was looking down at his hand, unable to credit the size of the gash he'd made there.

'Oh mother,' said a voice behind me. It was one of the Butler twins. 'I'll bet he's sore,' said the other one.

'I'll bet he's sore as *owt*,' said the first, and they turned and grinned at each other.

Behind them stood their older brother. Most of the battalion had seen what had happened to the kid, but Oliver Butler wasn't looking at the casualty. He was, as usual, eyeing me.

That evening, half of the battalion – A and B companies – had been given leave to go off into the town. Why *them?* The question was not to be asked. We were all at the mercy of the orderly corporals and the notices they pinned up in the dining hall. Some A and B blokes had been too tired after the march to take advantage, but most had gone, and come eight o'clock the reading room was practically deserted. A couple of blokes I didn't know played a quiet game of cards, and the Butler twins sat opposite each other. They weren't reading of course – I doubted they could. One – it might've been Andy – took out a Woodbine for himself, then passed one to Roy (if it was he).

Roy said, 'Fine style, Andy-lad,' then struck a match.

His brother, taking the light, said 'Fine style, Roy-boy,' in return.

They always did that when they smoked together. A little further along sat young William Harvey, reading with a bandaged hand. He looked particularly small, just then, the reading room being massive, like all the others. The place was filled with the sound of the droning wind, and the electroliers swung in time with the surging of the sea.

William sat on one chair with his feet on another, and a magazine across his lap. When he saw me, he took his feet down, just as though I *did* have a stripe on my arm.

'How's your hand, son?' I said, wondering whether they'd had to sew it, and he just nodded, evidently not over the shock yet. His bandage was stained with iodine. He stood up and made towards the door, moving at about half his usual pace. I walked over to where he'd been sitting, and I saw that it was the latest number of the *North Eastern Railway Journal* that he'd been reading. This was now almost entirely given over to the war, and had very little about the ordinary workings of the railway. You'd think the editors had been waiting all along for an excuse to drop railway subjects. Young William had evidently been reading the roll of honour, as mentioned on the march by Scholes, for he'd left the magazine open at that page. I picked it up, and read of the glorious deaths of railwaymen who'd gone to France at the earliest opportunity, prior to the formation of the battalion. Private Willetts, a labourer at Darlington Locomotive Works . . . a bullet had gone through his cap. Well, it hadn't only gone through his cap. There'd been the small matter of his head as well. But in the case of a Private Harrison, a shunter at York, the writer had written more plainly. Harrison had been 'blown up at Le Cateau'. But that wasn't quite the end of it. They'd amputated both legs . . . but he'd pegged out anyway. There was in addition a photographic portrait of a bloke who'd stopped something at Mons. He was reported 'as well as could be expected', but I doubted that he still looked as he did in the portrait.

Young William was watching me from a little way in advance of the doorway. He turned and made for the door as I looked up. The moving electroliers and the oil lamps acted in concert to make his shadow rise and fall as he walked. That, at least, was big.

Young William Harvey's hand did mend, and it might be that over the endless months of bull his chest expanded to the required thirty-four inches. He got back his martial spirit, or appeared to, and the blokes would ask him what he meant to do to Brother Fritz just to hear such bloodthirsty language coming out of such an angelic face – and of course with him, Britain was always 'Blighty'.

His jingoism put some of the blokes' backs up, but I didn't mind him, and he seemed to have quite taken to me. One evening he came up to me and asked me how I polished my cap badge. He seemed a bit shocked when I said it hadn't occurred to me to polish it at all. For something to say, I told him I'd seen Oamer going at his with some sort of white paste.

'That's toothpaste, Mr Stringer,' said Harvey, who never would call me Jim. 'Toothpaste is for teeth. Best thing is to use a dab of vinegar.'

'You sure, son?' I said, 'I don't want to smell like a pickled onion.'

'Vinegar,' he said, winking at me, 'it's the *army* way.'

He'd had this from his family, I believed. He had a number of relations who'd been in the colours before the war, and I'd heard that his father – currently working as a barman in the York Station Hotel – had won the Distinguished Conduct Medal in some long forgotten Empire Campaign.

We spent half of every day training, half of it drilling, and it got so you'd actually *think* about standing. I'd be out in Hull, waiting for a tram, and I'd be thinking: now I'm standing at ease; now I'm standing *easy*. The idea was that we would all move as one mechanism, but this never quite came about. We remained individuals, and most of us more railwayman than soldier. I kept cases on those particular individuals I have already mentioned, because we were all from York, and all in the same company. Anyhow these blokes interested me, and some of them I liked.

Oamer was about the best-liked NCO in the battalion, and the only mystery was why he'd not become an officer. I supposed he was seen as an oddity with his pipe, his thoughtful remarks, his rather too comfortable appearance. I recall one night in the dormitory watching him slowly applying foot powder while turning the pages of a difficult-looking book. He wrote a letter to somebody every night, and no man knew who. It did cross my mind that he might be queer.

My particular pal was Bernie Dawson (as I came to know him). His shadowy moustache survived the hatred of two sergeants and one sergeant major. He soon got a name for liking a drop of ale, and I believe he was involved in a bit of a barney in one of the Hull pubs, but I never saw any repeat of the Bootham Hotel sort of carry-on. He went everywhere with scuffed boots and – when we got our uniforms – pocket flaps undone, but he was amusing company.

My other mate was young Alfred Tinsley. Off duty, he and I would go and look at the engines at Hull Paragon station, and he would write down the numbers while telling me all about this footplate god of his – the York South Shed man – whose name, I learnt, was Tom Shaw. I'd never heard of Tom Shaw, and could scarcely credit his existence, since Tinsley only ever spoke to *me* about him, and the bloke seemed so perfect in all respects. But I was happy to go along with the lad's railway talk. (The footplate had been my original calling, and late at night in the dormitory, I would imagine myself driving engines for the army in France, and somehow saving the day by putting up some hard running of my own.)

Tinsley had a down on Harvey, who, he complained, was forever boasting of his army connections. Other blokes said the same, but I only ever saw the enthusiasm of the boy scout in Harvey; I found him amusing more than anything, and it counted for something with me that the Chief had liked him.

In February of 1915 I was called in again to see Butterfield, and he was still worrying away at the question of why I would not join the military police. At the end of our interview, he sat back, and said, 'I consider your decision unwise', and so there it was in the open: I could not hope for promotion on his watch, having twice defied his wishes. Scholes and Flower *had* come under the same sort of pressure, and Flower had cracked. His departure for the Military Mounted Police (where he'd be made straight up to corporal) left Scholes glooming about on his own, or sitting on the wall in the dock playing his flute.

When Oliver Butler heard of Flower's move, he approached me in the reading room, saying, 'He hasn't half the brains you have', which might possibly have been his genuine opinion.

I said. 'The army police operate at the back and that's no good for me. I want to have a slap at Fritz.'

'Where d'you get that talk from?' he said.

'William,' I said, turning the pages of *Punch*. 'He might be ten years old, but he's got some good lines.'

'Thing is,' Oliver said, 'some of the blokes do feel uncomfortable having coppers in the ranks. That's one reason Butterfield wants rid of you.'

'Well, it's hard bloody lines, isn't it?'

But what he'd said made sense; much the same had occurred to me.

In April 1915, we were told we'd had the great honour of being made a Pioneer Battalion. Pioneers were a kind of sappers:

shit shovellers as Oliver Butler bitterly had it; and we *did* dig a lot of practice trenches, and Andy and Roy Butler *could* each shift more earth than any three men, of which Oliver Butler was half proud and half ashamed. He himself – being ambitious, for all his sarcastic tone – aimed at the more technical side of pioneering, and had put in for a badge in field telephone operation.

It was known that pioneering might lead to railway construction at the front, but I couldn't see how it would lead to railway *operation*, which seemed all the province of the Railway Operating Division, a part of the Royal Engineers.

Anyhow, trenches were the thing mainly required. The *Yorkshire Evening Press* had stopped talking of 'steady progress'; it was more a matter of our boys having completely 'mastered' whatever was the latest German offensive. The other lot were making the running, in other words. Sometimes the paper would admit that the Germans had attacked 'in force', but then we would make 'a fine recovery'. A small line might be 'temporarily lost'. How did the bloody *Yorkshire Evening Press* know the loss was only temporary? Did they have the ability to see the future? You stopped believing it all. You'd look at the stuff not touching on the war – 'To-Day's Racing' or 'Schoolboy Thieves Arrested' – and wonder if *that* was all invented as well.

The fact that my path to promotion was blocked also depressed me, especially since the wife – on my leaves and in her letters – was forever asking when I was going to be made up. I banked on the early departure of Butterfield, for the officers did come and go at a hell of a rate. Second Lieutenant Quinn, for instance, was transferred to another regiment at the start of 1915, so that we had a different company commander during our first three billeting stints (six weeks at a time on the Yorkshire Moors, at Catterick and on Salisbury Plain), but in late summer he came back as *Captain* Quinn. He remained ever likely to say the word 'Unfortunately', and the men played a kind of game. You'd get points for overhearing him coming out with it. I 'bagged' one utterance. Quinn was coming off the square with another officer, and I heard him say, 'Unfortunately we've had some rather bad luck.' Well, I thought, bad luck generally *is* unfortunate, is it not? I speculated that he might have been talking about the whole situation on the Western Front, which now seemed one giant graveyard for British soldiers.

In the second half of 1915, we all expected our 'order for the front' every day, and even the most obviously fretful men – such as Scholes – wanted to get out there just so the waiting would be over. When, in late October, Oamer strolled up to me in the washroom and said, 'Confidentially, old man, we're out of here next week', I thought we were for France at last, but he meant only another billeting stint, this one at Spurn Head.

But Spurn Head would prove to be different. Everything that happened to us in France would be in direct consequence of events on that weird peninsula.

Spurn: November 1915

Spurn Head is about three miles long and in places not more than fifty yards across. On any map of Britain, they have a job making it thin enough without just drawing a single line. On one side is the North Sea, which (what with one thing and another) the army had stopped calling 'the German Sea'; on the other is the Humber Estuary. But what you saw if you stood on Spurn was just flat, shining sea, and if any ships happened to be on it, then they looked to be much higher than *you* were. At the northern end of Spurn stood the village of Kilnsea, and on the beach hard by, a huge, elevated bonfire burned day and night – a beacon for ships in a great iron goblet. It would warm you up from fifty yards off, that brute would.

The German navy had lately opened up with its twelve-inch guns on Scarborough, Whitby and the Hartlepools, and the army brass was now attempting to make safe the entire east coast. Accordingly, the Royal Engineers were going to secure Spurn Head, and so the Humber Estuary. This meant constructing gun batteries, which were to be linked with a standard-gauge military railway running along Spurn.

We went there as a section, detachment or working party, I'm not sure which. Our section commander (if that's what we were) was Corporal Prendergast, in other words Oamer. As far as I was concerned we were just a splinter of 'E' Platoon, various bits of which had been fired from Alexandra Dock in the direction of the east coast, all under the overall command of Captain Quinn.

At Hull we'd entrained for a spot called Patrington, which is the nearest railhead to Spurn, and which proudly stands in the centre of a network of mud roads. There, in late afternoon, we'd boarded two open wagonettes, and as these bumped their way east we sat first in greatcoats, then greatcoats and *horse blankets* – for the sea wind is murder in that territory. We saw the beacon from five miles off, growing brighter and bigger as the dusk fell.

Captain Quinn was in the first wagonette with Oamer, the two kids and one of the Butler twins: Andy. I was in the second with Dawson, Scholes, Oliver Butler and Roy Butler. At Patrington station, Oamer had deliberately separated the twins, and this, I knew, was done at the prompting of Quinn, who thought it bad for morale that they should be so thick with one another and hardly speak to anyone else.

I turned to Roy:

'What do you reckon's in store for us here, then?'

I knew I'd have to wait for my answer, and the wagonette jolted on for a good hundred yards more before he began, 'Should think . . .'

'What?'

'Bull,' he said, and it was something to get even that out of him.

'But what kind of *work*?' I asked Roy, who was gazing away over the fields towards the beacon.

Oliver Butler, who always watched closely my attempts to draw out either of his brothers, eyed me for a space after I'd given up. Then he said, 'Pick and shovel stunt – ten to one.' He had a copy of the *Press* on his lap. He was a big reader of that paper for some reason – had it on subscription whereas the rest of us would just pick up the copies we saw lying about. I read, 'York Officer's Big Pike'. It seemed to me that the paper was starting to lay off the actual fighting, ever since the battle of

Loos, the month before, which had been the first to involve the New Armies, the Kitchener boys I mean, sorts like us.

Word was, it had been a calamity. We'd used poison gas shells which meant the brass was getting desperate and that the war reports would no longer be able to call this a 'perfidious German method of warfare'.

To my right sat Scholes, who'd been silent since Hull. In his gloved hand, he held a sheaf of papers with music on them. He could read music just like words. You'd see him singing to himself as he did it. The week before, he and a shunter from Leeds who played the piano had given a concert in the reading room at Alexandra Dock, and I'd gone along just in case nobody else did. I was quite done in, so it had put me to sleep, but in a pleasant sort of way.

Bernie Dawson was sitting over opposite, alongside Oliver Butler. He'd been fishing about in his pack for a while, and now produced a canteen and a metal cup. He poured himself a tea, and drank it down fast; he poured another and offered it first to me. I took a swig, and Roy Butler most unexpectedly spoke up again.

'Owt like?' he said, meaning he wanted a belt of it for himself.

I handed him the cup and he downed it in a gulp.

The clouds in this place were like nothing I'd seen – like great black arrows swooping in from the sea. Presently, Roy Butler remembered about the cup, and passed it back to Dawson with a nod.

'Anytime, mate,' said Dawson, restoring the cup to his pack. He sat back in the bouncing wagonette, and pulled his blanket more tightly around him. 'Talk about a hole,' he said, taking in the strange beauty all around. Roy Butler was lighting a cigarette. He smoked more than his twin brother, I believed, and even though he usually appeared equally nerveless, he was more inclined to do so at anxious moments, so I had perhaps got him worried with my questions about our Spurn duty. I credited him with being brighter than his brother, and I fancied that, if kept apart from him for long enough, he would eventually become normal.

'All these fields,' Dawson said to Oliver Butler, '. . . could be just the place for some field *telephones*. You might be mucking in with the RE boys, Ollie.'

'We'll be digging their bloody latrines,' said Butler. 'You just wait.'

'Here,' said Dawson, 'where are we billeted?'

'At a farm, according to Oamer,' I said.

Suddenly leaning forward, Dawson enquired, 'At a farm-*house*, I hope he said.'

Well, the place was Cobble Farm. Quinn was in the farmhouse, the rest of us in the barn. For the first two weeks I never saw the farmer, name of Lowther, but sometimes at five in the morning I would hear the roar of a great petrol-driven tractor. The grub was served out to us from the back door of the farmhouse by Mrs Lowther, who was friendly enough, but wouldn't have the rank and file in her house. There were no animals to be seen, only half a dozen cats, and the whole place was clarted with wet mud – *shone* with it when there was any light in the sky, which there was for about three hours a day.

On the first morning, Quinn paraded us in the farmyard; then he started in on a little speech, with many a hesitation, and a glance towards the wide farmyard gate and the dead straight mud road stretching away to the beacon, burning even then at eleven o'clock on a rainy Tuesday morning like an advertisement for hell. Our time in the Alexandra Dock, Quinn said, had made soldiers of us. We may not realise it, but he could see that we were very different men. The work we were about to commence was of vital importance, but he hoped we would also enjoy and learn from it. It would be *hard* work, and he'd warned Mrs Lowther that it would put an edge on our appetites. (At this he grinned at us all, which meant he had told a joke.) He gave another glance over to the gate, and the smile gradually disappeared. I knew what was coming:

'Unfortunately . . .' said Captain Quinn, in his sad, dreamy sort of way.

He was gazing towards the mud road, and this time we all sneaked a look in that direction, for a motor van had appeared on the horizon. At this Quinn's smile, and power of speech, returned. With the van coming on quickly, he was talking about how the work in prospect would afford considerable scope for the display of initiative. '. . . And I am pleased to say', he continued, as an orderly climbed out of the van to open farm gates, 'that the shovels do now seem to have arrived.'

We would be constructing defensive earthworks in a vast field lying between Kilnsea and the beginning of the Spurn peninsula. The plans were in a piece of paper held in Captain Quinn's leather-gloved hands, but the paper and the field would prove to be two different matters.

The trouble (Oliver Butler had been dead right) was that for all our training, none of us could dig properly except for Roy-boy and Andy-lad.

I recall the end of our second week in that slimy field . . .

Fusilier Scholes – perhaps blown down by the roaring wind, or perhaps having simply missed his footing in the ooze – had lately fallen over, and Captain Quinn had watched him do it.

'After a very few days, Prendergast,' I overheard him saying to Oamer, 'I anticipate that things will be running like clockwork.'

As Scholes struggled to his feet, young William Harvey, trying to shake a clod of earth off his shovel, nearly brained young Alfred Tinsley, who shaped to give him a belt in return. They'd been needling each other for the past hour. Tinsley, as usual, had been talking trains, and William had said, 'The war's the thing now, not railways. Personally, I'm glad to be clear of them.'

Captain Quinn watched Oamer separate the pair. Then it was my turn to take a spill into the ditch we were accidentally making (for all the water in the field seemed to be running rapidly into our trench). Quinn climbed onto the horse with which he'd been equipped, saying to Oamer, 'In summer, Corporal, conditions here would have been very nearly ideal.'

After he'd departed, Oamer asked Andy and Roy Butler to give us all a demonstration of digging, which meant in practice that they gave each *other* a demonstration of digging. The first thing that told you they knew their way around a shovel was that they called it a blade.

'Tha needs ter clean t'blade,' Roy said to Andy.

'Aye?' said Andy, taking the role of the apprentice, and giggling back at Roy, 'Wha'ever fower?'

Roy then touched Andy on the shoulder, and half whispered, 'Ask me 'ow.'

''Ow,' said Andy. ''*Ow* do I clean it?'

Roy produced a wooden wedge from his tunic pocket, holding it up like a magician, which set them both laughing fit to bust. Oamer was looking at me and shaking his head, and Oliver Butler, who'd seen him do it, was scowling at both of us. But the twins were better at teaching digging than the army instructors. The main thing was to pat down the sides of the hole as you dug. Roy and Andy made a big thing of this, and turned it into a singing jig, which they performed while slapping with their shovels the sides of the trench. As far as I could make sense of the words, they ran along these lines:

'Batter 'em, flatten 'em,
Flatter 'em, splatter 'em,
Don't leave yer 'ole
'Til yer stuff's packed flatter 'n *that* 'n' mum.'

(Because as well as calling shovels 'blades', they called earth 'stuff'.)

The pressing question, it seemed to me, was: Are this pair actually dangerous? From the look on the face of William Harvey, he thought so, and I knew he'd spoken to Oamer about sleeping away from them in the barn.

Apart from digging, we were told off in pairs for sentry-go. A control point was made on the road leading onto Spurn consisting of three oil drums, two planks of wood and a charcoal brazier. Barbed wire was laid in the fields to either side. In this and the digging, we alternated with the other section from the battalion: we were Shift A, they were Shift B. Most of the traffic that came by was to help with the building of the railway along Spurn, construction of which had started from the opposite end – from the tip, Spurn Point.

The password was 'Skeleton'.

One morning, when I was doubled-up with Scholes, we were approached by a party of schoolkids from the villages of Kilnsea and its neighbour, Easington.

'Password,' said Scholes.

They didn't know it.

'Look here,' I said to the kid in the lead, '*is* there a school on Spurn?' (For we'd been told nothing about it.)

'Yes,' he said, 'otherwise we wouldn't be going there.'

I looked at Scholes, and he was standing with his eyes closed, as if he could transport himself elsewhere by so-doing. Scholes shouldn't have been a policeman, and he certainly wasn't cut out for a soldier. He was plum scared of going to France, I knew. He spent most of his guard turns staring out to the high ships and playing mournful tunes on the penny whistle that he'd brought with him in lieu of his flute. I let the kids through – if they were German spies, I would take the knock.

In fact, there *was* a school on Spurn, as we discovered when the master came along five minutes after. When that bloke had gone through, Scholes looked at the perfectly clear blue sky and said, 'A storm's due.' He'd heard this from one of the

B Shift men, who'd had it from the farmer they lodged with. Scholes then asked me what I made of Oliver Butler.

'Mmm . . . Tricky customer,' I said.

'Fascinated by you, he is. Always plugging me for particulars. What were you like in the police office? Were you up to the mark as a plain clothes man?'

'Snoopy bugger,' I said.

'And Dawson,' said Scholes, 'what about him?'

I said I considered him a thoroughly white bloke.

Scholes said, 'It's a bit weird being at close quarters with him. In York, I pulled him in twice.'

I asked 'What for?' but I already knew.

'Drunk and Incapable.'

'On the station?'

'Aye.'

'Has he ever mentioned it?'

'It's never come up, no. It's as if he's blotted it out of his memory.'

'Did he go away?' I asked, because you might get a week in a gaol for second time Drunk and Incapable.

'Fined thirty shillings the first time, forty shillings the next. The second time I had to blow the whistle for Fowler.'

'Resisted, did he?'

'Just a bit of lip, really. Not *much* more than that. Flower wanted him charged with assault, but I talked him round. Didn't seem worth getting the bloke lagged.'

Any other grade of railwayman would have been stood down for drunkenness, but the porters were all boozy, and known to be so. I reminded Scholes of the run-in the Chief and I had had with Dawson in the Bootham Hotel, and he said, 'Did you know he's been warned off half the pubs in York?'

'Well,' I said, warming my hands at the brazier, 'it's a good thing he doesn't hold a grudge.'

'But how do we *know* he doesn't?' said Scholes.

That evening, we were in our makeshift cribs in the barn, one oil lamp to every two men. Scholes was playing his whistle in the farmyard outside in the dark. He'd said the smoke from the brazier made his eyes smart, at which Bernie Dawson had muttered to me, 'You know, I don't think he's going to like the Western Front very much.'

We'd been warned by Oamer to expect news of a duty that would take us onto the actual peninsula for the first time. Meanwhile we were killing time, and listening to Scholes.

Young Alfred Tinsley, the next bloke along from me, was sucking a peppermint and reading the *Railway Magazine* – lost in it, he was. On the cover, I read 'Don't forget your friend in the services. Buy him a *Railway Magazine*!' I hadn't had that particular number yet. It would probably be waiting for me at Hull, the wife having sent it on from Thorpe. I was just then trying to write to the wife. In my last letter I told her that I was unable to disclose our location, and she'd written back saying, 'Would it be Kilnsea, East Yorks? Because that's what the postmark says.' I was now writing that it might be and it might not be, but she should keep in mind that incoming letters were soon to be read by officers as well as outgoing.

'Who are you writing to?' asked Oliver Butler.

'Mind your own fucking business,' I said.

'Everywhere one goes, the spirit of merry badinage in the air,' said Oamer, who'd just stepped into the barn. (Scholes had also come in behind him.)

'What's the special duty, Corporal?' came the voice of young William, who had his crib on the other side of wooden partition, next to Oamer's – his bolthole from the twins.

'Bide,' said Oamer.

This was the nearest he ever came to saying 'Shut up', and he was eyeing the twins, who hadn't yet left off with their secret whisperings. Presently, Oamer said, 'Be it known by all . . .'

which was his way of beginning an announcement. He then told us that the Spurn military railway very nearly was half completed.

'Oh good-o,' said Oliver Butler.

According to Oamer, it now ran from a railway pier at the tip of the peninsula to a spot somewhere in the middle. Tomorrow, we were to march to that spot, and there we'd board the train and be conveyed to the pier.

'That's a bit of all right,' said Alfred Tinsley, because here was a railway for him to look at.

'*Why* are we going to the railway pier, Corporal?' asked Oliver Butler.

'You are to unload a ship,' said Oamer, '. . . quite a small ship, you will be pleased to hear.'

Digesting this news, we all turned in for the night, and every lamp in the barn was soon extinguished except the one from Oamer's (and William's) side of the petition, which continued to burn low. Oamer would no doubt be writing to . . . well, whoever he wrote to.

I couldn't get off to sleep. I turned on my side; I heard a sort of grunt from the direction of Oamer, and then the noise hit. It did *hit* as well; the whole barn rocked, and every man instantly sat up. Every man was talking as well, but I couldn't make out a word; soft muffles seemed to fall from every mouth, even though I knew everyone was shouting. The Chief had once told me that a bloke in the Riflemen's Leagues at York had fired one of the big bore ones indoors without ear defenders. He burst both his ear drums, and the way he knew about it was that he couldn't hear the mechanism when he re-loaded the gun, and then he felt a tickling above his collar – the blood running down from his ears.

I put my hand up to my own neck, and there was no blood, but still my hearing wasn't right. After a space, the word being repeatedly spoken by Oamer, 'Bide . . . *bide*!' became clear, but it was no use against the shouting of the others, and one shout I heard above all: 'It's the bloody war,' said Scholes, 'it's come here . . . it's bloody come here.' Then the farmer came into the barn dressed in his night shirt with an Ulster coat slung over the top but no bloody trousers or underclothes on, so his privates were in plain view. In a right state, he was. Evidently half the windows in his house had smashed.

'What in hell's name's going on here?' he shouted at Oamer, but he'd been followed in by Captain Quinn, who addressed us while buttoning up his tunic. He would be riding down to the peninsula to make sure, but he believed that the Royal Engineers had fired one of their 9.2-inch guns – 'almost certainly not in anger', but merely to test it.

'Well, I'd say it was *working*,' muttered Dawson.

'Now if I'm wrong over this,' Quinn continued, 'and this *is* in fact a German battle group firing on us, then that puts a rather different complexion on matters . . .' We could rest assured he would be telephoning through to battalion headquarters from the Spurn redoubt directly.

He wheeled about and was gone, at which all eyes were fixed on Young William. He was sitting on the dusty flags and fighting for breath, just as though he'd run a mile at full pelt. Oamer made towards him, and the kid brushed him off, saying in an under-breath something like, 'Will you leave go of me?' in a way that could have landed him in very hot water indeed, if our corporal had been a different sort of person.

The Spurn railway terminated hard by a wooden hut that served as an officers' mess for the Royal Engineers. Someone had chalked a message on the bare wood of the shed door: 'Tom, Telephone down to Henry. Regards, Max', and that's the kind of set-up it was. The officers were easy-going blokes, more university professors than soldiers; they seemed to run Spurn like their own gentlemen's club.

The mess, and the temporary terminus, were bang in the middle of Spurn, in a part of it called the Narrows. There was beach at not more than thirty yards' distance on either side of the track. Just then the sea did not threaten the track, but I didn't fancy its chances in the event of any storm, such as that predicted by Scholes.

It was, in fact, a beautiful early-afternoon, the sea shining, two sailing ships off Spurn, both definitely not German destroyers. The day suited the cheery features of a certain Captain Leo Tate, who stood on the new-laid track, and addressed us as we sat on a sand dune. Our whole group was present save William, who'd been detailed to bicycle between the cottages and the farms around Kilnsea and Easington, giving out a schedule of the times when the Spurn gun would be tested again. He would then return to Cobble Farm in the evening.

Captain Leo Tate was a little older than me – somewhere in the middle thirties. He told us he'd been delighted to hear we'd been given this detail because he was from York himself. Well, he certainly didn't sound it. He was also a good friend of our own Captain Quinn's, both of them having been at St Peter's School, the Eton of the North. As he addressed us, Tate seemed fascinated by the sight of the twins, and kept sneaking sly looks at them.

'Did you know Spurn is eroding at the rate of a yard every year?' he began.

'Yes,' I heard someone say. (Probably Oliver Butler.)

Tate told us something of what he and his fellows had been about, adding that we would shortly see for ourselves. After talking for five minutes, he asked if we had any questions.

'What class of engines do you run on the railway, sir?'

It was Alfred Tinsley, of course.

'Well, you see our modest engine shed,' Quinn said, pointing to what looked like a glorified beach hut at the end of a siding a hundred yards distant. Steam *was* leaking from it, and more from the walls than the chimney. 'At present, it houses just the one locomotive,' Tate was saying. 'A Hudswell-Clarke standard, and I don't need to tell you men the specifications.'

Dawson leant into me, and said, 'He does need to tell *me*.'

'Outside cylinder 0-4-0 saddle tank,' I said, and Quinn heard and pointed at me, 'Quite right, there. Are you an engine man, fusilier?'

'I'm a railway policeman sir,' I said. 'Detective division.'

But Captain Leo Tate didn't seem to have heard me. He was looking along the line, with a big grin spreading over his features; then there came a gasp from Alfred Tinsley. Something was skimming towards us at a hell of a lick. It was two men sitting in something between a railway wagon and a yacht – for it was propelled by sails.

'What *is* it?' breathed Tinsley, and he was looking the question directly at Tate, even though a private soldier is not supposed to address an officer, but must wait until spoken to.

'Pump trolley converted by the addition of a lug sail,' said Tate, beaming, 'and these chaps are on a broad reach.'

Even he seemed amazed by the speed of it. When the thing came close it looked jerry-built, ridiculous, but you couldn't help liking the looks of the two blokes who stepped off it – two junior officers in the Tate mould: a pair of overgrown boy scouts. They put their funny little bug in a siding, and at that instant, the barking of steam was heard from the little engine shed, and the Hudswell-Clarke rolled out. 'Anyone fancy a footplate ride?' enquired Tate. Alfred Tinsley's hand was up directly. Mine would've been too, had I not been on my dignity. There were no other takers, but Tate pointed to me, asking, 'How about our railway policeman?'

The engine – which could have done with a clean – was a Standard 14, to be exact, that maid of all work, often to be seen at pit head and factory. It was still in North Eastern Railway colours, and had kept its name: *Lord Mayor.* We watched it collect an open wagon and take a drink from a water siding. Then we climbed up. It was a tight squeeze on the footplate, since Tate evidently proposed riding there too. The rest of the party climbed onto the open wagon, and all our packs and rifles were slung up there as well. We set off, with our smoke and steam darting crazily in the blustery wind that was getting up. But the sky remained a beautiful pale blue, with just two or three white clouds turning over and over.

'You can see half the world from here,' said our driver, a sergeant from his uniform, and evidently a poetic one. Captain Tate, not so poetic, said, 'Strictly speaking, Spurn is what's called a Sand Spit . . .' and started on another geography lesson. When he'd finished, I asked the sergeant whether the regulator gave gyp, since he did seem to have to wrestle with it. Tate, who'd learnt my name by now, said, 'You take a close interest for a railway policeman, Stringer.' I explained that I'd been trained up as a fireman, at which our own fireman stepped aside without a word, and handed me the shovel. I put a bit on, and it did go more or less where I'd aimed it. As Spurn Point was approached, I'd graduated to the regulator, and Alfred Tinsley was trying his hand with the shovel. Well, *Lord Mayor* was a pretty good steamer, and we were both practically wriggling with happiness just then (although I was trying to hide the fact).

We passed a small boy signalling a semaphore message with two flags much bigger than he was; very soon after, we passed the small girl he was signalling *to*. Tate informed us that the Spurn schoolkids practised semaphore every day. On our right hand side, the estuary side, was a new sea wall about two hundred yards long, and six feet wide on top. Iron bollards, mushroom-shaped for the tying-up of boats, were placed along its length, and I recall noticing that a length of rope ran from one of these into the water.

'That's where the sea does its worst!' Leo Tate called over

the beating of the engine. 'In the school they call it a promenade. Of course, technically it's a revetment!'

The end of our ride was the railway pier, and we took our engine onto it after collecting two more open wagons. The steamer was there waiting, just in from Grimsby, and bucking about on its moorings. Around the pier stood three gun batteries, with only one gun as yet in place – the one we'd already heard from. The other emplacements were signified by concrete dishes. There were the makings of what would be a signalling station; also shelters, magazines, workshops, and a largish wooden hut – about the dimensions of a village hall – with the words Hope and Anchor painted in giant white letters on one of its roof slopes. This was the RE boys' wet canteen. The name was another of their little jokes, the pub in Kilnsea being called the *Crown* and Anchor. At about twenty yards' distance from this stood the jakes, which took the form of one single outside lavatory, and another with washroom attached. Both were of a primitive appearance but were brick-built, and so more solid than the hutted village around them, having once belonged to a row of lifeboatmen's cottages that had stood on the site.

'You might think it looks like a shack,' said Tate, indicating the Hope and Anchor, 'but we have at present . . . I believe five barrels of John Smith's bitter in there. Since you're all here for the night,' he continued (which was the first we'd heard of it), 'you'll perhaps sample a glass or two yourselves.'

I eyed Bernie Dawson as Tate spoke. He looked his usual good-natured self, leaning with folded arms against the boiler frame of *Lord Mayor*, but I was thinking: we could be in for a bit of bother here.

As we commenced the unloading, the weather gods were putting on a good show. The clouds were mainly black, but there was a kind of light resembling golden smoke whirling underneath them.

That ship held a regular hotchpotch of goods, all too small to be lifted by crane – including shells that we carried one at a time, and very carefully even though the detonators weren't in. We didn't know much about shells as yet; I imagined we'd be getting better acquainted in France. As we worked, the wind rose, the pier stakes set up a fearful groaning, and the ship clattered against the side, making the gangplank a dangerous place to walk. Some of the stuff was to be loaded onto the train – which made two trips back up the peninsula as we worked – and some passed hand to hand along the length of the pier to the stores round about. We worked under the direction of another RE sergeant who apparently knew field telephones inside out, and so found a friend in Oliver Butler who would quiz him in between carrying jobs.

We worked right through to evening without a break, for the ship had to get back to Grimsby before the storm came. About five o'clock, by which time all the gold had gone from the sky, we saw the headlamps of a War Department van coming up to the Hope. It had driven the length of Spurn – which would've been fun for the driver, since there were no roads to speak of – and held the food for our suppers. (The same van, we were told, would be returning in the morning with our breakfasts.)

Come six o'clock, a fast rain was falling, but the storm hadn't quite got started. *Lord Mayor* was pulling away from the pier and moving fast, anxious to get away. All the RE blokes returned to their redoubt at the top end of the Narrows, and they'd taken Captain Quinn with them. He was to be wined and dined on the officers' table at some function in Kilnsea for every RE man on the peninsula, officers *and* other ranks. The entry point to the peninsula was being guarded by our opposite numbers, the B Shift. The arrangement of men on Spurn would be a matter of importance come morning.

I was one of the last ones off the pier, and into the Hope and Anchor. The main part of it was a hall with a stove and makeshift stage. There was pile of kindling next to the stove, and Alfred Tinsley was using it to get the fire going. I put my pack and my rifle where the other blokes had put theirs: on the stage. There was a regular warren of little rooms at the back of the hall, behind the stage, and we'd have one of these apiece for kip. After a bit of sluice-down in the jakes it was seven o'clock, and I was ready for my tea. As I walked back into the hall, young Tinsley – who looked odd with a pint in his hand – was talking to Scholes about our absent friend, young William.

'If he tells me one more time that throwing a bomb is easy as anything . . . I swear I'll brain him,' Scholes was saying.

Tinsley nodded: 'And if *I* hear one more time that story about how he had bad teeth, and was worried he'd be rejected as unfit for service, so he went to the flipping dentists, and they pulled them out for free so's he could do his patriotic duty . . .'

Oamer strolled over to them, pipe on the go, and Scholes asked him, 'What exactly is Harvey telling these farmers?'

'The times when the guns go off,' said Oamer.

'But what can they do about it? Clap their hands over their ears?'

'They've to open windows in their houses,' said Oamer, '. . . it's to equalise the pressure, you know.'

'He'll be popular,' said Scholes, '. . . weather like this.'

The place was village hall-like. I could just see the RE boys holding smoking concerts here. There was a piano on the stage; propped at the back of it was a giant mock-up of the Royal Engineers' crest, and our packs and rifles were clustered around that. On the front edge of the stage the beer barrels – branded with the word 'Smith's' – rested. Dawson was alongside them, superintending. I eyed him carefully; he looked all right so far. As a unit we'd drunk together only once before – at the abovementioned Crown and Anchor in Kilnsea – and on that occasion we'd put the peg in after two pints apiece.

There was a stove in the centre of the room, a pile of papers and a basket of coal next to it for fuel, our supper bubbling away in a dixie on top. Alongside this, a trestle table was loaded with cutlery and enamel plates; jumbled round about were little wooden chairs, some with newspapers on them. From the roof beams hung Union Jacks and hurricane lamps in alternation. There were chalk marks on the floor, which was gritty with sand; these marks had numbers next to them, for the playing of some game made up by the RE boys – and there was a hoops board on the wall nearby, with a full complement of hoops hanging from the hooks.

We all had a couple of pints before setting about the food. Alfred Tinsley served it out, and it was either soup or stew depending on what his spoon brought up. I asked Dawson, who'd spoken to the bloke who'd delivered it, 'What'd he say this *was*? I mean, did he give any clue?'

Dawson shrugged. 'He said it was "something in the way of grub".'

'That's a very good description of it,' I said.

I was already feeling slightly canned. The beer was John Smith's strongest variety, or had been made so by the way it was kept. Scholes was at the piano now, playing something slow and grand, which made a bit of a mockery of the clattering of cutlery as the blokes at the trestle table put away their stew.

'Liszt?' Oamer called over.

Scholes replied, 'Sonata in B minor – don't know it all.'

And he broke off in embarrassment.

'I've heard Egypt's on the cards for us,' said Oliver Butler, mopping his plate with bread, and eyeing every man in turn.

'*Egypt?*' somebody said, flabbergasted.

'Fighting the darkies.'

'What darkies?' Scholes called over, taking a pull from his glass before placing it on the piano top.

'*I* don't bloody know,' said Butler. 'Full of darkies, is Egypt. Some of them are Turkish. Overrun with the bloody *Turks* just at present, is Egypt.'

I was watching Oamer. He'd been smoking his pipe after his meal – his 'post-prandial' smoke, as he called it – but he now removed it from his mouth and stood. Dawson called out 'Bide!' on his behalf, and silence fell.

'Your conversation, gentlemen,' said Oamer, 'has anticipated an announcement that Captain Quinn has asked me to make this evening.'

Scholes shut the piano lid, and walked over to the trestle table.

'We *are* off to Egypt?' someone gasped.

'You are *off*', said Oamer, speaking in such a way as to prove he didn't normally use that word in that way, 'to France – because that's where the war is. And you are going next Thursday, when, after three days' home leave – '

(A small cheer at this.)

' – you will entrain from Hull to a sea port I am not at liberty to name, before proceeding to . . . somewhere I am also not at liberty to name in France.'

Oamer took two papers from his tunic pocket, and glanced down at the first, saying, 'Captain Quinn has asked me to read the following: "Tell the men that I wish them all a very happy time on leave, short though it is. I know they will honour the battalion and the brigade in France, and I hope they may all come through the whole war safely." He has also asked me to pass this amongst you.' So saying, he handed this second paper to Scholes, who looked at it with a face like yesterday. 'Captain Quinn will be here to address you himself in the morning,' Oamer continued. Then he looked at his watch: 'We turn in at ten o'clock, gentlemen.'

Silence in the room as each man figured his own picture of life at the front. Presently, the second paper came my way. It was a list, badly typed, giving further instances of North Eastern railwaymen serving with other battalions who'd shown valour in the field. One of them, a fellow called Arnold Hogg, I knew. He was a clerk in the York goods station. He was serving with the West Riding Royal Field Artillery, and he'd been awarded the French *Médaille Militaire*. It didn't say exactly what he'd done, but it must have been in aid of the French. At the presentation, a French Infantry Regiment had given him a guard of honour. I thought of Hogg: a big, round-faced bloke puffing and blowing as he rode his bike against the wind along Station Road. I could not imagine that guard of honour. Or at any rate, I could not imagine the blokes in it keeping a straight face.

I'd now had three pints and needed to drain off. I put on my cap, and opened the door of the Hope – with difficulty, for the wind was going all out to keep it shut. There was a great roaring that was either the sea or the wind, or both. The first lash of the rain nearly felled me and I was sodden by the time I reached the dark jakes. I knew there were candle stubs littered about in the place, but the flames had burnt out; the matches in my pocket were now useless, and there was no moon. The wind echoed strangely inside the brick cubicle, and made the sound of the flushing undetectable.

When I regained the Hope, a general chatter had started up again, and the twins were walking over to the hoops board. I watched them while drying at the stove. One of the pair – the brightest, Roy – made two chalk marks at the top of the little blackboard fixed alongside. These marks might have said 'Roy' and 'Andy', although not in a way generally recognisable. Roy took aim first. He threw three hoops. None landed on a hook, and after each one, Andy called out, '*Missed*, Roy-boy!'

Was this how the beer took the twins? (They'd put away as much as anyone save Dawson.) Or was it just their usual, wild way of going on? The queer thing was that they *were* both soon playing to a decent standard, and I recalled that they'd shown themselves decent marksmen at Alexandra Dock. (Well, it was known that platelayers, since they worked in the fields all day, spent half their time taking pot-shots at rabbits.)

Come nine-fifteen, Oamer was sitting on the edge of the stage with his pipe and a book, and Dawson, self-appointed custodian of the barrels, was filling glasses. The storm was blasting away outside. At the table, the topic of discussion was how the RE men would keep cases on the ships entering the Humber Estuary.

'They send a man out, don't they?' said Scholes.

'I wouldn't fancy that job,' I said, 'going up to a dirty great German destroyer in a little rowing boat.'

'But it might *not* be a German destroyer, remember,' said Alfred Tinsley.

'I suppose, if the blokes on the ship sink the bloke in the rowing boat, then that's a bit of a giveaway.'

We'd both gone a bit daft with the beer.

'Know nothing about signals, do you?' said Oliver Butler. 'They use a light. They ask for a password, just as we do here – only it's done by flashes.'

At quarter to ten, every man was dead drunk, especially Dawson, and his face had that peeved look it had worn in the Bootham Hotel, but so far he had kept his behaviour in bounds. He was observing young Tinsley: 'Thought *you'd* have turned in long since,' he said. 'Quite a stickler, ain't you, son?'

'Mmm . . . not *quite* the right word,' said Oamer, who had rejoined the table, and it might be that Dawson gave this remark the go-by (for it was certainly meant in a spirit of amiability), or it might be that he gave a rather narrow look to our over-educated Corporal. At this point, Oliver Butler stood, and fixed his cap on. He looked about the room, and picked up one of the newspapers. He was off to the jakes.

In drink, Tinsley had become even more of a railway nut, and he now started in about how, when he graduated to driving, he'd oil round his engines not only at the start of a run, but at all principal stations *on* the run. After a few minutes of this, Dawson, who'd made two visits to the beer barrel since Tinsley had started on his speech, looked over and said, 'Stow it, kid,' and I thought: right, he's *turned*.

I said, 'Lay off him, won't you?'

Dawson, who was walking over to the beer barrels yet again, turned and said, 'Watch it, copper. I'll stop the bloody clock on you.'

The room fell quiet at that, and there came only the sound of the storm. Scholes was eyeing me, looking apprehensive. I saw that Oliver Butler had returned, and that he was soaking wet but grinning by the door as he looked back and forth between Dawson and me. Dawson necked another pint rapidly as Oamer called, 'That's enough, Dawson. Time for some shut-eye.'

Dawson turned a questioning scowl on Oamer.

'Bed,' said Oamer.

'*Bide*,' said Dawson, shooting Oamer's favourite word back at him.

I said, 'Turn in, Dawson,' and it was a deliberate provocation, since I had no authority to order him anywhere.

'I don't see *your* fucking stripe,' he said.

Well, we were right back in the Bootham Hotel, with Oamer in place of the Chief. The difference was that the Chief could lay out any man. I walked towards Dawson; he walked towards me. I heard the ocean creaking, the wind ramming the walls, the strange whirlings of hot air within the stove. Part of me thought: I'll be in France within the week. I had my passage booked. Giant fucking Saxons will be waiting to put my lights out. For a certainty, one of them's going to succeed – and the condemned man doesn't have to take lip from anyone. As we closed, Dawson said, 'Here comes the constabulary,' and he was holding his pint glass in such a way that I couldn't tell whether he meant to drink from it or crown me with it. I ducked back; he ducked back; I came forward again with fists raised; Dawson came forwards likewise, but then he ducked *back* again for no good reason, slipped and cracked his head on one of the barrels.

'You'll pay for that, copper,' he said, and I was caught between laughing and looking out for a bit of assistance, because Dawson had smashed his glass in the fall, and he was coming at me with the jagged edge of it.

'You should never drink,' I said.

'It's the likes of you that drive me to it, copper,' said Dawson.

I looked down at my hands, and spat on them as we closed again. I didn't know why, but I'd seen the Chief do it. I put my fists forward, and the broken glass, which Dawson happened to be swinging at that moment whisked against the edge of my right hand. There was a line of blood over the two outermost knuckles. Dawson had seen it; he looked . . . I would say surprised. I don't believe any other man in the hall had noticed the blood, but a moment later it was just . . . people in motion, the room turning round, boots trampling on the broken glass, the roaring of the storm all around. I couldn't get a belt in at Dawson, and he couldn't get one in at me. The two of us were muffled by others . . . and it was Oliver Butler who was between us: Oliver Butler and Oamer, and I believed that even young Tinsley was involved. But it was Butler who'd come in first, and kept Dawson from me.

Dawson sat down on the edge of the stage, dazed, shaking his head. Oamer walked over to him, and a deal was struck between them. Dawson would have one more pint then go off. Meantime, Oliver Butler walked (dead straight, for he could hold his beer) over to his brothers, who were wrestling near the stove – which seemed to have been brought on by the sight of the other scrap. Butler said, 'Time for the boys to turn in now,' and a deal was struck there, too:

'One more go on t' 'oops, Ol,' said Andy, or Roy. (They called their brother 'Ol', his full name being too much of a mouthful in their rapid patter.)

The two hurried back to the board, and played again in the way they'd started out the last time. Andy pitched his three hoops as Roy yelled, 'Missed, Andy-lad . . . Missed Andy-lad . . . Missed Andy-lad,' then Roy started *his* turn. When the first hoop missed, and Andy shouted, 'Missed, Roy-boy!' Oamer held up his hands:

'We'll take the rest as read, I think.'

They paid him no mind, and completed the ritual. Oliver then asked them, 'Do the boys need to pay a visit?'

The pair clapped their caps on their heads, then one of them turned and opened the door. When they saw the storm, they both said 'Oh mother!' before dashing out into it with great enthusiasm. A few minutes later, they came back laughing (and sodden), and trooped off to the back rooms, with Oliver Butler following.

'Rum,' observed Oamer, who was standing near the stove, pipe in hand, and I wondered what it would take to stir him up. Nothing had done so far.

At quarter after ten, he and I put out the lamps, all except one, and when Oamer went off to his kip, I settled down by this remaining light with the *Yorkshire Post*, since I was too squiffed for *The Count of Monte Cristo*, which I had in fact yet to start reading.

But I couldn't concentrate, so I examined my cut knuckle. The cut would be practically gone by morning. My mind was full of thoughts of France. I stood up, rounded up the stray glasses and put them near the barrels on the stage. The stove was still burning, and the door was open. I closed it, in case sparks might blow out. Oamer had left the message from Captain Quinn about our posting, and the list of valorous railwaymen folded together on the table top, and I didn't touch those. I then made for the warren of rooms at the rear. The men slept on their groundsheets with greatcoats over, and folded tunics for pillows. I searched out an unoccupied room with a lit candle in my hand. All the doors were ajar, or not there at all, and it was like a little exhibition of sleeping men. Young Tinsley and Dawson were both well away in the first two booths, while Scholes slept with a sort of smile on his face – music running through his head, perhaps, and not thoughts of France. I'd not seen him smile since the day of his enlistment. One thing Oamer and Butler had in common: their quarters were neat, and they both kept hair brushes by their pillows. The next room was empty, and that was because the twins had shared, and they both occupied the next one along. They lay down next to each other, but were not asleep. They had *not* made pillows of their tunics, and their discarded uniforms lay in a trail between the door and where they lay. There was a candle stub between them, and as I looked in (neither saw me, I was certain of it), one of the pair blew it out.

'I see it's gone dark in here,' said the other.

'You can't *see* in the dark,' said the first, and that set them both spluttering with laughter.

My own room smelt of distemper; it held three pasteboard boxes full of old screws. It had a little window, too. I looked through it, and the storm was still there.

I was woken by the sound of a motor; I stood and walked over to the window. There was a guilty look about the weather, as though it was aware of having overdone it the night before. I wouldn't have been surprised to see the tangled wrecks of half a dozen ships on the sand, but there was only the gentlest breeze, a milkiness to the waters, and a War Department van pulling to a halt. It was the breakfast bloke from the farm. I was bursting for a piss, but otherwise feeling not too bad, considering. I pulled on my boots and walked out, past the gallery of sleepers. All the blokes seemed arranged as when I'd turned in, down to the trail of clothes leading between the door of the twins' room and the twins themselves.

The bloke had the back of his van open and the hot boxes were stacked in there.

'Want a hand bringing it in?' I said.

'Aye,' he said, in a thoughtful sort of way.

'Hold on, I'll just go to the jakes.'

Three minutes later we set about it.

'How's Cobble Farm?' I enquired, as we loaded the stuff onto the trestle table.

'Well, it's covered in shit,' he said. 'Otherwise I like it.'

Two empty beer glasses stood on the table. I thought I'd cleared the lot away the night before – I was *certain* I had done. Also, I had left the two papers – Quinn's message and the list of valorous railwaymen – together, but they were now separate on the table top.

'Bit blowy last night, eh?' the bloke was saying.

The stove door was open as well, yet I'd closed it the night before. It was all ashes in there – all except a scrap of paper at the front. I fished it out. There were printed words on it: 'London, E.C.', then, underneath, 'Telephone – 2087 HOLBORN'. The address was familiar, somehow. I looked up at the stage. All the kit bags and rifles were there as before.

'Oh,' the food bloke was saying, 'question from the sentry blokes up top: did the kid get here all right?'

'What kid?'

'Kid on a bike.'

'William Harvey? He's at the farm.'

'No, pal. *I* was at the farm, and I had the barn to myself.'

'He was meant to go there.'

'Well *he* thought different. He came by the sentry post here last night, or this morning anyhow – half past midnight sort of time. Said he was under orders to rejoin his unit after completing a special duty. He was on a push bike. Hold on . . . Did he not pitch up?'

The blokes were filtering in from the back rooms, putting on their tunics: Oamer, Scholes and Oliver Butler. A little while later came the twins and Alfred Tinsley, all fixing their caps on their heads. Roy Butler had a fag on the go. 'Anyone seen Young William?' I called out, and we went through it all again. He wasn't *supposed* to be here. When Dawson appeared, he admitted to feeling 'pretty cheap'; otherwise he was amiability himself. Had he seen William?

'No, mate, I've been asleep.'

Half an hour later, breakfast had been eaten at the trestle table, but Oamer did not feel able to light his pipe. By all accounts, nobody had seen the boy, or heard any disturbance in the night. All the blokes looked grave, except the twins, who were out of hand as usual, occasionally laughing. Quinn then appeared, together with his opposite number, Leo Tate. As they entered, Quinn was saying to Tate, 'And this morning not a cloud in the sky! Couldn't be more splendid!'

But the moment he saw us, he was in fits, and he told Oamer to fall us in. Quinn held a cap in his hand. It bore the badge of our battalion, and the man who'd lost it would find himself on a charge. Quinn had discovered the cap near the sea wall, or, as he put it, 'Captain Tate's revetment'. It was one of the small-sized ones, and it was a disgrace that no name was written inside it, but this was not such a disgrace really: every man was supposed to have written his name on the band of the cap, but the ink would be repeatedly wiped off by sweat. Quinn surveyed us. Every man present undoubtedly had a cap on his head. Quinn enquired, 'Corporal Prendergast, where's Private Harvey?'

So Quinn, too, had expected the lad to be with us.

'If I might have a word with you about that, sir,' said Oamer.

We were put at ease, and I heard snatches of the conflab. Oamer explained that the boy had come past the sentries in the small hours.

'Well yes, I know that,' said Quinn. 'The sentries told us all about it when Captain Tate, myself and the other officers came back from the village. He'd gone through a little while before.'

I thought: they must have been going some at Kilnsea, to be returning at that hour.

'He was under a misapprehension as to his orders, sir,' said Oamer.

'So it appeared to me,' said Quinn, 'so it appeared to me. But he's not here now, you say? How is that possible? Once on Spurn, he can't have left it. I mean, the only way off is via the sentries . . . except by *boat*, of course.'

He eyed Oamer sadly for a while, before saying, 'I think we'd better have a scout about.'

As Oamer was giving orders for the search, I saw Quinn looking down at the cap in his hand. He looked up and said to me – since my eyes just happened to meet his at that moment – 'You know, there's *blood* on the inside of this cap.' I thought of the bit of Latin on the cap badge. Oamer had translated it for me: 'Whither the fates call.'

Under the high blue sky, we combed the peninsula – us and the RE men both. We searched individually, so that every man was alone with his thoughts, and I wondered how many were inclining my way – towards a suspicion of foul play.

I searched both sides of the peninsula up towards the Narrows, and there were two more of the kids from the school practising semaphore. I watched, mesmerised, as they whirled their great red flags into position and then froze, blank-faced, before whirling them into a different position.

It was about half after midday when I heard the first shout, which came from Scholes. He'd found the bike – it had evidently been lying in a dune a little way inland of the revetment.

We all had a look at it for a while, leaving it in place for whoever would be investigating (our regimental military police, as I imagined). Then, on Quinn's orders, we spread out again for a further search.

The second shout went up half an hour later, and it came from Oamer, who'd been walking along the revetment. He was bending over and looking into the sea. He bent rather than crouched – bent as a woman does, and I could see his great, khaki-covered arse. Walking fast over the dunes towards him, I thought: you don't normally look at the sea in that way. Oamer was making rather a dainty inspection, of the sort more suited to the examination of frog spawn in a village pond; he was next to one of the iron bollards, the one with a length of rope attaching to it. I followed the rope with my eye as I took up position next to Oamer, and looked where he looked.

In the water, the rope held the just-submerged body of Harvey by virtue of having twisted itself once around his middle. It held him with no effort in the beautifully clear water, which slopped against the sea wall in a relaxed and casual sort of way. The motion of the waves would carry Fusilier Harvey two feet or so away from the wall, then two feet back – out and back, out and back, but never more than two feet either way. Oamer was saying nothing, but breathing hard, either because he was concentrating, somehow, on the body in the water, or just because he was not in the peak of condition. Five minutes later, we had the entire unit around us, and Harvey was stretched out on the sea wall.

The twins, between them, said:

'Oh . . .'

'Muth . . .'

'Ah . . .'

So making 'Oh mother' their favourite expression.

Harvey was very dead, and had apparently been given a new head. He looked to have been clobbered mightily at least twice, for he had the appearance of a sort of a bug. His left eye was black and swollen, and the right one was quite lost in a bulge of purple-coloured flesh, from which the lashes sprouted at wrong angles, so that it was like a kind of anemone. This eye, which had winked at me, was now locked in a *permanent* wink, as though Harvey had just let on the biggest secret of all. As for the rest of him . . . all that seemed smaller; and the seawater seemed to me to be acting upon him even as he lay on the dry stones, shrinking him fast before our eyes.

Of the kid's pack, rifle and cap there was no sign.

He was the first casualty of the battalion. Would he figure in the roll of honour? Could it be said that he'd died in the course of duty?

Come two o'clock we were all back in the Hope, drinking tea – all save Quinn, who'd gone off with Tate to make telephone calls. Fried bread and jam was going for those that wanted it, but at first nobody did. People seemed minded to avoid the subject of the actual corpse, so it fell out that Scholes was the star turn, telling everyone about how he'd turned up the *bike* . . . Practically tripped over it, he had. It had been half buried in the sand, which Scholes reckoned must have been wind-blown sand. The events of the morning seemed to have galvanised him. Perhaps they'd come as a distraction from thoughts of France, or was he just glad not to have copped it himself?

With his pipe in his mouth, but not lit, Oamer called me over to him.

'You're a detective,' he said, now examining his pipe, 'what do you make of it? Confidentially, I mean.'

'The essential data . . . ' I said. 'Our lot were the only men on Spurn when William pitched up. There's been no lifeboat crew since the military came here; the school is the only civilian operation – it's a day school and no one lives on the premises. I don't believe any boat could have landed in that weather. As far as I know all the RE men went up to Kilnsea last night. Their story is that when they came back, the sentries mentioned that the kid had come by. That was none of their affair, and they went directly to their billets and to sleep. The story from this end is that all the blokes were in by bed by half after ten. I can verify that, since I was the last one to turn in. Every man says he slept through the night, and saw nothing of the kid.'

'You think *Dawson* slept through the night?' enquired Oamer.

It was the obvious question, given what had gone on the night before.

I said, 'He seemed dead to the world when I turned in.'

'Anything else?' said Oamer.

I didn't mention that, whatever the situation at ten-thirty, it seemed unlikely to me that no man had got up in the night to visit the jakes or, more likely, take a piss directly outside the door of the hut.

'If the bike had been on the sea wall,' I said, 'there might be grounds for thinking Harvey had tried to ride it along there, and come off it.'

I didn't want to say that the kid might have made away with himself by *jumping* in the sea, because that seemed even more of a slander than suggesting he'd be thick-headed enough to bike along the revetment in a storm. There was a small chance he *might* have jumped though (smashing his head against the wall in the process), because he was in a funk about going to war. It might be that he'd been the one who disturbed the papers on the table. Perhaps he'd read of our posting, and of the plucky railwaymen, and knew he wasn't up to the mark.

Scholes had made a start on the fried bread, which had been prepared by the van driver. He – Scholes – was also scared of going to war, but at least he was open about the fact. He went glooming about the place, but the other blokes didn't mind that. It made them feel braver. William, on the other hand, with his talk of what he was going to do to the Hun, which everyone knew was complete rot – he annoyed most of the blokes. I didn't see how any of it could lead to murder, but I could see how it would lead to rows.

For example, Scholes: being a bit yellow himself, he particularly resented the kid's war-like talk.

As for Tinsley: he and William were rivals – two young bloods – and made no secret of it.

Bernie Dawson? Sober, he was the straightest of fellows, and good company with it. Drunk, the man was a liability, and he *had* been drunk, and spoiling for a scrap before lights out.

The twins? They seemed at times a pair of wild men, barely kept in check by their older brother. Their feelings about William, or any other matter, were a mystery to me, but William had certainly been unnerved by them.

Oliver Butler . . . He seemed to have *me* in his sights, not William Harvey. When he'd come to my aid against Dawson, I'd thought that might indicate a change in our relations, but evidently not. At any rate, he was glaring at me from over near the stove at that very moment. But I didn't see what he could have against Harvey. The kid would be beneath his notice.

I kept all this back from Oamer, together with the disturbance of the papers on the table; the beer glasses; the door of the stove. Somebody – or two people, in view of the glasses – had been up in the night, and that was fact. Why did I keep all this back? To give me time to think, and out of loyalty to the section. I would be fighting alongside these men in France within a matter of days. Also because . . . well . . . was the fellow questioning me above suspicion? Who *did* Oamer write his letters to, not being a married man, and having, as far as was known, no sweetheart? And why wasn't he an officer? What kept him back? Was it something known to the army brass? All his usual jollity seemed to have drained out of him as he stood before me.

The glare Butler was sending my way had redoubled. He

didn't like to see me so thick with the NCO.

'Another thing,' I said. 'Did the kid come past the sentries with his pack and his rifle?'

'His pack's still at the farm; that's where it was left, as arranged. On his bike he carried his rifle and his haversack, with a bite to eat in it and a map of the farms. He had both on him when he passed the sentries.' Oamer was still examining his pipe, as though it belonged to another man altogether. 'It's going to be the devil of a job to get to the bottom of this,' he said. 'Half the battalion's already in France, and we'll be there ourselves in no time.'

What he meant, I thought, was that a lot more deaths were coming, in comparison with which the present one would no longer signify.

'That's this war all over,' I said, without quite knowing what I meant.

'One trouble compounds another,' said Oamer.

I fancied that I saw water in his eye, and it occurred to me that he and I had been the only two in the unit not openly hostile to Harvey. The kid liked army types – not pressed men, so to speak, and not railwaymen. I was 'army' in that I was a copper. (Yes, plain clothes, but the Chief *would* parade us every once in a while on the main 'Up' platform of York station, much to the amusement of the other blokes.) Oamer had been in the Territorials, and was an NCO. He was a military man in spite of not looking the part; in spite of not being naturally suited to it. Harvey was perhaps a similar case in that he'd gone into a world where bravery was all in spite of not being overly brave. That took courage. He'd worked hard at keeping up an illusion – which, perhaps, accounted for that water in Oamer's eye.

Butler, Scholes, Dawson and Tinsley were near the stove. All had now made a start on the grub. The twins sat on the edge of the stage. Andy was playing with his rifle in a gormless sort of way, and Roy was smoking.

Butler addressed every man in the room – although he was eyeing me in particular – as he said, 'What do we think then, boys? Suicide?'

Dawson nodded to himself. Scholes did likewise, muttering, 'Made away with himself, that's it.'

Tinsley said nothing. He was inspecting his cap. On the stage, Roy Butler stared straight ahead, and continued to smoke as his brother – larking about – repeatedly banged him on the arm with the butt of his rifle. A great engine roar came from beyond the window. The breakfast van was starting up, and taking William Harvey back to Hull, along with the empty food boxes.

Thorpe-on-Ouse and York

I arrived back at our house in Thorpe late in the evening. Only a few chinks of light showed in the village, and both the pubs were closed even though it was not yet ten o'clock. On walking through our front door, my first duty, after kissing the wife, was to be taken into the children's bedrooms. They had been expecting me, and would on no account go to sleep until I arrived. Harry climbed out of his bed, and met me in the hallway, holding a candle.

'Dad,' he said, 'what do you think of *The Count of Monte Cristo*?', asking the question as though it was a matter of the greatest urgency and importance, and the trouble was that he'd actually read it himself, after a fashion, and been very taken with the whole idea of it.

I ruffled his hair, and said, 'Ask me another', and he didn't see the joke at all, but just walked away.

I followed the boy into his room, saying I was saving the book for France, at which he bucked up slightly. His room was fuller of books than I remembered. Harry was shaping up as an intellect. I went through to Sylvia's room; she was half asleep. She opened one eye, and, looking at me rather narrowly, said, 'I've been talking to Daisy Backhouse about you.' Daisy Backhouse was the daughter of Lillian and Peter. 'She says your best bet is to get wounded.'

'Really?'

'Quite badly. Then they'll send you home.'

'Tell Daisy Backhouse she's being far too gloomy, and she doesn't know what she's talking about.'

'I might tell her the first part,' Sylvia said, and then: 'Give me a kiss anyway. I'm rather tired.'

'She seems to have become rather a cool customer since I saw her last,' I said to the wife, as she turned down the gas on the landing.

'It's how she hides her feelings,' said the wife, who, after having a last look in at Harry, returned to the Count of Monte-bloody Cristo. 'You *have* had it for a year, Jim; it *was* a special edition and he did buy it with his own money.'

Later, in our own bedroom, the wife made herself available to me. Well, she was doing her bit for morale, but it was an awkward business, which might have gone off better had she produced my coming-home present – two bottles of Smith's purchased at the employee's preferential rate at the Co-Operative Stores – before rather than after. As we sat side by side on the bed, she let on that, what with half my wages (which the North Eastern Railway was paying at the full rate), the separation allowance, and her own pay from the Women's Co-Operative Guild, she was better off than ever. So there were no worries on that front. She then asked me about life in the billets.

I said, 'On Spurn Head, you mean?'

'So that's where you were?'

'You better forget I said that.'

I told her what had happened to Harvey, angling the account to make it look like suicide.

'The poor boy killed himself,' she said obligingly, then, 'I'm not going to think about it any more.'

She started talking about her own work. She herself was still in favour of the war, so she wasn't a peace activist exactly, but the concern of her committees was that the war should be fought 'fairly'.

'What does that mean?' I said, and she told me it meant that men or their wives should not lose out by enlisting, and that the food price rises should be kept in check. She had also helped to set up – together with the Church of England Men's Society (or some such outfit of do-gooders) – a 'Soldiers and Sailors Buffet' in an old carriage that had been shunted into place at the bay platform number eight at York station.

I said I didn't like the sound of the Church of England Men.

'Why ever not?' said the wife.

'There ought not to be any of them left. They ought all to be in France.'

'Their average age is fifty.'

'Oh.'

'And some of them are *awfully* handsome, considering.'

This, I knew, was my cue to have another go at love-making; and a more satisfactory result was obtained this time.

The next day, I went into town with the wife, and she marched me straight up to Walton's, the outfitters on Parliament Street, where they had mannequins in the window showing officers' service dress. Officers, the wife informed me, were able to choose their own colours for their shirts and ties, within reason. She'd been in and asked about this. She thought the set in the window would suit me. It was labelled 'Mustard'.

'But I'm not an officer,' I said.

'But you will be.'

It was a bright day, if cold, and York seemed full of slackers. Of course, it always *had* been, but you noticed them now there weren't supposed to be any. They'd all have some tale about why they'd put off joining the colours; special circumstances would have urged them to hold back: 'I'm worried about me old mum, you see. She can't be left for a minute.' The usual loungers stood at the gates of the Museum Gardens, smoking away, and not in the least put out by the sight of men going past in uniform, because there were plenty of those, York being a garrison town. All the pubs were open, I was relieved to see, but they had funny little notices posted on their doors, these being to do with new regulations of the York Licensing Justices. They would be closed by nine – and this was why Thorpe-on-Ouse had been dark the night before. The shops were all trading normally, if anything looking busier than before. There were more flags about, but fewer horses (horses had been commandeered) which meant more motor vehicles. I looked at the city in a different way. The Victorian War memorials meant something more to me now. In truth they made my stomach lurch, and the beauty of the whole place, with its picturesque buildings, chiming churches and festive air seemed something precious, something that might soon be lost, or lost to me at any rate. The cocoa smell was in the air from the chocolate factories, and that too made me feel nervous, but then it always had done for some reason. The scene in every street reminded me of the postcards sold from Field's, the stationer in Stonegate, which showed York scenes and were all inscribed 'Old York', whether they showed the particularly old buildings or not.

On Ouse Bridge, I spied Black Leonard, the darkie who advertised pleasure cruises on the vessel called *The River King*, which was known as *Black Len's Barge*, and was the only pleasure cruiser to run all year round. Black Leonard wore his sandwich board as usual, giving the prices, and at the bottom was a new notice, 'Wounded Soldiers Go Free'.

The wife looked with approval at that. It was 'only fair'. As we turned into Coney Street, she told me that the Co-Operative ladies were proposing to dig up the cricket pitches of the city, so as to grow food for the returning and wounded soldiers. I said, 'I think they'd rather watch the cricket'. But the wife knew nothing of cricket. If a man knew as little about Women's Co-Operation as the wife knew about cricket she'd be down on him like a ton of coal.

On Coney Street, a bill for the *Press* read 'N.E.R. BATTALION MEN OFF ON ACTIVE SERVICE', which somehow gave the impression that we were all dead *keen* to be off. I didn't buy the paper. It would be all about the successful conclusion of operations at Gallipoli, just as though the object of the attack all along had been to retreat. I stood and watched the traffic of blokes going in and out of Sinclair's, the tobacconist. That was the Chief's favourite shop, but I did not want to strike the Chief on my ramble about the city; I wasn't up to hearing him talk of the new machine guns. I would come back and see him when I had a decoration or a commission.

The next day was my appointed one for rejoining the battalion, and the wife accompanied me to the station in the early afternoon. Here again, I avoided the Chief – in fact, the police office seemed closed down entirely – and the wife offered to show me the famous Soldiers and Sailors Buffet on platform eight. I of course had my uniform on, so the ladies inside were pleased to see me, and to serve me tea and a bun, which I did not want, having lately eaten sausages and fried potatoes in Thorpe-on-Ouse, but they were *particularly* keen to see Lydia, who talked to them all until my train time.

We naturally had a bit of a choky moment as I leant down to her from the carriage window. With the train pulling away, she called out, 'I'll send you a hamper, Jim!' I believe because it seemed to her the safest thing to say just then.

PART TWO

France

Albert: December 1915

We went round the houses to get to France: Southampton to Le Havre (a four-hour Channel crossing) as against the holiday-makers' route, Dover to Calais (two hours).

Dover to Calais, Oamer said, was 'taken', what with all the men and supplies going over every day. Oliver Butler, who was sick on the steamer, moaned about it, and Oamer (who recommended a pipe for seasickness) said, 'Anyone would think you wanted to get there fast.'

But there wasn't much talk on the way. The day before leaving Hull, we'd all been questioned in the adjutant's room on the ship *Rievaulx Abbey* by the regimental police of the battalion. These were a couple of quiet NCOs who seemed embarrassed at the whole business. One of them – a bloke called Brewster or Baxter (he was not the sort whose name stuck) – went so far as to say that he felt sorry for us chaps. He and his mate wore the letters 'MP' in red on black brassards, but didn't have the red cap covers that marked out the Military Mounted Police as men to be feared. Captain Quinn had sat in on the questioning as our 'accused adviser'. None of us had yet been accused, but this term was rather anxious-making. Also, we had been told that the case papers would be passed *on* to the Military Mounted Police for their consideration. There would be no public inquest, the military activities going ahead on Spurn being hush-hush, but we were informed that an army doctor had found the cause of death to have been a blow to the head, or rather to the eye. It was admitted on all sides that Harvey might have jumped, or fallen, into the sea, and then been clashed against the sea wall. He might have collided with an iron ladder that was fixed to it, before becoming entangled in the stray length of rope. This theory was favourite among the section – or so we all pretended.

As far as I knew, no man had yet admitted being up in the night. I myself said little more to the regimental police than I had to Oamer in the Hope and Anchor. I did not try to cast suspicion on any man. I admitted the tussle with Dawson, but made light of this as far as possible: 'Horseplay. We were just larking about. I admit we'd had a drink taken.' I did mention that I had gained a cut on my knuckle in the skirmish, although I held off from saying exactly how.

But Quinn, like Oamer, had been mindful of the fact that I was a trained detective, and after saying, 'It's all too perplexing' over and over, had taken me into his confidence: 'What about Private Dawson?' he said. 'Apparently the man fights like a tiger when drunk.' I made some remark of a neutral kind.

Marching us off the ship, Oamer had assured us that the matter did not seem to merit further investigation, and that Quinn believed it would not come to anything; that he would do his best to write down the death as a suicide.

At Le Havre, early in the afternoon, it was snowing on the grey docks, but as fast as the snow came down it melted. The troop train we boarded was made up of coaches from every system in France – not their best specimens either, but we'd heard that many blokes had gone to the front in horse wagons, so we were better off than some.

'It's vestibuled throughout,' said Tinsley, as we found a compartment.

'But springless,' said Oamer, as we creaked away from the station, almost directly on boarding. I was sitting with Oamer (with pipe, poetry book and magazine), Tinsley (with notebook on knee, observing the railway scene), Scholes (who sat silent), and a reasonably cheery Dawson. Presently, Scholes and Dawson seemed to doze. At intervals, Tinsley would make a note and a remark, usually to do with railways. The trains we passed seemed to be civilian-operated, but approaching Rouen, Tinsley twice observed 'Hospital train', and the second time, Scholes stirred and shook his head sorrowfully. Tinsley also made a note whenever he saw one of 'ours' – that is, the engines run by the Railway Operating Division of the Royal Engineers.

When there was nothing to see but dull, flat fields under grey sky and falling rain, Tinsley said, 'Look at that farmer – funny sort of cart he's got.'

'He's a peasant, in fact,' said Oamer.

I happened to have writing paper and one of the franked army envelopes on me, and I had the idea of killing a bit of time writing a letter to the Chief, since I was feeling rather guilty at not having looked him up in York. In the letter, I explained briefly what had happened on Spurn, and told him I thought any promotion would be held back as a result. I suppose I was half hoping he'd step in on my behalf, but I knew he didn't really have any authority to do so.

At a spot called Romescamps, there was a great military siding, and I pointed out some North Eastern Railway engines to Tinsley.

'I wish we could go slower through here,' he said.

'We're going slowly enough, mate,' said Dawson, who'd now stirred.

Just then we lurched to a halt in a mass of sidings.

'This is likely to be a two hours' business,' said Oamer.

He said he was getting out to stretch his legs. He had a letter of his own to post, and offered to take mine, so I addressed it: 'Chief Inspector Weatherill, York Station Police Office, York, Yorkshire, England' and handed it over. I noticed that he paid no attention to the address as he took the letter.

In fact, we were only one hour at Romescamps, during which Tinsley and I climbed down, and looked over the wilderness of rainswept sidings. Tinsley was very taken by the French engines. 'Look at that!' he'd say, 'Square funnel! What I wouldn't give to have a camera just now.'

I told him he'd very likely be shot if he started taking pictures here. We both saluted as we passed Captain Quinn, who'd also climbed down from the better class of carriage in which he'd been riding. He was speaking to some of his fellow officers, and I heard him say, 'I believe it's snowing heavily in Scotland at the present time.'

When we climbed back up, I reported this remark to Dawson, who said, 'Snowing heavily in Scotland, eh? That's *unfortunate*.'

Oamer came in on the joke, saying, 'Captain Quinn does have a penchant for that word. But over here it's going to have to be in French, thus *malheureusement*.'

Dawson shook his head, saying, 'Don't see him getting his chops around that.'

We set off again, and Tinsley said to Oamer, 'We're for Albert, aren't we?' which he pronounced like Queen Victoria's husband.

'Whatever makes you think that?' said Oamer, for our destination had not been officially disclosed. But Tinsley's habit of cocking his ear to every rumour where the subject was railways had paid dividends, and he blurted it all out, as Scholes listened, horrified.

Albert, Tinsley said, was a 'rather forward' railhead. It was in the Somme department of France, and had taken a lot of punishment from shellfire, but was still heavily populated by French civilians and Tommies both. We were approaching it from the south-west, via Amiens. It was not possible to approach it from the north-east, via Arras, which would have been quicker, because the line between Arras and Albert had been cut by the German advance.

'Hold on,' said Scholes, 'how far is Albert from the front?'

'About three miles,' said Oamer, who by his answer told us that everything Tinsley said had been true.

In the light of this knowledge, silence fell again for a while.

We were slightly bucked by the sight of Amiens station. There were plenty of soldiers but plenty of civilians as well, and some very pretty samples of French womanhood.

'Look like cats they do, the French doxies,' said Dawson.

'And is that a good thing?' enquired Oamer.

'It is to my mind,' said Dawson.

But I believed Oamer to be indifferent on the point.

The next station was all army, however. It had no name, but Tinsley knew it for a spot called Corbie. Two minutes after we pulled out, we saw a wrecked cottage. After a few more of the same, Dawson said, 'House roofs seem to be at a premium around here.'

It wasn't just the houses; the trees were broken too, and the fields under the darkening sky were fields of mud, with clusters of ponds everywhere – ugly black ponds that might have held monstrous creatures. We came through another mass of sidings, and beyond these were whole *crowds* of wrecked buildings, as if they'd all banded together out of sympathy with one another – a wrecked town, in fact.

'Albert,' said Oamer.

'Jesus Christ,' said Scholes.

Albert station had survived, which only made it look the more ridiculous. You thought: why does this place merit a station? Why don't the trains just go on until they come to a proper place? As I climbed down, with the engine blowing off up front, and all the blokes shouting, I saw that the station building was like a town hall, with a clock tower, and the time on the clock was about right: six p.m. But that was the only thing that *was* right. At the sight of this place, I was scared shitless but I wasn't about to lie quaking on the ground. The only thing to do was muster around the 'E' Company sergeant major as directed. After we'd told off into our companies, a silence fell. The engine had stopped blowing off steam, and was now simmering; all the slamming of doors had stopped. A new noise could be heard, and every man was listening to it. This was the most infernal and continuous crashing, screeching, howling. In this noise there was everything bad: old ladies screaming, mighty waves breaking, whole train crashes happening out of sight in the sky.

'Hold on a minute,' said Scholes, who was standing alongside me, a look of horror on his face.

Two minutes later, we were marching, in extended order, towards the noise. Oliver Butler was behind me. 'Got the collywobbles, Private Stringer?' he called out. 'It's got me spooked, I don't mind admitting.'

His brothers were alongside him. As a great jabbering arose amid the stream of din, I glanced back at them. 'Oh mother,' they said in unison . . . Only they were laughing at the same time.

We went first through the centre of Albert. It wasn't a ghost town because – Tinsley had been right – the ruins were all rampacked with Frenchers and soldiers. It was as though everyone had decided: *All right, the place is wrecked, but let's pretend it's not.* In what appeared to be the central square of Albert, a lorry rumbled past us with trailer attached. The trailer was full of Tommies, and one of them called out, 'Just arrived mate? Rather a hot shop, this is.'

And it *would* be Scholes that he'd spoken to. Scholes was breathing too fast.

'I'm not good here,' he said, 'I'm strained all to pieces.'

I was thinking it would have been well worth jumping in

the sea off Spurn to avoid, but I said, 'It's not like this all the time, you know', and as we approached the noise it was changing, the screaming din being replaced by periodic bangs, with sometimes the more continuous noise of a machine gun, like a sort of virtuoso player in an orchestra. All the while, the sky would continually change colour, from a deep blue, to green, to red, and back.

We left Albert behind, guided by Oamer and the battalion billeting officer. This bloke was coming with us rather than any other unit because we would be in the furthest billet, the one nearest the front, and I thought: is this deliberate? Are we being put in harm's way because, after what happened on Spurn, we're considered a liability? Were the Brass, or the regimental police, trying to 'sweat' us, so that a confession or an accusation might emerge?

We went along rough chalk roads that shone with a moonlike glow in the darkness. Some of the fields were ploughed, as far as I could make out, but others contained upended or broken carts, as though the farmer had suddenly come to his senses and fled the district. There were more of the ponds I'd seen from the train, and I seemed to make out black flying things skimming back and forth across them, like evil sprites or spirits. At one point, I thought, we are now entering a wood, but the wood never came *on*. We just kept walking through widely spaced, broken trees.

We were still in the wood, if that's what it was, when the billeting officer came to a halt. He indicated a large building and a small one, the only survivors of a group of ruins. He said, 'You're barely a quarter mile from the reserve trenches, so it's pretty well sniped by the whizzbangs.'

'Nice,' said Dawson.

At that moment, I wanted to get my head down, no matter where. I turned towards the main building, and saw in the moonlight a French word, or part of one, painted in a sort of red, fairground lettering. The word was: 'T–VERNE'. Dawson was looking the same way. 'There's an "A" missing,' he was saying, frowning; then he turned to me with a grin. 'It's a pub, mate!'

We went inside and got some hurricane lamps lit. It *was* a pub, of sorts: there was a bar, with posters of some strange-shaped green bottles behind it (although no actual bottles). The place was filled with a petrol-like smell, and the floor crowded with furniture – couches and cupboards mainly, that had perhaps been rescued from the ruins round about. In one corner was a trapdoor leading down to a cellar. Dawson was all for kipping down there, but the billeting officer, addressing Oamer, said that if a five-nine hit us directly we were done for anyway. There was no food in the place. That would come in the night, we were told, together with our trench kit. Meanwhile we had our water bottles, and Oamer handed out some hard biscuits. He made a sort of cubbyhole for himself behind the bar, and rest of us lay on the floor at crazy angles, one couch and one cupboard apiece.

I was asleep in an instant, and I dreamt of a ghost train. A train made of light, and not running on rails, but flying through the air at a great speed. I woke with a start when the noise of its chuffing became faster than was possible, and I sat up on my couch. The noise was still there. Scholes was staring across at me, mortified. The twins were awake and listening too, both with heads propped on hands. They had two candle stubs burning between them. One said to the other: 'Heavy shower's coming.' Lined against the wall beyond them were picks and shovels, and other bits of kit that had not been there when I'd turned in. I noticed an opened window. All this I saw in less than a second. The shell hit, and the ghost train crashed, leaving a darkness and a ringing in my ear. The concussion had blown out the candles. I heard Oamer's voice, quite steady from behind the bar: 'Speculative, I would say. Back to sleep, boys.'

If I did sleep, then I was woken soon after by another noise. Sitting upright, it took me a second to work out what it had been. It was a fart. One of the twins had let one go, and was putting his head under the blanket to sample the smell.

'It's quite a stifler,' he said, making a surprisingly good job of putting on an officer-like voice. I looked at him – I believe it was Roy – and he most unexpectedly met my eye across the dark room, and spoke back: 'What are you gaumin' at?'

He looked tough as nails just then, and I thought: this pair spook me no end; I wouldn't mind if a shell put their lights out before too long. I eyed Roy, who'd gone back to larking with his brother; then came a machine gun rattle. There was no dream about it; the war was still there, a quarter of a mile off. It had introduced itself to us the night before, and now waited for us to pay a call.

An hour later, with bacon, bread and tea inside us, we approached the trenches, Oamer in the lead. He told us that we'd been guarded in the night by sentries from the battalion, but from now on we'd be doing our own sentry-go. Battalion HQ was near a spot called Aveluy. Our billet, the tavern, was near a spot called Méaulte. Captain Quinn was at battalion HQ, looking for a horse. He would be joining us that evening.

'That's if we live 'til then,' Scholes put in.

We walked slowly along the white chalky road in the grey light. It was still far too early in the bloody morning. We walked slowly mainly on account of the waders that came right up to our arses. You'd think we were fishermen except that we carried picks and shovels in place of rods. Our rifles were on our backs. We carried our haversacks and not our packs; we'd also been issued with tin helmets, respirators against gas, and ammunition. We'd put all this kit on in silence, unquestioning. Normality had gone completely out of the window.

Oamer turned about, saying, 'Voices down, boys. We're in machine gun range now.'

I thought of the Chief on Station Road, talking to me about how the Germans didn't bother with rimmed cartridges, which made their machine guns all the more efficient.

'Everything just keeps getting worse,' Scholes whispered to me, and he was obviously in a terrible state.

Right on cue, a machine gun rattle started up. But we were beginning a descent . . .

'Is this a trench?' enquired Tinsley.

'Yes,' said Oamer, as we all began to walk bent double, 'that's why you're alive.'

It was more like a little valley cut by a beck – a natural formation – but then I saw sandbags on top on either side. The machine gun rattle came again.

'But where's the enemy?' said Tinsley.

'Don't be so fucking naive,' snapped Oliver Butler. 'This is a communication trench. You're at right angles to him.'

We intersected first with the reserve trench, then the support trench. The first of these seemed deserted; the second held a few men sitting on shell boxes eating breakfast. I saw a man drinking from a Rowntree's fruit gum tin, and he gave me – or more likely young Tinsley – a wink as we went past. He must be a Yorkie! But then I recalled that Rowntree's fruit gums were sold all over Britain, and not just in the city of their making.

I asked Oamer, 'Who are this lot?'

'First West Kents,' he said.

We pressed on along our ditch, and presently intersected with another trench.

'What's this one?' asked Scholes. 'Is it the front line?'

Well, I knew that trenches came in threes, and we'd already

passed the reserve and the support, so the front was all that remained, but Scholes had a look of panic about him, so I said, 'Seems quiet anyhow', and there were in fact no guns or artillery to be heard just then.

Oamer was talking to a sergeant. Men were dotted along the fire step of the trench, but this couldn't have been the morning 'stand to' that we'd all heard of, since half of them were sitting down. Oamer, having finished his conflab with the sergeant, sent me, Scholes and the twins one way along the trench. We were to ask for a Corporal Newton who would detail us to our jobs. Oamer and the others went the other way.

We went in the direction indicated, wading through mud, but so far no water. We couldn't say what was coming up though, for the trench zig-zagged, just as we'd been told they would. A bloke put a fag out as we came up, and said, 'You the digging party?' He indicated that we were to go with him, but before we could do that, two blokes pushed past us, and disappeared around the corner of the trench.

'Where are they off?' asked Tinsley, and Corporal Newton said something like, 'Power pit'. We knew what he meant a minute later when the bloody machine gun racket started up again, and it was those two blokes who were making it. When we turned the corner – with Tinsley leading the way – we saw one of them sitting at the gun in a kind of bay cut into the front of the trench. The other was behind him, passing up the belts of ammunition. A third man held a trench periscope, which we'd all heard of but never seen, and he was shouting instructions at the gunner. There'd been no machine guns involved in our training. Even from ten feet away, I could feel the heat coming off the bloody thing, and the avalanche of spent cartridges flowing back down into the trench off it was hypnotising. After a while, the gunner left off, but only to light a cigarette. He was then straight back at it. He and his two mates between them were blocking the trench, and Newton, from behind me, called out to Tinsley, 'Push on there.'

With the gun still going like the blazes, I heard Alfred Tinsley saying, 'Excuse me, could we get by?'

I heard Newton saying, 'Christ almighty', and from behind him, the twins were saying 'Road block' over and over again, the word rebounding between them. Newton turned and clocked them, frowning.

When we'd finally got past the machine gun position, he said to me in a low tone, 'If your mates are nutty like that now, what are they going to be like after a week in the section?'

I said, 'The same, I should think . . . You'll see the point of them when they get their shovels going.'

'The key is to notice the small faults before they develop into serious ones,' Newton was saying as we turned a corner of the trench, 'but we haven't really been doing that.'

The traverse we had now entered looked to have been abandoned. The parados – that is, the embankment on the friendly side – was collapsed in places, and there weren't enough sandbags at the top on the *other* side. The stakes that were meant to support the trench walls were sticking out at all angles, or floating in the filthy water.

'What happened?' I asked Newton. 'Did a shell hit?'

'No,' he said, 'It just rained for a long time.'

The duckboards, which were supposed to be on the bottom of the trench, floated about in two feet of water.

'It's all yours,' said Newton, and the twins were already going at it with their shovels, digging into the mud under the water, to create sumps for drainage. Young Tinsley and I worked at a slower pace. I thought Newton would have cleared off directly, but he sat for a while on what little bit of the fire step remained and smoked a cigarette. He'd decided to give us a little lecture.

'That', he said, indicating forward, 'is the dog's leap. No man's land. On the other side of it, you have the Alleyman.

The German. That's where he comes from you see? Allemagne. I can't say it, but I don't suppose he can say Bromley. That's where I'm from. Been shelled yet? When you hear one coming over, tip your hat to keep the splash off your face . . . So you're New Army . . . The Railway Pals, eh? I expect you're a train driver,' he said, pointing at me, 'and you're a fireman,' he added, pointing to Tinsley.

'Soon will be,' said Tinsley, digging, not looking up.

Presently, Newton departed and we worked on. He came back with bully beef in bread and hard biscuits at about midday – also water, with a nasty chemical in it, to fill up our water bottles. He told us to keep at it; the answer to the water was to dig deeper, creating sumps at intervals. Then he went off again.

In the afternoon, the twins would occasionally sing bits of their digging song, sometimes both singing different bits of it at the same time, and that was the only sound to be heard all afternoon. It was just like one of those hazy York days with nothing doing, but an occasional clanking in the far distance, which in York would have been a factory at work, or wagons being shunted, but hereabouts was probably something worse. We might have been digging on the railwaymen's allotments at Holgate, and we seemed to have this stretch of trench to ourselves. After a couple of hours, with the light beginning to fade, Newton came back once again with a trench cooker, and all the doings for tea. As he brewed up, the twins went over to him, and Roy said 'Where's t'shitter, boss?' only Newton, not being a Yorkshireman, couldn't make him out.

'They're after the latrines,' I said.

So Newton led them off back the way we'd come. When they'd gone, Tinsley took out his paybook, and removed a photograph from it. It showed a collection of railwaymen sitting on a platform bench somewhere. A smart, small bloke sat in the centre. He had his legs crossed, and looked away from the camera, as though he knew he was the main object of interest, but couldn't get excited about it. The other blokes, sitting alongside him or standing behind, all grinned.

'There he is,' said Tinsley, indicating the central bloke.

'Who?' I asked, sipping tea.

'Tom Shaw,' he said, 'if you recall.'

And he seemed hurt that I'd forgotten about his hero driver.

'Always beautifully turned out, he is. He can be five hours on the footplate, and there's not a speck of coal dust on him. It's almost magical, Jim. To keep himself in trim, he comes into work on his bike rather than take the train, and he'll come along all these muddy lanes . . . The bike will be absolutely clarted Jim, but Tom Shaw's suit'll be spotless.'

I didn't recognise him, but then I didn't know all the York drivers – not by a long chalk. In truth, I didn't much like the look of the bloke.

'I didn't expect him to be small,' I said. Most drivers were thin, but tall.

'He rides the engine with a light touch,' said Tinsley. 'Like a jockey, you know.'

'Why did you enlist, Alfred?' I asked Tinsley. 'I mean, *he* didn't.'

The Company, and the government, had to keep the trains going, so drivers and firemen had the best of excuses for not joining up. Given that plenty of them *had* enlisted even so, a youngster could expect to move up from cleaning engines to firing much quicker than normal.

'Tom Shaw', he said, putting the photograph back in its place, 'got over the obstacles that were put in his way, and I must get over the ones put in mine. You can't expect to get on the footplate without facing down difficulties, whatever they might be. My difficulty is this war, do you see?'

'It certainly is,' I said.

'And I mean to face it down.'

I took out a packet of Woodbines, and offered one to Tinsley. He took it.

'You must never light three fags from one match,' said a voice. It was Newton, back from the jakes with the twins.

'We're not,' I said.

'I know,' he said. 'But I'm just warning you. It gives away a position – the third bloke always gets it.'

Even I'd heard that tale. Newton didn't seem to have much that was *new* to offer, but he evidently wanted to play the old army hand. He fell to telling us what had happened to his best pal the week before. He'd been on sentry-go in the trench at two o'clock in the morning when a German raiding party had come over. They'd made no fuss, never fired a single shot, but had just taken Newton's mate – and him alone – off with them. 'It's not as bad as being shot, of course,' said Newton, 'but a good deal *stranger*. Here,' he said, 'do you want to go out?'

'How do you mean?' I said; but I thought I knew.

'See a Fritz,' said Newton.

'A dead one, you mean?' said Tinsley, before blowing smoke in such a way (he looked like someone whistling) that you knew he'd never done it before.

'Course not. Follow me.'

'I don't fancy going into the dog's teeth,' said Tinsley.

'The dog's *leap*,' said Newton, and we followed him past the twins, who'd gone back to digging, now both grunting and humming instead of singing, being, as I supposed, that bit more tired, but still going at it like a pair of machines. At the end of the bad bit of trench there was a ditch going off at right angles into no man's land.

'This is a sap,' said Newton. 'Now keep your head down for Christ's sake.'

I knew it was a sap, and I didn't really want to follow him, but I wouldn't funk it; Tinsley, I guessed, felt the same. There was nothing in the sap at all – no sandbags, no duckboards, just two banks of mud about four feet high, and a queer smell coming and going: as if there was some strong cheese lying about somewhere – cheese-gone-wrong. It was mixed with a floating smell of woodsmoke. We're gone about twenty yards, and my back was killing me from the crouching walk. But just then we were at the end of it, and here was a little cockpit made of sandbags and a tarpaulin.

'Now you lie down flat on this tarp,' said Newton, 'and just have a peek over.'

Tinsley was looking at me, uncertain, but half grinning.

'Come off it,' I said to Newton.

'It's quite all right,' he said. 'They don't know about this. They're looking at our trench, not here. Except they're not even doing that, you see, cause they've got a brew on.'

'They have a fire going,' said Tinsley.

'Exactly,' said Newton. 'Always do at this time.'

'They're not cooking cheese, are they?' said Tinsley. 'I mean, sort of toasting it?'

'What do you think this is?' said Newton, 'Wilson's bloody Tea Rooms?'

I thought that must be some place in Bromley that he knew of. The bloke was getting agitated now, in a way that I didn't quite like. 'No,' he said, 'that cheese smell is Rogers, and he's dead. He died yesterday on a raid. He's about twenty feet over that way, but you don't want to look at *him* do you?'

At that instant, he put his head up and down.

'Big fucking Alleyman in plain view,' he said, but even though he tried to keep an even tone, he was panting as he spoke. It had taken a lot out of him to put his head up. 'I don't know what it is, but when they have a brew on it's always the same. You can see 'em.'

'I mean to have a look,' said Tinsley, and he was eyeing me because he knew I'd object. Perhaps he wanted me to, but I didn't think so. This test was another one he had to pass if he was ever to make it to the footplate of an express engine. It was a bloody game of dare – that's what Newton had got us into.

I said, 'You'll not.'

I turned to Newton, saying, 'I've to look out for this kid.'

'What *kid*?' said Tinsley. 'No you haven't.'

And his head, too, was up and down in an instant.

'I *saw* him,' he said, but I wasn't sure I believed him, and in the end it was pure curiosity that made me stick my own head up. I saw a line of scribble that was German wire, then a wall of sandbags, a gap in the sandbags and a small moving face in that gap: a Fritz, talking to another Fritz who was out of sight. It was as if they were in a different century over there. I detected a big moustache on the man; his helmet had a spike it in – just as promised in the manuals – and a white band wrapped around it. I thought: he's a Prussian, not a German, and having ducked down again, I was all for crawling back fast to the trench, since it was properly evening now, and the 'hate' would soon be starting. But Newton was saying, 'Who wants a pot?'

Well, we all had our guns on our backs. That was the thing about being a soldier on active duty. You could shoot anybody at any time. But I didn't mean to open up with this idiot as officer commanding. He was addressing Tinsley.

'It's not many who bag a Fritz on their first day at the front, kid. He's still there.' And as Newton lifted his head for a second time, there came a fast whistling, like the sort of whistle a man might give when he's just had a narrow escape. But Newton hadn't escaped. The whole side of his face was red – the left side. Tinsley was in shock; he almost laughed, gasping out, 'Holy smoke!'

It was his ear; I couldn't account for all of it – part of it was gone. Seeing me move towards him, Newton said, 'No, don't touch. It's all right, just don't touch it.'

'Take your tin hat off. It's your lobe . . . your ear lobe.'

Well, I was in shock too. His ear lobe had gone, and all I

could think was that, however long he lived, he'd never get it back.

'Field dressing,' I said, remembering about it just then. But Newton had turned about and was beginning to wriggle fast back along the sap, with blood flowing all down his collar on that side and painting his left shoulder red.

'It's quite all right,' he was saying, 'it doesn't hurt in the least.'

When we got back to the trench, Andy and Roy were waiting there, taking a breather; one held a pick, the other a shovel, and for once they were on the sensible side of things. Well, not quite, for they were into their old routine:

'I'll bet he's sore,' said Roy.

'As *owt*,' said Andy.

It had been a bloody stupid stunt to go along that sap, and we were lucky no other men of the West Kents apart from Newton had seen us do it, but just at that moment, the shout went up of 'Stand-to!' and those same West Kents came flooding from both sides into the broken – or half fixed-up – trench. A sergeant – a big, tough-looking customer – was the first one to see the state of Newton's tunic, and his ear. This bloke was on the point of utterance when Newton spoke up.

'I've copped it, sarn't,' he said, 'just now, just by this stretch here where the bags are down,' and he indicated a gap in the sandbags. 'The railway blokes hadn't got round to fixing that part yet – that right, lads?' he said.

So it appeared that, having risked three lives in his attempt to show off, he was now blaming us for what had gone wrong, and asking us to back up his lies into the bargain. As the West Kents took up firing positions, the sergeant glared, and Newton repeated, 'That's right ain't it, lads?'

The twins stared at Newton dazed, with perhaps the beginnings of a smile on their faces, while young Tinsley and I also looked dazed at him, but with no hint of a smile in either case.

I nodded at the sergeant, and Tinsley, willing to follow my lead in this at least, did the same.

We knocked off at six, when Oamer came for us. His waders were muddy up to the knees. When we converged in the communication trench with the others of our gang, I saw that they all had mud right up to the *top* of their waders. As we came out of the communication trench, the evening hate started. The mad animals, the screaming women, the flying locomotives all came back. But Oamer, walking in the lead with his pipe on the go and a hurricane lamp swinging in his hand, paid it no mind. That was called leading by example, and I wouldn't have minded trying it myself. I did think I had it in me, and it would give me a reason to be brave, or to pretend to be.

We were into the thin, grey wood now, along with other broken-down wanderers. They came and went to either side of us, heavy-laden with all kinds of digging kit. They were from our battalion: blokes from 'D' Company making for their own billets, seemingly with no NCO of their own at that moment. I recognised a bloke from the York railway offices although I couldn't have put a name to him. The last time I'd seen him, he'd been eating a sandwich on that patch of grass under the Bar Walls over opposite from those offices. He'd been neat in a good suit, with his grey felt hat by his side. Now, his uniform was invisible beneath mud, so that even when he came close I couldn't see if he had a stripe. The mud hadn't affected his brain though. He had all the gen. 'A' Company, he told our lot, were working on a road pushing east from somewhere north of Albert. This would connect two other roads that went north–south. 'B' Company were 'doing railway work', and at this Tinsley's ears pricked up, and he asked what sort. Well, I couldn't quite follow the geography of it, but they were building branches off the surviving lines around Albert. These would be standard gauge, but there would be narrow-gauge lines coming off them, and extending nearly to the front line.

'Three-foot gauge?' said Tinsley.

'Two foot,' said the bloke, and I immediately thought of the comical little railway that carried fruit and vegetables through the York railway nursery at Poppleton.

'It's all in aid of the big push that's coming,' said the knowledgeable bloke; then he drifted off, half staggering under the weight of mud on him.

'Two-foot gauge,' said Tinsley, coming up to me, 'I'd settle for that. They'll want drivers and firemen. Have we to put in for it?'

'Well,' I said, 'let's let 'em get it built first.'

But I did fancy the notion.

We pressed on through the haunted wood, and after a while it fell out that I was walking with Dawson, the others having disappeared from view ahead of us. His face was filthy – looked as though his muddy moustache had spread over all of it. Some shells were falling quite near; every so often you'd catch the force of one, and feel a little winded, as though you'd just run ten yards.

Dawson said something I couldn't catch, and I saw he was indicating a bloke on a white horse in the trees. He looked as though he'd always been there. He was calling to us.

'You there!'

Dawson said to me, 'That's not a very military form of address, is it?'

We walked up to the bloke, and we both saluted (in a ragged sort of way) since he was on a horse after all, and he wore a cap instead of a tin hat. It seemed odds on that he was an officer. In fact, he was just about as perfect – up there on that horse – as any toy soldier. He had a waxed moustache; his well-pressed uniform was offset by a gleaming thin white rope about one shoulder – a lanyard. He took out a paper, and struck a match, the better to read it, and by the light of this flame, I saw his red cap cover. He was a member of the Military Mounted Police – a monkey, as they were known to the men – and he had three stripes on his sleeve. Compared to him, the regimental police in our own battalion had just been playing at the job.

'Are you the 17th Northumberland?' he said. He spoke like a machine. 'I'm looking for a Captain Quinn. Quinn of 'E' Company.'

I knew he'd come about William Harvey. I saw in my mind's eye the sodden dead boy, left out to dry on the sea wall at Spurn . . . and the bug-like eyes. The matter had followed us to France, and it broke in on me for the first time that I had no more means of proving my innocence than any other man in the section. All that could be said in my favour was that I had no obvious motive for killing Harvey.

We indicated the direction of the tavern, and the ruin next door that would be housing Quinn. The bloke turned his horse and went off that way, and we trooped after. Dawson smoked in silence as we walked and I thought how this wasn't like him: the smoking was, but not the silence.

When we got back to the billet, we saw Quinn, sitting on his own horse (he'd evidently just got back with it), talking to the Military Policeman on *his*. They were in between the tavern and the ruin next door. Every so often the horses would twitch or start at the wilder noises coming from the front line. As Dawson and I made for the tavern, I could make out Quinn's voice.

'My men have had a very hard time of it today,' he was saying, 'or so I should imagine. I myself was in Albert trying to find a horse, and then lunching with the adjutant.'

Well, at least he was honest about it. Another thing: it was funny to hear him say 'My men'.

Inside the tavern, I discovered that orderlies from battalion HQ had visited earlier in the day and not only located a stove, but filled it with coal. A dixie of the usual sort of stew was boiling away on it. Everything was now focused on that stove. The men had shifted their couches towards it, and tunics and trousers were draped over chairs and stools and pushed towards it for drying. Two hurricane lamps burned on the bar, and all the blokes were stripping off prior to going out back where, Oamer promised, there was a pump and a bucket. The twins, I noticed, wore nothing underneath their rough tunics. Roy Butler smoked while contemplating the hard muscles of his stomach; he didn't seem proud, just interested. Their brother, on the other hand, was combing his hair in a fragment of mirror that he'd got hold of. Scholes was sitting on his couch, and taking his penny whistle from his pack. There was quite a happy undercurrent of conversation because at least we were all out of the rain. The fact that something a bit heavier might fall on us at any moment seemed generally forgotten about. Scholes began to play his whistle – just a short burst of something fast and complicated. When he'd finished, Oliver Butler, stowing his mirror back in his pack, said, 'It's good, is that. Carry on.'

He could be a decent sort sometimes, and I noticed the expression on Scholes's face. Chuffed, he was – and perhaps for another reason as well: he'd gone to the front line and come back, proved himself up to the mark.

But his happiness didn't last, for Oamer walked in just then, went directly over to Scholes and had a word in his ear. Looking dead white, Scholes put down his whistle, and walked out of the tavern.

I collared Oamer as he followed Scholes out, saying, 'What does that red hat want?'

Oamer replied without stopping, 'Spurn. New evidence come to light.'

That was at seven o'clock. At quarter past seven, Scholes came back, sat silent on his couch, then took his whistle from his sack and didn't play it but sat there holding it. At twenty past, Oamer returned. The twins were to go over to the next-door ruin for their turn at being questioned.

'What's this about?' barked Oliver, as his brothers were marched off.

When they'd gone, Oliver Butler turned his anger on Scholes: 'What did you tell him that he's called Roy and Andy in?'

Scholes just shook his head, could barely bring himself to speak. At length, he said, 'He's had a report from our regimental police.'

'What's his name?' said Butler.

'Thackeray,' Scholes muttered, 'Company Sergeant Major Thackeray.'

'What did he say?'

'That he thinks William Harvey was done in by one of us; that he doesn't mean to let the matter drop, just because we've come out here. That no man will be promoted within our section until he's got to the bottom of it all.'

'What did he want with you?'

Scholes just shook his head, still staring at nothing.

'Why does he want to see the twins?'

'Why do you bloody *think*?' said Scholes. 'Because they're not right in the head.'

'They're my brothers,' said Butler, furious.

'That's *your* look-out,' said Scholes, and he thought: yes, that's just what it is. Oliver Butler is perpetually looking out for his brothers. Scholes had had enough of our stares. He picked up his whistle, and quit the room, with Butler looking daggers into his back.

At seven-thirty, the twins returned, grinning – but then that meant nothing in their case – and Oliver took them into a huddle in the corner. He wanted to know if they'd been seen separately or together. Evidently, they'd been seen separately. Young Tinsley had taken refuge in the *Railway Magazine*. Dawson lay flat on his couch, which was next to mine. I looked a question at him.

'I'm looking at that bottle, mate,' he said, indicating with his stockinged foot the poster behind the bar, 'and I'm thinking I'd like to go large on whatever wine is left over in this place.'

'Like a drop of wine, do you?'

He nodded.

'Beer for preference, but I do like a drop of white wine. Van Blonk,' he said, 'Point *blank* . . . Or cider, of course. I like a drop of that.'

He gave me a queer smile, the meaning of which I would only understand later. I wondered if it was only beer that turned him into the *other* Dawson, the wild man, as he'd been turned on Spurn Head – and only John Smith's bitter at that.

'Not bothered about the red cap?' I said.

'Ah,' he said. 'Now this is you with your detective hat on. No, I'm not bothered about him. He's part of the future, and I don't really think about the future.'

'Because you might cop it at any moment, you mean?'

'No,' he said, after a while. 'As a *general rule* I don't think about the future.'

He reached under his couch and caught up his water bottle; he passed it over to me.

'Cider,' he said, 'from the basement. It's dark down there, but I found a crate of this.'

I took a pull. After receiving another nod from him by way of encouragement, I took another, longer one. It was a strong brew of cider, and it affected me directly.

'So even in the past you didn't think about the future?' I said, giving it back.

Dawson nodded. 'Even *then*.'

Oamer returned, and this time he marched Tinsley out. When he'd gone, I walked over to his couch, and picked up the *Railway Magazine* he'd left lying there. I wanted to see the words that always appeared at the foot of the back page – and they appeared in full this time: 'The Railway Publishing Co., Ltd., 30, Fetter Lane, Fleet St., London, E.C. Telephone – 2087 HOLBORN'.

Tinsley returned looking white-faced. He too had evidently been given a roasting. He collected up his rifle on coming back into the tavern, and went off again to do his sentry-go. Next it was Dawson's turn with the red cap, and when Oamer returned him, he called for me.

Quinn stood outside the small ruin. The red cap, Thackeray, was evidently within.

Quinn nodded as I approached, saying, 'You will address the Company Sergeant Major as "sir"', which had me wondering whether one of the blokes had tried to 'sarge' Thackeray.

The small ruin held a kind of coffin-like box bed – Quinn's. Beside it was a rickety table with Company Sergeant Major Thackeray sitting at it. Quinn himself remained hovering outside, and since the door of the ruin was kept open, he would have heard what took place inside. This was a sort of compromise. He would be a witness to the questioning but would not quite sit in on it.

'You are Fusilier Stringer,' said Thackeray, in his clattering, mechanical way. 'Do you have anything to add to your statement?'

'No, sir.'

'You were the last man to go to bed.'

'Yes.'

He stared at me for a while.

'Do you have any grievance against any man in your section?'

'No, sir.'

'Does any other man in your section have any grievance against any *other* man?'

'Not that I'm aware of,' I said.

(Which wasn't exactly true.)

'And yet you were involved in a fight during the evening.'

'More of a scuffle, as I said in the statement. It never came to blows.'

'Every man had been drinking,' he said, and I knew at that moment: this bloke's teetotal. 'In the fight, you sustained a cut to your right knuckle.'

I nodded. This was rather concerning . . . but it had been a tiny cut, and Dawson would testify that I'd got it from him, and not through striking William Harvey. Anyhow, I *believed* he would, and perhaps he already had done.

Thackeray stood, proving there was not a single crease in his uniform.

'No,' he said, 'because you are all *pals*. You are part of a whole battalion of pals, in fact.' He was standing, more or less to attention, by the side of the table; even so, his riding boots creaked a little. 'Chums,' he said, with disgust. 'You have left your homes, wives, children, jobs to come to the aid of Blighty in her hour of need; and for no more in return than twice the pay of a regular soldier, and the status of national hero.'

'Is there a question?' I said, having decided to stop sirring him.

With a great squeaking and creaking of boots, he sat back down again, saying, 'You were a policeman of sorts.'

'Detective sergeant on the railway force.'

'Where were you based?'

'York station,' and at that the moustache fluttered, signifying a laugh.

'And did your power of arrest extend beyond the ticket gate?'

'It extended over all the railway lands.'

'The railway lands' – and again the moustache went up. 'That sounds like somewhere in your imagination.'

'They are set out in *The North Eastern Railway Police Manual*.' I eyed him for a while, before adding, 'It's not an *over*-imaginative book.'

'Why the hell aren't you in the Military Mounted Police?'

'I can't ride a horse.'

'No,' he said, after a space, 'I'm not surprised.'

'And I wanted to see action.'

'Alongside your pals?'

'And others besides.'

'Your pals and your *chums*.' He leant forwards. 'What do you suppose this is? A war or a social outing?' He leant further forwards. 'Even though you are unaccustomed to army life, you are hoping to have the nerve to keep your head up.'

'Something of that.'

'Well, a boy is dead, and it appears to me that you or one of your drunken pals is responsible, so you *will* be seeing some action, that I guarantee, fusilier.' I thought that might have been it, but he eyed me for a good long while before adding, 'In his report the doctor said he'd never seen a greater injury of that type. You might think the eye – the right eye – was coming out of the boy's head. But it went in – all the way *into* his brain. Do you suppose he *saw* his brain? Do you suppose he had sight of it just before he died?'

But I was not meant to answer this morbid question.

'You are free to go,' said Thackeray. 'For now.'

When I stepped out, Quinn was still hovering, and looking none too pleased.

An hour later, after our feed, Oamer stood in that apology for a wood, on the dark border of our camp, and lit his pipe. It was his turn for sentry-go. He passed the match to me, and I touched it to the end of a Woodbine.

'What was the new evidence?' I asked him. 'I never found out.'

'Regarding Scholes,' said Oamer. 'It was the manner of his finding the bike . . . And it was a question of nuance.'

'Of what?'

'You recall those children with the flags on Spurn? It seems they have the power of speech after all, and they've given their version of events.'

'But they'd cleared off by the evening,' I said.

'But they came back the next *day*,' said Oamer, 'and they saw the search.'

I recalled that he was right; that I'd seen them myself while searching.

'One of the two – name of Lucy – said she saw a man finding the bike. She was asked about that, and she said, "I saw him pick it up. I don't know that he *found* it." So naturally she was then asked, "Did he *look* as though he'd found it?"' Oamer sighed and looked at his pipe. 'She said "no", and was quite insistent on the point. The man she'd seen – Scholes – had, it appeared to her, known where the bike was when he made towards it.'

'Rum,' I said.

'It's quite a subtle distinction for Lucy to make,' Oamer ran on. 'But they turn out some bright sparks at the Spurn elementary school.'

'So the position is that we're all in it, but Scholes is the number one suspect?'

'That's right.'

A thought struck me. I asked Oamer:

'Were you questioned?'

'I was . . . Pleasant sort, isn't he?'

'Not a crease in his uniform.'

'I think that may be the entire point of him. I hope so, anyhow.'

In fact, the point of the red cap, Thackeray, was that he was one of those regular army types who saw the volunteers as merely civilians in uniforms – so many slackers and wranglers, given an easy time of it so as to encourage others to join up.

It was a common sort of prejudice, I believed, and now we'd come up hard against it.

I took over from Oamer as sentry, walking in the wood,

listening to the fireworks of the front, and thinking hard. One question particularly bothered me. On Spurn . . . why would Tinsley have put an edition of his beloved *Railway Magazine* in the stove?

When I was relieved, by Dawson, I went straight to sleep, but dreamt again – this time of the trenches. It appeared that the war invaded sleep as well as the waking hours. I was just dangling about in no man's land waiting to be shot, looking out for an opportunity to die with no particular feelings about it either way. Corporal Newton came up to me and said, 'You're in the wrong place, mate. You ought to be over here.' Then the red cap, Thackeray, was before me on his horse. A voice – it was Bernie Dawson's – said, 'You can tell he's a bastard just by the expression on his face – on his horse's face, I mean.' The horse, and Thackeray, moved off, and I was awake. In the light of the candle stub that still burned by Tinsley's couch, I inspected the tavern room. Two couches were empty: Oliver Butler's, and Scholes's. Oliver Butler would be standing sentry, but Scholes, I knew, did not have a sentry duty that night. He ought to have been sleeping. His kit bag was there, and his rifle ought to have been propped against it, but I couldn't make it out. Then again, the room was half enclosed in darkness. I went over and picked up the candle, looking harder. I then put on my trousers and my boots; I took up my own rifle, and walked out. No sound came from the direction of the front. I heard a cough, and there was Scholes on the margin of the wood, sitting on a broken tree. He wore his uniform, with tunic unbuttoned. 'Where's your rifle?' I said, walking fast up to him.

'Under the couch. Why? Did you think I'd make away with myself?'

I leant against the tree.

'Thackeray gave you a tough time of it.'

'He tried his best,' said Scholes. 'Tried his best and succeeded.'

'What about the bike?'

'You've heard about that, have you? Evidently, I didn't find it, but put it on the dune. Fact is . . .' he said, finally looking up at me, 'I *did* come upon it earlier. I'd seen it ten minutes before and I was just wondering what to do about it – if anything. I just knew that some copper would take that line if I spoke up about seeing the bike. That's the thing about this war, isn't it? The world's gone out of balance: there's no *good* luck any more.'

'Did you explain that to him? About the bike, I mean?'

Scholes nodded. 'I think I'm off the hook for now. I told him I'm a policeman myself, I don't commit crimes. He said, "You *were*. You *were* a policeman. I'm the law now." I haven't seen the last of him, none of us has. He means to keep cases on all of us. He has a down on *all* our lot.'

'Our unit?' I said, 'The Northumberlands? Railwaymen?'

But I knew the answer.

'Volunteers,' said Thackeray. 'The New Army. He calls us the militia. He says we might have the grateful thanks of the public, but we don't have his grateful thanks. He wanted to make that quite clear. He said, "Do you understand?" and he wouldn't let me go until I said "Yes". Quinn was decent about it. He took me aside afterwards and said this was all "rather irregular", and he'd do his best to look out for me.'

I offered Scholes a Woodbine. Two rifle cracks came from the direction of the front. A low rumble followed.

'No thanks,' he said, and he looked too depressed to smoke.

'He plays the cello,' said Scholes, kicking at the hard mud.

'Who does?'

'Quinn. He told me.'

I said, 'I can just see him doing that.'

'How do you mean?'

'Frowning over it, you know.'

'Oh.'

'Thackeray . . .' I said. 'He has the twins in his sights as well, evidently.'

'He said they're a pair of loonies. He'd been told that by our regimental police . . . Well, they are aren't they? How did they get past the recruiting sergeant?'

An owl hooted from somewhere among the broken, ash-coloured trees.

I said, 'It must be fucking mad, that owl, to be hanging about here. Do you remember that one in York station?'

'That's just it,' said Scholes. 'You've got to say *York* station because it's all gone now . . . I tell you what,' he said, looking hard at me, and with a kind of desperation, 'if Thackeray does come back for me, I'll tell him what I really know.'

For the first time in his life, Scholes had surprised me.

'You mean you didn't?'

'No.'

'Will you tell *me*?'

'I will not.'

I lit my Woodbine, and at the very moment of the match striking the box, I heard another sound. We both turned about, and there was a figure in the trees. He held a rifle, not in the firing position, but I had the idea that he wouldn't have to adjust the position of it so *very* much to loose one off. It was Oliver Butler. I called after him, but he just turned and walked back towards the tavern, in the doorway of which stood Oamer, half dressed, and with folded arms, looking somehow like a mother about to reprimand her children for staying out late.

West of Aveluy Wood: The Last Day of June and the First Day of July 1916

As we – that is, the 17th Battalion of the Northumberland Fusiliers in its entirety – made towards our assembly point for the big push, marching in fours along a straight, dusty road, some of the blokes were looking at the flowers growing in the margins of the fields of hard mud. Mustard flowers were identified and certain kinds of poppy. But Alfred Tinsley, walking alongside me, was looking beyond the flowers and instead gazing into the field on our left, where he had some time ago detected a railway line, albeit a little one. As we pushed on, the railway line gradually coincided with our road. The rails were newly laid, and had been put down directly on the baked grey earth. They were only two feet apart.

'There you are, Jim,' said Tinsley, indicating the line. 'That's *us*.'

He meant that we would soon be working on it, or one similar – or he hoped we would. If we came through the push, we would certainly be applying.

That morning, when we'd set off from our latest billet, Oamer had read out a circular, beginning: 'Particulars of NCOs and men required with experience of railway operating and railway workshops, and the following railway trades . . .' It was signed, Oamer had told us, by Captain Leo Tate, that cheery Royal Engineer late of Spurn Head. It appeared that narrow-gauge railways were the coming thing on the Western Front: the latest way of taking men and materiel to forward positions.

The line accompanied us, in a companionable sort of way, for perhaps half a mile of our tramp, then we diverted towards our assembly point while the track aimed itself at one of the broken woods on the horizon.

Also that morning, Oamer had told us that Sergeant Major fucking Thackeray of the Military Mounted Police had written to Captain Quinn saying he meant to question once again some or all of the section. It seemed he was based at Albert, where the military police detachment of the Fourth Army had its headquarters – so he was handily placed for making our lives a misery. We had been informed, in turn, that Quinn had written to the army legal service requesting representation for any men so questioned – and it was made quite clear to us once again that Quinn believed the death of Harvey to be an accident; and that he did not approve of Thackeray's continuing with the matter.

Some lorries came past us, some London buses, and I thought: yes, the front line is the terminus. The buses got a cheer, although we didn't know who was in them. It was just the thought of every last British thing being pitched in against the Boche. We were to take the pressure off the French at Verdun, or something of the sort. After the buses, the artillery blokes kept coming: six horses at a time, harnessed in pairs and kicking up dust, a man riding each left hand horse, the gun and the ammunition limber being towed behind. According to Tinsley, it was no way to take artillery forward. Narrow-gauge railways were the answer.

Our assembly billet was a little cluster of ruins on the margin of a worked-out limestone quarry. After the stew had been served out from the hot boxes, the blokes had spread out in the quarry, playing football, cards, dice, reading, larking about. From the direction of the front came the continual crashing that had evidently been going on for days, the idea being to do for Fritz for good and all this time: cut his wires, bury him in his dugouts, generally scare the shit out of him, and leave him defenceless before our charge at his trenches. The sound came in waves, as did clouds of haze, sometimes of a pinkish colour, sometimes yellow-ish. None of it was gas, but only dust, floating in the light of a beautiful summer's evening. As a battalion we were to be 'in reserve' for the push. This meant we would not be in at the start, which would be at half past seven in the morning, but would move forward later – after a leisurely breakfast, sort of thing. Captain Quinn, addressing us, had been very clear about our role in the coming fight:

'We are to wait for the breakthrough; then we are to move forward to open up communications between our lines and the positions won. We are to do this by the rapid prolongation towards the enemy lines of saps already prepared by the Royal Engineers . . .' At the end, he'd said that Oamer would answer any questions we might have, then he'd fled the scene, sharp-ish.

Dawson sat alongside me on the top edge of the quarry. Tinsley was with us, and we were trying to pick out the York station men.

'There's the porters, see,' said Dawson, and he pointed to six blokes sitting or lying on the ground, all smoking.

'What's the skill of being a porter?' asked Tinsley.

'Skill?' said Dawson. 'None.'

'But not every man who applies is taken on,' said Tinsley, 'so there must be something to it.'

It was a good point; Dawson was forced to consider it.

'Well,' he said, 'when I was taken on at York, I was interviewed by Braithwaite.'(Braithwaite was the deputy station master, and now a platoon commander of 'B' Company, and no doubt somewhere in one of the clusters of officers among the men below.) 'He asked me: "How do you know when you've come to the end of a train?"'

'*I* know,' said Tinsley.

'I hadn't bargained on being asked that,' said Dawson, ignoring Tinsley, 'so I said, "You come to the guard's van." Braithwaite said, "But how do you know when you've come to the end of the guard's van?"'

'I know *that*,' said Tinsley, and again Dawson ignored him:

'So I hazarded a guess: "Would it be by the red light hanging off the back of it?" and that was the right answer. Braithwaite then asked me, "How do you address a male passenger of the superior classes?" I said, "Sir". He said, "And how would you address a male passenger of the inferior classes, a chimney sweep, for example?" I said, "Sir also". Right again. I knew I was getting everything right, because Braithwaite was getting really annoyed. He didn't much like me, you see. He asked me, "And why must you address all passengers, of whatever class, in that respectful manner?" Now I'd been warned of this by Palmer.' (He indicated one of the smoking porters below.) 'Palmer told me that if you answer that question, "To get tips off them", you're out on your ear. Palmer had been coached up in the right answer by one of the older lads, and he passed it on to me, so I looked Braithwaite in the eye, and I gave it him straight: I said, "Because you are the public face of the Company. If you are rude, or scruffily turned, the Company is likewise; if you smell of drink, the Company smells of drink; if you're smoking on duty, the Company is smoking on duty. "All right, all right," said Braithwaite. He'd had enough of me by then you see, but of course he had to give me the job.'

We all looked down at the quarry. I saw the twins, playing some scuffling game of their own. They looked like two dogs: mongrels of a long-legged sort.

'Two of the top link drivers from the North Shed,' said Tinsley, indicating two blokes in a football game.

'I wonder what your man Tom Shaw is doing just now?' I said.

Tinsley looked at his watch: 'He often takes the eight forty to London, so he might just be coming into Doncaster. Wherever he's going, he'll be going *fast*.'

'What if he's in the pub?' said Dawson. (And I believed it was the first time he'd heard of Tom Shaw, but he'd caught on fast.)

'What if *who* is?'

The voice came from behind; someone had crept up on us: Oliver Butler, of course.

'We're talking about engine drivers,' said Tinsley.

'I can't stand 'em,' said Butler. 'You'll find that all guards hate all drivers.'

'Why?' asked Tinsley.

'The guard must ask permission to go onto the footplate, but the driver can climb up into the guard's van whenever he likes. Where's the fairness in that?'

'It's the driver's train,' said Tinsley.

'Wrong,' said Butler. 'It's the guard's train. He holds a document saying so on every trip.'

Tinsley said, 'But without the driver there wouldn't *be* a trip.'

However, the question of the ownership of a train was put paid to by the blowing of a whistle in the quarry. We were to make for our billets, and lights out.

'Anyhow,' said Dawson, pitching the stub of his cigarette into the quarry below, 'we're all in the same box now.'

I don't believe that any man slept that night – not properly.

The dark, hot building I lay in had once had a high, pointed roof, going by the few rafters that remained, over which some filthy tarpaulins had been hung. Two companies of the battalion were crammed into it. The officers and NCOs were in the more select ruins round about. It came to me at about two o'clock in the morning that the building was a church, and not only that but I was sleeping on the altar of it. This in turn reminded that I had promised the wife in a letter that I would attend a service of communion before the big push, and I now recalled one particular gathering of officers and men down in the quarry that might have been that very service in progress. A week earlier, I had written out my will in my paybook, on the page reserved for that purpose. I had left everything to the wife, except my revolver. That I had left to the Chief, thinking he might have more use for it. The thing lay in my drawer in the York police office in any case, so he might as well have it. I knew that Dawson had left 'everything' – meaning whatever pay he was owed, since he didn't actually have anything – to a girl called Betty who he'd met in a pub in Hull. Butler, I imagined, had left everything to his wife; I knew for a fact that he'd asked Oamer permission to fill out his brothers' will forms. He would have arranged, I supposed, for the one twin to leave whatever he had to the other. Of course, just because identical twins were born at the same time, that didn't mean they would also die at the same time, but I couldn't imagine it any other way in the case of those two.

It was not compulsory to fill out a will. Oamer had said, it was for 'the pessimistically inclined', which had evidently included himself, for Oliver Butler had seen him filling out the page after lights out. However, Butler had been in agonies over the fact that he hadn't been able to see who Oamer was leaving his worldly goods *to*. Scholes was the most pessimistically inclined of us all, but he'd left the page blank on the grounds that to fill it in would be tempting fate.

Tinsley had left everything to his mother except his *Railway Magazines*, which he told me he had left to me. I had then put a footnote onto my own will – Oamer told me that would be in order, and he called it a 'codicil' – leaving *my Railway Magazines* to Tinsley. My collection went back further than his, but Tinsley's were bound in the red cloth. However, I supposed that one number would be missing. Or was it another man's

Railway Magazine that had ended up in the stove at Spurn? I had seen no other man *reading* the *Railway Magazine*, but it was perfectly possible that one of the RE blokes had been a subscriber.

I had mentioned the will in my last letter to the wife. I had tried to do it in a light-hearted way, but it had been a poor sort of letter all round, and had finished with an outright lie: 'Tell Harry that I am well on the way with *The Count of Monte Cristo*, and it is every bit as good as he says . . .' Might I be spared to finish that book, or rather to start it? I began the Lord's Prayer in my head, but was interrupted halfway through by the voice of an officer, which I could hear clearly over the rumbling guns, there not being much in the way of wall. It was Captain Quinn, and he was saying (probably to Oamer), 'How do you think the men have enjoyed their six months of pioneering? It does seem to be rather dirty work, doesn't it?'

I couldn't settle on any subject to think about. If I thought of the wife and children I became choky. If I thought of the pubs of York, I became likewise (which was rather shaming). I thought of the dozen or so dead men I had so far seen in six months of repairing trenches. They had all been different colours: one completely white; one blue; one brown, which was the dried blood that had formed into a mask on his face. But none had looked as dead, and as *unjustly* dead, as William Harvey.

I did get off into a sort of kip eventually, and woke to find the church filled with light and the sound of shells of all calibres being set off, a sound not only deafening but also confusing, and almost amusing, as when a match is dropped into a box of fireworks. As I set off to the latrines, one of the mines we'd all been warned of went up. This was the Royal Engineers, not content with the noise of the shelling, trying for the biggest bang ever heard on earth. Everything shook: the bright blue sky, the stones of the upper part of the quarry; the latrine tent, and Bernie Dawson, who was entering it at the same time as me.

'To think it's Saturday morning,' he said.

It was a beautiful one at that.

The incredible racket continued as I breakfasted in the church on a tin of Maconochie steak and kidney, hard biscuits and tea with rum in it – a lot of rum. Then Oamer came round with a jar of the stuff, offering extras. I took some. I noticed that Dawson did not. They ought to give him a pint of John Smith's bitter. He'd tear into the Hun after that all right. In the latrine, I'd noticed a sinister smell, which I put down to the chemicals used in the long ditch beneath the shitting planks. But the smell was now in the church.

'It's gas,' Dawson said. 'But don't worry, it's ours.'

Oamer told us, 'It's dispersing, Jim. That's official.'

There was a lot of chatter in the ruined church – relief that the day had finally come, even if we weren't going forward quite yet. The men were clustered around their NCOs, dependent on them now for a word of guidance or encouragement even if they couldn't stand the sight of them in normal times. Everybody was on the look-out for someone who had faith in the plan, or had any proper idea what it was. I pictured the men going over the top at that moment, and in a way I'd rather have been with them than dangling about waiting.

Officers would come and go from the cottages, speaking in low voices to the NCOs. Not having anything to read (except *The Count of Monte Cristo*), I wandered out of the church. I couldn't see the front, just fields separated by low ridges like railway embankments, but of course I could hear it: a noise like a giant gorilla rattling the bars of its giant cage while a million women screamed. I sat down, and a voice called over, 'You're sitting in a graveyard.'

It was Oliver Butler. Oamer was at that point crossing between us, going from the officers' mess into the church, and carrying a sheet of paper, which meant an order for us. He said, 'I'm sure the irony is not lost on him.'

But it was. I hadn't realised.

The twins were standing at the church door, and Oamer, on his way in, turned to them, saying, 'Ready to go lads?'

They stared at him, and when he'd gone into the church, Andy turned to his brother, saying, 'Ready to go, Roy-boy?' which Roy took as a playful insult, so he pitched away the fag he had on the go, and they fell into one of their sparring bouts. Two minutes later, every man was called into the church, and the announcement was made. We were going forward at last.

We trooped into the communication trench, joining a flow of men. Every few seconds, the flow was interrupted and we stepped aside to let Royal Army Medical Corps and their stretcher cases come past. You'd hear the screaming and groaning before you saw the man, and you'd wonder what it would signify. But I tried not to look at the ones being carried since, very often, important parts of them would be missing.

I carried my rifle with fixed bayonet, two hundred and fifty rounds of ammunition, pick, shovel, haversack. This was battle order; it was meant to be light but was not. I was far too hot. About half the men moving forward carried bombs in addition, and you'd look at them thinking: is that bugger going to trip over and blow us all up? Whenever the communication trench came to a junction, there'd be signs, letters of all different sizes – like children's writing – daubed in black paint on planks: 'Moorside . . . Bank Top . . . Park Terrace'. These must be streets in the home town of whoever'd made these trenches. By the sounds of it, they were from a Northern town. But some were in French. One said 'Arrêt', and Oamer, leading the way, pointed to it, saying, '*Don't*, on any account.'

At every junction, more men came in, and I tried to think who they might be. We were in with the 32nd Division, alongside two regular battalions – at least one was Scots, I couldn't recall its name – and half a dozen others from the New Army like ourselves. The Salford Pals – that was one lot. But how did you know a Salford man by looking at him? I had now lost touch with Oamer, but relied on being re-united with him in the front trench.

When I reached the final junction, a subaltern stood there silently (because nobody could be heard without screaming) directing the flow. He was like a human signal post: as each man approached, his left arm or his right would go up. I was sent to his left, and I wondered how he knew where I was supposed to be going. We'd never clapped eyes on each other before. But I found Oamer and our digging team directly. They stood at the entrance to the sap, which was a ditch connecting with the upper part of the trench. You'd scramble up an earth mound to get into it. The twins were there, shovels ready, eager to get going. Scholes was looking not so eager, and I noticed he was mumbling to himself as Quinn addressed an RE man.

'So to recap,' Quinn was saying, 'the sap is literally stuffed with dead bodies?'

The RE man nodded. ''Fraid so.'

'Mmm . . .' said Quinn. 'And what about further along?'

'More of the same,' said the RE man.

'What? More dead bodies?'

'And a shell's done for the final part.'

So the sap had become a grave many times over. I supposed dying men had rolled into it for cover. This didn't affect the twins. They wanted to be in there a digging, and Quinn nodded at Oamer, who took them aside and talked to them very softly, which they seemed to be able to hear and understand in spite of the stream of din overhead. They were to clear a way through the sap as best they could, make good the end of it, and then extend it if possible.

I had become aware, as this little conference took place, of the short ladders in the trench making a claim on my attention. Where had *they* all come from?

The twins had scrambled off into the sap. Quinn turned to the rest of us.

'Now I'm afraid there's been a change of plan,' he said, straining to be heard over the high screaming of some eighteen-pounders that our side happened to be sending over just then, 'Owing to unforeseen circumstances . . .' Quinn was saying.

Behind him, the RE bloke was grinning. He was another captain. He carried no gun. None of the RE blokes did, just as though the war, to them, was not about death but just about building things, making loud bangs and generally having a ripping time of it. Quinn was still talking but I couldn't hear a bloody word because of some deep-booming Howitzers that were having their say. I knew that it would end in us going up the ladders though, and so it proved. When Quinn had done, the RE man summarised the orders in a brighter sort of voice that I *could* hear. Indicating the sap, he said, 'Rather congested in there lads, so you'll push on towards the end of it in the open.'

He meant in the dog's leap – in no man's land.

'. . . There you'll rendezvous with the two queer chaps . . .'

If this man did have any nerves in his body, which he appeared not to, then the glare that Oliver Butler was sending his way might have found them out. But he wasn't looking in that direction.

'. . . You'll sap forwards by digging between shell holes. That make sense?'

It made sense in that I understood it, but not in any other way.

'Good luck!' he said, and he indicated the ladders. Any one of them, it seemed, would do just as well as any other.

Quinn, in fact, was already halfway up one of them, and he was the first over, going into that great storm with just a revolver in his hand. Oamer went directly after him, his big behind squeezing with difficulty through the gap in the sandbags. I turned towards another ladder, at the top of which Scholes was pausing, taking in the scene. Whatever he saw made him shake his head: then he rolled forwards, like a reluctant swimmer entering a pool, and he disappeared from view.

As I approached the top of the ladder, I did so with the idea that everyone knew more about what to do in this battle than I did myself – the action in the trench had seemed to indicate as much – but the picture disclosed when I raised my head above the topmost sandbag put paid to that notion. I saw the remains of a bad idea: a vast acreage of baked earth; lines of men, half on the ground, half walking forwards. This was what remained of 'open formation'. Sometimes the ones moving forward went suddenly down to the ground; sometimes some of those got up again. I knew that in one glance I had taken in hundreds of dead men. Smoke rolled over the picture, revealing new scenes of chaos, then hiding them for decency's sake. In its higher levels, rotating lines of denser smoke forged upwards, and dissolved as they fell – and these were the shells of our barrage. That was part of the noise, but there was another, sharper sound: machine guns, but so many of them that they merged into one continuous explosion. It was a triumphant kind of noise: look what we can do when we band together! And they were German machine guns.

I rolled over the sandbags. I wriggled forwards, stood, ran, stopped, turned. For the moment, I had quite forgotten about the sap. A man was shouting, 'Get down!' so I did. In fact, I now realised, most men were down, one way or another. Ought I to reach for my rifle, and take a pot at the German lines? These appeared as a low, dark tangle about three hundred yards off. But there were only our own men before me, and the thing was . . . There was nowhere for them to go – nowhere but the tiniest dips in the hard mud; some trees hardly worth the name; patches of yellowness that looked like sand and that might have been bunkers on a golf course. But there was one private soldier who *did* have a fixed idea about what to do, and he was going the wrong bloody way: a runner with a message, making for our lines at a hell of a lick – and zig-zagging like a fucking rabbit. He flew past me into the smoke.

I resumed looking forwards. Only one position commanded the battlefield: a ruin rising above, and somewhat to the rear of, the German lines. This must be the Chateau of Thiepval. The village that had once stood around it had gone but it was our target all the same. In the whirling smoke to my right, Bernie Dawson turned, lighting a Woodbine as he did so. He'd been standing, and when he went down, I thought for a minute he'd taken a bullet, but he continued to smoke on the ground while peering forwards. I heard a singing noise very close; then it came again; the noise might have been in my head, like a disturbance in the ear. They were bullets, missing – as I supposed – by inches and perhaps by less than inches. Dawson was roaring: 'Get down! Get down!' But I was already down. I looked beyond Dawson. On the other side of him stood Scholes, and that's who he was shouting at. I too called to Scholes to get down, but he was beyond hearing. He was wandering away to the right, into the smoke. I told myself I was not scared; it was just that I'd somehow got hypnotised. I might die *now*; or I might die *now*. If I lifted my hand, a bullet might go through it; or my hand might dodge the bullet that would've hit it if I'd kept the hand down.

Dawson watched me for a moment, then said, 'There's the job, mate,' and he pointed with his cigarette a little way ahead. I saw two bobbing tin hats – bobbing faster than any other two in a line of digging men. I believed that cigarette smoke came from underneath one of them. It was the twins, working at the head of the sap.

'Let's go then,' I said, which took a big effort to say.

'You reckon?' said Dawson.

'Get those shovels going,' I said, and the close whistling came again.

Dawson was nodding.

'Zig-zag,' I said, and we stood and we pelted.

When were about six feet short of the hole we both leapt, so that it would have looked to the twins like the arrival of two long jumpers – if they'd paid any attention, that is, which they did not seem to have. They just carried on digging. Oamer and Oliver Butler were already there, digging behind them. Captain Quinn was lying behind these two, on his front. He appeared to be writing a bloody letter. The men deepening the sap behind him were all RE blokes, but no . . . Tinsley was in there digging with them. Good. I didn't want his *Railway Magazines*.

I crouched down, shaking my head at Oamer. Beyond him, Quinn was giving his letter to Tinsley, sending him back along the sap with it. Quinn then crawled over towards Oamer, Dawson and myself.

'This is a very fluid situation,' he began. 'I don't want to risk you men trying to work outside this sap. I've sent young Tinsley back to seek clarification. We dig until I hear back.'

As Quinn returned on all fours to his former position, two more men leapt into the sap, nearly braining him.

'Could you try to be more careful?' he said, but they couldn't hear him above the racket. The men were strangers, not part of our battalion, and I liked the way Quinn let them stay and take cover. I unhooked the shovel from my webbing and fell in behind the twins. Once they saw that I was in position, with Bernie Dawson alongside, they began pitching the earth – the 'stuff' – backwards so that we might chuck it up over the sides. This was according to our training as pioneers. (It was hard work to dig the leading edge of a sap *and* to pitch the earth out of it.) We pressed forward at a good rate. At first I was digging half lying; then I was digging half standing. I would keep glancing over the top. I couldn't help it; it was that fascinating.

The twins didn't trouble at all to keep their heads down. Every so often they'd see a man hit, and one would say to the other, 'He's 'appened an accident' or, '*He's* petered *right* out.'

After a long while, I sat on the bottom of the sap, and took a drink of water.

I wore no watch. The twins were now singing, some song about making money on the railway: 'An' the brass in our pockets, it's shinin', shinin'.'

Later, when we'd advanced perhaps forty yards, I asked Oamer, 'What *time* is it?' and he laughed at the question.

He said, 'Come what may, time and the hour runs through the roughest day.'

'Eh?' I said, and he repeated it.

Then he said, 'Two o'clock.'

Later, when we were all drinking water, and shells were coming close, I asked Oamer:

'Do you think they've found our range?'

'Nothing to be done if they have,' he replied.

'You see, that's why they call you a philosopher,' said Dawson.

After we'd eaten our emergency ration, Tinsley came back, and reported to Quinn that we were to press on, digging connections with advanced shell holes. With his tin hat removed, so that he might mop his brow, and with mud falling into his beautiful hair from some nearby explosion, Oamer reported the position to us. 'The situation', Captain Quinn had decided, 'was still not under control.' Any forward move would be risky, but it must be done. Oliver Butler would remain in the present sap in order to take delivery of, and to operate, a field telephone that Quinn had asked to be brought forward. At last he would be making use of the badge he'd earned at Hull. We were evidently one of the most forward groups in an entrenched position. The German front was now only a matter of a hundred and seventy or so yards off. We were to remember that the machine guns were still going like blazes over there.

Another shell came near, and ten seconds after it had gone off, I felt what I assumed was sweat running down my cheeks. I put my hand to it, and it was blood.

'We might be better off out of here anyway,' said Oamer, and at that I realised he meant to come with us. Eyeing my cut, he took out the gauze pad from his own field dressing, and pressed it on to my cheek for me – a very strange moment. Dawson was making ready to leave, easing himself up and over the side like a snake. I did likewise and, once again at risk of bullets as well as shells, we crawled, faces an inch above the hard mud, on to which drops of blood from my cheek periodically fell. My neck chafed against my tunic collar: I was being burnt by the sun.

During our crawl forward, I saw no man standing on the battlefield. The only difference was between those that moved and those that didn't.

We came to a shell hole perhaps fifty yards beyond the end of the sap we'd left behind. It was a circle fifteen feet wide, and one foot deep. It afforded hardly any more protection than being out in the open. We rolled into it, and lay on our stomachs, breathing dirt, and with our heads to the side, since that made them smaller to the machine gunners than if we'd lain face down. Our faces faced one another.

'This hole,' said Dawson, 'it's too fucking small.'

'Yeah,' I said.

'When you *want* a big shell to have landed, it fucking hasn't. How many Woodies have you got left?'

'One.'

'I've two.'

After a short while, in which we watched two Scotsmen (well, they wore kilts) fall to the cracks of rifle bullets a little way off, Dawson said, 'I have a plan.'

'Let's hear it then,' I said, my mouth distorted by being pressed so hard against the ground.

'We share one Woodbine now, and have one apiece later on.'

'Later on,' I said, 'I like that.'

'Gives us something to look forward to,' said Dawson.

He lit a cigarette sideways, drew on it twice, and passed it over to me. The smoke gave me courage, and I lifted my head and looked over the edge of the hole.

I saw a man upright about thirty yards off to the left: Scholes. I called out to him to get down, at which Dawson twisted about so as to look in the same direction. Scholes looked back our way, but only as if we were an annoying distraction from some other business. He re-fixed his gaze towards the enemy lines. At the sound of a bullet crack, he closed his eyes, as though he'd seen all he wanted to, and then the shell that I believed he had been in search of met him. I watched the smoke clear. It took its time, but I knew from the start that Scholes would not emerge from it. I thought of his hunt for the owl carrier on York station; he had not found him, and he'd been fighting a losing battle ever since. Scholes had missed his way, ought to have been a musician, and would have been if he'd been born into the right class. Dawson turned back towards me.

'It's a shame about him,' he said at length, 'but he'd have ended in a mental home the way he was going.'

There was nothing for it but to start digging, and we began by scraping at the earth with our boots, then running the blades of our shovels over the surface of the clay so as to get it down bit by bit. After half an hour, we might have been two inches further down. We lay flat as before, facing one another.

'It's a dead loss,' I said, 'the ground's baked hard.'

Dawson was removing his Woodbine packet from his tunic pocket, or trying to. He was having difficulty extracting it, so he rolled onto his back.

'Watch it,' I said.

He'd fished out the packet and was holding it just above his chest. There came a whistling sound – as a man might make when he sees a good-looking woman – and the packet was somersaulting in the air, knocked by the flying bullet. It landed beyond the hole, and bounced away.

'Reduce your smoking bill by about half,' said Dawson. It was the slogan on a poster that had been near the ticket office in York station for years. I lit my own Woodbine by the sideways method, and we shared that one.

'We're for it,' said Dawson.

We were in a fix, no question. We couldn't dig without standing, and we couldn't stand without being shot. I was all-in, and this tiredness took the edge off my fear. It was hopeless to try to avoid death in a place like this. It would be a matter of hoping for special treatment from God, and no man has a right to expect that. I tilted my head up slightly, and looked back towards the sap we'd lately vacated, which came and went according to the swirling of the smoke. Just then I could see it fairly clearly and there was movement over there. The twins were emerging. They faced our hole, and they came running, holding their rifles as though on a bayonet charge, and – I swear – laughing, with their spades (or 'blades') flapping behind them and tangled up anyhow in their webbing. They must have been sent by Quinn. A whizzbang came down close as they approached, and the twins landed in our hole together with the dirt blown from it, both shouting at exactly the same time, 'Heavy shower!' Not that they looked at either of us; they just unhitched their shovels and dug. We all dug, and we had four foot of earth in front of us in next to no time, three of those four feet having been created by the twins. Even on their knees they dug with a proper swing to their shovels; the clay seemed to cause them no trouble, probably on account of the sharpness of their blades. Every so often they would stop and take a belt of water – until their bottles ran out – or they'd observe the landing of a nearby shell, and make some remark while facing the German lines such as 'Are you trying to wake a dead *'orse?'* always as though this was a terrific lark.

Even so, I ought to have thanked them for pitching in, and I daresay Dawson felt the same, only they would not look at us, so we had no opportunity. Now we only had to connect back to the sap. I risked another look at it. I thought I saw Quinn's head, looking over. Oliver Butler was there behind him, and Tinsley. But I couldn't see Oamer. As I looked on, Tinsley rose, came out the sap, and started charging. He was coming our way. I watched him, roaring at him to come on even though he was already going full tilt. He seemed to start his leap about twenty feet short of our hole.

'What are you lot doing?' he said, when he'd landed.

'Playing fucking sardines,' said Dawson.

'Message from the Staff,' Tinsley said, and he was breathless, so that he gave the message as it might appear on a telegram, '. . . no hope of taking Thiepval . . . Their front trenches and wire all intact . . . our digging useless . . . hang on here for now . . . return to own lines . . . under cover darkness.'

When he'd got his breath back, he gave more news.

'Oamer's copped it. He's all right though. He was on the edge of the hole, letting fly with his rifle . . . Been at it all afternoon . . . And he was just reloading when a piece of shell case took the top off his middle finger. He was cool as you like about it. He just said, "Now *that's* rather singular." Quinn sent him back to our lines.'

'What's Oliver Butler up to?'

'He's been taking a few pots as well, and he's turned telephonist. Very proud, he is, of being able to wind that little handle.'

'Did you bring any water, son?' asked Dawson.

'Oh,' said Tinsley. 'Quinn told me to bring some over, but I forgot.'

'No bother,' said Dawson. 'We can last out until dark.'

'He said I should bring a packet of cigarettes, but I forgot that 'n' all.'

Dawson scowled at the kid from behind his back.

'Well, cigarettes are detrimental to health,' I said.

After a while, Tinsley perked up again, saying, 'You know . . . the 14th Northumberlands went over kicking a football!'

Well, that was the 'pals' for you. I thought of Thackeray's words: Was this a war or a social outing?

'. . . About half of them have copped it,' the kid added.

The sun was fading now. I thought: what a waste of a beautiful day. I couldn't stop calling to mind the image of Scholes on the look-out for a shell to take him away, or had it been a rifle bullet that had got him first? *Had* he done for young Harvey on Spurn Point and then hidden the bike, only to pretend to find it later? Perhaps he thought, with Sergeant Major Thackeray on the case, that there was no point in surviving the war? I figured again the moment of his death.

He had closed his eyes at the sound of a near bullet.

. . . Wait a bit. Had he been shot from the rear, a moment before being shelled?

'Railway topics?' Tinsley suddenly said.

'Oh,' I said. 'Go on then.'

'When you were on the engines, Jim, how often would the boiler plates be scraped clean? As a general rule, I mean?'

'Can't recall,' I said.

'Can't *recall*?' he said, and he looked so downhearted that I said, 'But look here. Tell me about your man, Tom Shaw. Have you been on a run with him?'

'I have that,' said Tinsley, and a shell came, and we all pressed down that bit lower. 'I was third man with him on a run to Leeds – him and his regular fireman, Percy Aspinall. Lovely sunny day it was, just like . . . Well, not like this *exactly* . . . Coming out of the south shed with dampers shut, jet off, and the firehole door wide open . . . gauge showing 175lbs . . . That was one of the best moments in my life so far. I got down when we came to our train, and Tom Shaw let me couple on and tighten up the shackle. I called up to him "Blow up!" and he started to create the vacuum.' Tinsley inched closer towards me. 'Tom was dead set on doing the run in under the half hour . . . Against regulations, mind you, but . . .'

The boy talked on, and I let him because his voice covered up the cries from the other shell holes that were becoming more noticeable as the light faded. Our barrage had long since dropped off, and there were more rifles to be heard amid the machine guns, which must have meant that that *fewer* machine guns were being fired. But still it was not safe to stand, and even the twins were lying quite flat. The lack of water, and the strain of waiting for the fatal shell to come began to turn me a bit funny. Under the flickering colours of the Verey lights, I started to think that because our hole was practically a perfect circle, it might keep me alive by magic. I would hear the twins muttering, and couldn't tell whether I was hearing right or making it up:

'The witch falls into the candle wax,' I seemed to hear one of them say, while the other replied, 'And that's the thief, brother.' One of the pair had a hard biscuit left, and they passed it between them saying, 'Take a bit and leave a bit' until it was all gone. Dawson had obviously gone queer as well, because he was talking about going out to find the Woodbine that had flown away. But as the evening wore on, all my thoughts turned towards water. I could not think of York station without picturing the drinking fountain in the Gentlemen's lavatory on the main 'Up' platform. To think of all the times I'd walked past there without making use of it. I closed my eyes, and, for all the noise of the battle, I might have slept, only some vision of water would keep waking me.

Dawson had turned towards me.

'Do you realise', he said, 'that even if we get out of this, the odds are seven to one for each of us against being tied to a post and shot by firing squad.'

He meant on account of Harvey's death.

'They *were* one in eight,' said Dawson, 'but then Scholes bought it.'

'But Scholes might have *done* it,' I said.

'Makes no difference, does it?' said Dawson. 'If Thackeray thought Scholes was the culprit, he wouldn't drop the matter just because Scholes was dead. He'd just find another mark. He has to have someone who's alive, you see. Otherwise he can't kill them . . .'

'When Thackeray questioned you,' I said, 'did he ask you about the cut on my knuckle?'

'What cut, mate?' said Dawson. He frowned, which somehow nearly made his moustache disappear. 'I believe he asked me whether you'd got injured in our little . . . whatever it was . . . It's a bit hazy, Jim . . . I said no, not as far as I could – '

A dirty face appeared over the lip of the hole.

It was Quinn, lying down. Straining to be heard over the sound of explosions, he said, 'The present lull affords an opportunity to withdraw.'

He passed out water bottles from his haversack; we all drank, and made ready to follow Quinn, wriggling, back to our own front lines. Dawson had set me calculating odds, and I reckoned they were very much against our safe return.

Aveluy Railhead: Late July 1916

Aveluy was the railhead for the light railway operation got up by Captain Leo Tate of the Royal Engineers, who in fact had lately become Major Tate, but he was no more military – that is to say, bullish – than he had been on Spurn. I threw down my Woodbine and saluted him as he came out of one of the little shacks that served as the office, but I don't know why I bothered. He'd seemed to be about to step over the tracks and come towards me, but he merely held up five fingers, calling, 'Five minutes, Stringer! I'm off to see O/C BAC,' and ducked into another of the shacks. O/C BAC . . . Officer Commanding Brigade Ammunition Column. He was the bloke from the Royal Artillery, who talked to the Royal Engineers about where they should send their train-loads of shells.

So I was left dangling about, circling the little locomotive that fumed away in the fading light of a rainy afternoon, impatient to be off along the line towards the villages recently taken. Here, new gun positions were to be installed for new bombardments in the push, the first phase of which had proved to be not so big a push after all, but more like the start of a slow crawl east that was costing, some said, two dead men for every yard gained.

I had been at Aveluy for two days, having been detached from my own battalion and attached to Tate's new Light Railway Operating Company. It was a typical village of the Somme district, which is to say a cluster of smashed buildings with a crucifix at its main crossroad, and a collection of shell-damaged trees on its fringes that looked like half-burnt telegraph poles. There were more of these to the north than the south of the village, and someone had had the nerve to call them 'Aveluy Wood'. Tate's operation was in a clearing in this Wood. It was approached by two standard-gauge railway lines – the nearest they dared come to the scenes of the Somme battle. One came in from Acheux, which lay directly to the west. The other approached from the south, from Albert, the hub of the central Somme region. This track from Albert to Aveluy was the first stage of the line that had once run north-east to Arras, but it wasn't safe – and in fact no longer existed – beyond Aveluy.

Any journey leading any way eastwards meant trouble, and it was to the east that the little locomotive was just then pointing. It was a black tank engine with two big domes above the boiler. The engine itself was comically small, and the domes were comically big, as if somebody's pencil had slipped, twice, in the drawing room.

The narrow-gauge line on which it sat began a few yards opposite to the buffer stops of the big lines from Acheux and Albert. At midnight every night a long, dark materiel train brought shells or entrenching equipment from Acheux or Albert, and these goods were stored on the sidings of what was called the Yard, in which standard-gauge and narrow-gauge lines were tangled according to some system understood only by Captain Tate. Most of the shells were on pallets in between the lines of the Yard, but one narrow-gauge flat wagon was loaded with a dozen six-inch shells, and this would form our load for the evening. A dozen shells would be chickenfeed to the three guns in the section we'd be delivering to. They'd get through a hundred and twenty in a night with no bother, but it was by way of a trial run: the first delivery of ammo by narrow-gauge rail rather than the cratered roads that presently served the forward positions.

All around the Yard was a jumble of tin shacks with splayed-out walls and little bent chimneys, the purpose of each being indicated in paint on the door: 'Workshop'; 'Office'; 'Canteen', and so on. The whole set-up was called Burton Dump after Burton Junction north of York station. This was Tate's doing, him being a York man. All in all, it looked like a picture of a town in the Wild West of America such as you might see in a boy's paper.

By day, Burton Dump slept, as did the blokes stationed there. Such men as *were* at large in Burton during the daytime were under orders to look out for Boche balloons or aeroplanes, and Jerry *had* put some 5.9s down in the vicinity, one of which, a dud, was propped outside the canteen as a souvenir and a warning. The men also kept an eye out for rats – of which there'd been plenty from the word go – and shot them when they could.

A red dusk was falling over the tracks and buildings of the Dump just then – a blackness floating within it. From our forward lines, four miles to the east, came the sound of the usual screaming match, but I had learnt to ignore it by now.

I heard bootsteps, and Tate came around the side of the engine.

'Where are the others, Stringer?'

'Should be here directly,' I said. 'They knew the time for the off.'

As I spoke, I saw Tinsley stepping out of the engine men's mess, and fixing on his tin hat. He began walking towards us, grinning fit to bust, yet trying to look serious as he repeatedly saluted Tate, who was crouching down at the engine's wheels and muttering to himself something like, 'Trouble with these brutes is . . . always having to nip the bearings up.' Standing up and turning about, he at last saw one of Tinsley's salutes, which he ignored.

'You two ever pair up back in York?' he enquired, looking from Tinsley to me.

He seemed to have forgotten for the moment that I was a railway policeman, and Tinsley only an engine cleaner, but no matter. He had seen us driving and firing on Spurn, and that was enough for him. He seemed to have taken a fancy to our little lot, in spite of whatever might have happened to young Harvey on Spurn. I supposed it was the York connection that made him stick with us; and that he'd put the boy's death down to suicide. Anyhow, he was, generally speaking, not much interested in anything that was not mechanical.

The three of us climbed up onto the footplate. It was a tight squeeze, not least because Tinsley and I were being required to operate the engine while wearing tin hats and respirators with rifles to be kept within arm's length at all times. Tinsley opened the fire door.

'Needs a bit on,' he said with satisfaction. Practically shoving me out of the way, he turned to the coal bunker, where he picked up the little shovel, which was just two feet long, and used it to put three lumps of coal – one at a time so as to savour the job – into the whirling flames. He might as well have pitched them in with his hand, but that wouldn't have been fireman-like. Everything about the controls was the same as for a normal engine, only about half size, so I felt like a giant up there as I performed my checks.

'Sorry to hear about old Squint,' said Tate, who was studying the catch on the footplate locker. I had examined the engine myself but not yet looked in there.

'Squint, sir?' I said.

'Captain Quinn,' he said.

In the small hours of July 2nd, when we'd been about six feet away from our home trench, shrapnel had broken Quinn's left arm. It had been a bad break, but he would be rejoining the battalion – presently quartered at a spot called Bouzincourt – before long, and then coming on to Burton Dump as liaison officer between the Royal Engineers and the other units that would be required to work the small-gauge railway. We discussed these matters for a while; then I respectfully asked Tate why he called Quinn 'Squint', since he didn't appear to have any trouble with his eyes.

'He doesn't have a *squint*,' said Tate, who was now reaching inside the locker. 'Of *course* he doesn't, but one of his middle names is Stephen, so it's S. Quinn . . . Squint, you see.'

It struck me that we were not the beneficiaries of the York connection so much as the St Peter's School connection – the old school tie. I thought back to my own school at Baytown. Not one of the people I'd been there with had come up again in my life. Tate had shut the locker door and was turning around. He held a crumpled canvas bag, and he took out of it a grenade – a Mills bomb. As he held it up, Tinsley, at the fire door, took a single step back. I managed to hold my ground, but only just.

'Before we set off,' Tate said, 'a little word about the procedure should the Hun try to capture the engine. You put this,' he said, indicating the hand grenade, 'into there.' And he indicated the firebox. 'Then get *right* out of it.'

Well, the Germans did have their own lines of the same gauge, so they would have a use for our loco. But Tinsley, I could see, was appalled at this waste of a good engine.

'Now where's our guard?' said Tate.

I indicated Oliver Butler, who'd crept up from nowhere, and was standing on the ground by the engine, a martyr to the fading light and falling rain. He saluted Tate, not overenthusiastically. But it would take more than a scowl from Butler to stop the smiles of Tate. Just as though we were all playing a party game, he asked Butler, 'And where's our train then, guard?'

With a sigh, Butler pointed to the one loaded wagon in the Yard.

'Let's go and get it, Stringer,' said Tate, at which Butler began walking over to the wagon.

Since he was a man for correct form, albeit in a joking sort of way, I asked Tate, 'Permission to perform a shunting manoeuvre, sir.'

Tate waved his left hand. With his right, he was oiling the reversing lever. Tinsley was peering at the fire again.

'Think we need a couple more rocks on there?' he asked.

I didn't like to disappoint, so I gave him the nod.

'Brake please,' I said, and Tinsley turned from the fire and unscrewed the handbrake. Instinctively, I put my hand up to the whistle, and froze in mid-motion, grinning at Tate.

'It's no easy matter to drive a steam locomotive discreetly, Stringer,' he said, 'but this we must try.'

I put the gear into reverse, and eased the regulator open – it was a queer, lateral job. As I pulled on it, I couldn't resist saying, 'I'll just give her a breath of steam' and we eased away very satisfactorily. All our lives would shortly be endangered – already were, in point of fact – but I had no thought in my mind just then apart from avoiding wheelslip at the 'right away'. We buffered up to the loaded wagon as Bernie Dawson came strolling across the siding.

'Ah,' said Tate. 'Our loader. I was wondering where he'd got to.'

Porters were 'loaders' at the Burton Dump; they ought really to have been 'unloaders', since their work would be carrying the shells to the gun placements in the forward areas. Dawson made for the cab, and saluted Tate, who appeared suddenly fascinated by Dawson's face, which was half in shadow under the tin hat.

'Fusilier,' said Tate, 'I can never make out whether you have a moustache or just haven't washed properly.'

'Bit of both, sir,' said Dawson. 'If I could lay my hands on a cake of soap, sir, I'd – '

'Have a shave?' Tate cut in. 'Is that a promise?'

But while he was 'army' enough to have mentioned Dawson's appearance he was not that way strongly enough to keep on about it. He now asked Butler to couple up the wagon, and I could see that our guard didn't like that one bit. He *did* take care of his appearance, and coupling up would put dirt on his hands. As Butler laboured to hook us up, Tate gave me a little lecture on the coupling pin, which he was very proud of, and which he'd improvised himself from an ammo box pin, having found the original design unsatisfactory. Butler and Dawson now lifted up the drop-down side of the wagon and locked it into place. It was important that the shells did not roll off. Yes, the fuses had been stowed in separate boxes (the shells had wooden plugs in their tops instead), but any shell suffering an impact might still explode.

In very short order, we were rolling away from the Burton Dump, heading in what was known to the men of the Dump as the 'Up' direction: towards the front, and the flashes and screams of the Evening Hate. The tracks put down so far led into the village of Ovillers, what was left of it, then into the more easterly village of Pozières. Ovillers had been captured a couple of weeks before, and while Pozières had lately come into our hands, the Germans hadn't yet given up on it, and were shelling it nightly, so it was a pretty hot spot to be riding towards. On the other hand I was at last employed in the job I had aspired to since boyhood. (Of course, I should have known that it would come about, if at all, with complications.)

We were now running surrounded by skeleton trees with a look of winter even in late July. The tracks had been put down quickly and roughly, and we were shaking about a good deal. The narrowness of the line gave a heightened idea of speed, and we would seem to rush up to a smashed tree at a great rate before diverting away at the last moment. Tate was giving us a lecture about the engine. It was a Baldwin, built in America; a pretty good steamer, but the high boiler made it unstable and liable to tip over, which gave cause for concern if you might happen to be pulling, say, three tons of high explosive shells, which might become a normal sort of load in time. I looked back over the shaking coal bunker. Dawson sat smoking on the wagon. Oliver Butler stood on the coupling unit at the rear, holding onto the wheel of the handbrake, and not seeming to enjoy the ride over-much. After a while, he returned my gaze, saying, 'Keep your eye on the road, mate, will you?'

He was exposed to the rain, and he minded that, or perhaps he minded that I had the protection of a cab roof, even if it did extend only halfway across the footplate.

The man Butler . . .

According to Tinsley, he had been firing from the sap on the first day of the battle. Scholes would have been within his range, and it had seemed to me that he might have taken a bullet before the shell hit. Scholes had threatened to speak out about what he knew – whatever that might be – if Thackeray returned to give him another roasting, and it seemed that Thackeray did intend to return, and we all knew it. Oliver Butler had certainly overheard Scholes's threat. He'd been standing behind him when he made it.

Might Oamer have heard it as well? He had stepped out of the billet only a moment later – and he too had evidently been firing from the sap.

Thackeray had not yet come to the Dump, but he had been seen about in Albert. Well, Tinsley – sent there on an errand – had seen him, on his horse outside the cathedral, apparently watching every private soldier that went past. Blokes fighting and dying for their country . . . You'd think he'd lay off . . .

We were rolling past a bloody great shell crater. The edge of it was about six feet from the tracks, and the rain was trying to fill it.

'Crikey,' said Tinsley.

Tate, following his eyes, said, 'Jerry's got some pretty big stuff pointed this way.'

'How close would a Boche shell have to be to set off our load?' Tinsley enquired.

'About as close as that,' said Tate, indicating the crater under discussion. I was glad when we'd left it behind – out of sight out of mind. Except that Tate didn't drop the subject. 'You see, our shells don't have their fuses fitted, but what *is* a fuse? Heat and air pressure. An enemy shell could easily provide that.'

'Watch your level,' I said to Tinsley, because the water gauge was a little low; and he practically leapt on the injector. Tate was nodding in an absent sort of way. I didn't doubt that he could have driven this engine half asleep, and it annoyed me to think so. Was he really superior, or just of a superior class? After a brief pause he took up his lecture again, all about the difficulty of getting stuff to the front by MT. This stood for Motor Transport: lorries. But Tate preferred to say MT. Horses weren't *in* it, and he never gave them a mention. Horses were the past. He hoped to have a dozen trains a night running to the front before long. At this, I thought again of Oamer: he would be returning to the line over the next day or so, minus his finger, and would be joining our detachment at Burton Dump as supervisor of the running office, which would control the movements of the little trains. His experience in the York ticket office fitted him for that role; and his all-round braininess.

We were shaking in a different way now, climbing out of the wood. More coal was needed.

'Steep hill,' said Tinsley, swinging his shovel.

'Now locomotives don't really go up hills, do they?' said Tate. 'I would call that . . .' And he thought for a good ten seconds. 'I would call it a knoll.'

The engine danced in a yet different way, and harsh rumbling came from underneath.

'Girder bridge,' said Tate. 'Would you believe our boys put that up in less than two days?'

I would've actually, since the thing moved as we went over it. I looked down and back as we came off it, and saw a demoralised-looking black river that had given up flowing anywhere.

'The River Ancre,' said Tate.

It certainly wasn't up to much. The big river hereabouts was the Somme, but that was off somewhere to the south and I'd never seen it. We went past a wooden post with a sign on it.

'That was the first of our stations,' said Tate, facing backwards on the footplate, and looking back at the post with affection. I hadn't been able to make out the name.

'Old Station,' said Tate. 'We made it ten days ago. There were gun positions either side – behind that hummock, and in that ditch.' He pointed to shadowy features I could barely see in the dark. 'Abandoned now, they've done their work.'

The noise of the Hate was becoming louder as he pointed over to a wrecked house. The queer thing was that the roof remained, supported by only two and a half walls.

'Holgate Villa,' Tate said, grinning. 'Part of Ovillers, technically.'

I was getting the idea now. There was a Burton at York, also an Old Station. And Holgate Villa was a grand old house that had been swallowed up by the York railway lands, and was used – last time I'd been in there – for storing masses of dusty restaurant car crockery.

I looked back at Holgate Villa. The Verey lights flashing on it – red, green, yellow, flickering red again – and I knew the situation was unstable. I didn't believe it could be there for too much longer.

We rolled slowly past another post.

'New Station,' said Tate. 'German second line, as was. Gun positions . . . there!' And at that instant the gun position in question – out of sight behind a low hill – loosed off a shell. A whistle came from the German side; then another whistle, then the two crumps. In the field next to us, two trees made of mud arose and collapsed. I heard again the steady beat of the engine. Tinsley eyed me, nodding.

'Steaming nicely,' he said, in a confidential sort of way.

One hundred and sixty pounds of pressure; faint ghost of smoke and steam over the chimney. Tinsley and me . . . We trusted the engine to take us through the scrap over Ovillers. But then came another Boche shell, and two more sent over from our side; we were approaching another of the Somme woods, another graveyard of trees. I pulled on the regulator. I would feel a bit safer in the trees, such as they were, but as we closed on them under the falling shells, the engine gave a lurch. Tate crashed into Tinsley, and called out, 'We're over!' But we stabilised the next moment.

'Track gang missed that spot,' said Tate.

Our track gang was Andy and Roy Butler – they'd gone ahead in the afternoon to walk the track and make good. We were to collect them at the dropping off point for the goods.

'They've done a decent job up to now,' I said, for we'd had a smooth ride given the conditions. Tate began to speak but a shell came down, so he stopped and then started again: 'Rather uncommunicative, that pair.'

The trees came around us, and formed up either side in their dead parade; a shell came into the woods causing a disturbance in the rear ranks of the trees and setting two fires. I was sweating. It was a hot night, though still raining somewhat. I looked back at our two passengers, and both Dawson and Butler gazed in the direction of the burning trees with a look of wonder. I was feeling a drag on the engine; I could see no incline, and I wondered whether Dawson had screwed down the brake a little, having been scared by our near-spill, or just in order to spite me. He was more of a brakesman than a guard, and his control of the brake was the only power at his command.

I saw a moving light ahead and what appeared to be the side rails of another girder bridge.

'This is us,' said Tate.

I knocked off the regulator, and we cruised up to the light, which gradually turned into a hurricane lamp held by Roy Butler – or was it Andy? Impossible to tell in the dark. The lamp gave a whitish glow. In their ganging days back in York, there would have been red and green filters. There would have been a 'responsible person' to stand in advance of them on the line, and they would have carried twice as many tools as they presently did. One held a shovel and fish bolt spanner, the other a mallet and a track gauge, for making sure two feet stayed two feet.

Oliver Butler braked his wagon, and climbed down to his brothers; Tate also jumped down, and he addressed the twins, I noticed, as though they were normal.

'Well, we've had a fairly smooth run out . . . Anything in particular need of attention?'

The twins gave a shrug. They looked sidelong at their brother.

'Come on now,' said Tate, 'what did you have to do?'

'Tightening,' said Andy, who held the spanner.

'Flattening,' said Roy, who held the mallet.

And then Andy, turning to Roy and laughing while squirming strangely, said, '. . . *Frightening*,' drawing the word out.

Tate looked up – I remained on the footplate – and frowned.

Tate said, 'You've been having a warm time of it, have you?'

From behind the twins came a great bang – like somebody deciding that enough is enough – and a shell went climbing, scrambling into the air at hundreds of miles an hour. It was one of ours, there was a battery hard by but out of sight in the trees.

'Place is in uproar!' said Roy, and for once he did offer a direct glance at Tate.

Another shell was loosed from a bit further beyond.

'Oh mother!' said Andy, and now he too was looking directly at Tate, while grinning. Tate turned back to me, evidently knocked by the sight of Andy's face. I heard the whistling in the black sky, over the broken trees. One was coming our way. I counted to five, and it came down a hundred yards off, and the only effect on us was a quantity of sticks blown towards the engine.

I heard the cracking of tree branches, and saw men coming towards us, rifles in hand. Four silent men, soaked in sweat and with tunics undone. They were from one or more of the gun placements. They contemplated the Baldwin with amusement, as it seemed to me. At the sight of the blokes, Tate called out, 'Fusilier Dawson!' and Bernie Dawson, who'd been sitting on the edge of his wagon, scrambled to his feet, saying, 'Right, who wants some bombs?'

Tinsley was brushing some coal dust off the footplate, which was hardly necessary, and I contemplated with anxiety the thin twists of smoke and steam coming up from the chimney.

'You know, I can't believe she'd give us away,' said Tinsley, seeing where I was looking. 'Daft isn't it?'

It was, but I knew what he meant. On the other hand, we were just another fire in the woods. There seemed to be several going on about us. The gunners, Dawson (with Woodbine on the go), and the twins had begun carting the shells to the guns. One man could lift one shell, just about. Oliver Butler was standing by his wagon. Lugging shells was beneath him, or so he thought, but Tate, who'd been scrutinising the wheels of the Baldwin, suddenly eyed Butler.

'What are you doing, man?'

'I'm superintending the train,' came the reply. 'It's the first duty of the train guard.'

'Well this is not the Scotch Express,' said Tate. 'Lend a hand with the shells.'

And so Butler picked up a shell, or tried to. He had a job to keep hold of it.

'Want a hand?' I said, my aim being not so much to help him as to save us being blown to buggery if he dropped it wrong end first. But he'd got a grip on it now, and fairly staggered off into the woods without replying. Tinsley, meanwhile, was peering at a particular tree, which I now saw had a short plank nailed to the upper trunk. He caught up the lamp that was hooked on the locker door. He jumped down from the footplate and held the lamp up before the tree. There were two words painted on the sign, and they came and went as the lamp swung.

'Naburn Lock,' he finally pronounced, in triumph.

Well, I knew Naburn Lock. It was only a mile or so south of Thorpe-on-Ouse – a popular spot with picnickers. The village of Naburn was picturesque, and there was a tea place at the lock. People would sit by it and watch the boats go through, marvelling at the pleasure cruisers of the York swells, and hoping one of them would collide with the lock gates, or somehow come a cropper.

The shell carters were now returning, having cleared the wagon. Tate, standing by the side of the Baldwin, had satisfied himself as to the soundness of the wheels. He said, 'Naburn Lock, that's right. Let's have the lamp, and I'll show you why.'

Tinsley handed him the light, and Tate walked over to the little ditch traversed by the track. The lamp showed a quantity of smashed and rotten wood in the black water. 'A gate,' said Tate. 'A gate in the water – that's what a lock is, so . . . Naburn Lock. My mother would take me there. We'd have ices at Martindale's, and I'd watch the operation of the lock gates.'

That was the name of the tea rooms, and it was operated by a little old woman with a sweet face but a hunched back. She had some young assistants – generally one or two lasses who were real lookers – but I recalled that old Ma Martindale looked so frail, yet so anxious to please her customers, that you felt sorry for her rather than the opposite when the place was full.

Tate was climbing back up, and I was readying to pull the reversing lever (we would be returning to Burton Dump backwards), when I happened to glance over to Oliver Butler, who was standing by the wagon, eyeing the plank nailed to the tree, his brothers either side of him. All three looked mortified.

One – Roy, as far as I could make out in the gloom – was saying, 'What's going *off*, our kid? What's to *do*?' and both were looking to their brother in search of an answer to something. Oliver Butler seemed about to speak – to address some remark to Leo Tate, as it seemed to me – before deciding at the last moment to keep silence.

Was it the naming of the halt that had bothered him?

'Know Naburn Lock, do you?' I called out, and the three Butlers turned to me as one man, while making no remark. 'It's a pretty spot.'

Of course, every railwayman in York knew the *village* of Naburn because the London line was carried over the river Ouse by a swing bridge just a little way outside it. 'Decent pub in Naburn,' I called out (for I seemed to be able to hold the three of them in suspension just by speaking of Naburn), '. . . The Horseshoe. It had a dining room and a dram shop but . . .'

Shells came flying, landing either side of us, as if telling me to get on with it. Everyone climbed up; I gave a tug on the regulator and we began rolling back towards Burton Dump. I had been about to say that for all its good points, the jakes at The Horseshoe was at the bottom of the garden, which was a bugger when it rained. I'd sometimes bike along the river for a pint there when the children were in bed, and I'd hear the roaring of the weir – which was next to the Lock – from half a mile away.

On the rattling wagon, Dawson sat smoking again, while the twins stood, exchanging whispers. Roy was nodding at something Andy was saying, at the same time fishing about in his pockets, perhaps looking for his own fags. Oliver Butler was at his post on the coupling gear, and since we were rolling backwards, he was now at the front, like the figurehead on a ship. Even though I could only see his back, I somehow knew he was thinking hard. Leo Tate, cause of all this disturbance in the Butlers, was now climbing over the coal bunker, and down onto the wagon. He stood in the centre of it, perfectly balanced and looking to left and right. He'd long since forgotten about Naburn and its lock, and was on the look-out for . . . what? Some new problem to solve. Something out there in the ruined trees he could set to rights. We came out of the trees, and rolled past Old Station – I only saw it because I was on the look-out *for* it – and then I knew where to look for Holgate Villa. It still stood. Then came the New Station, followed by the different rumble of the girder bridge over the Ancre. What had been an ascent was now a tricky descent, and I knocked off the regulator, so that we coasted down towards Aveluy Wood, rattling and clanking in the sudden silence. There hadn't been a shell for five minutes and we'd shortly be back at base, but I didn't care for the way that Tate was prowling on the wagon, looking to left and right.

He turned and raised his hand to me, indicating that I should stop. He was walking forwards to Oliver Butler, to warn him of same. He'd found something to fix. He was speaking to Dawson, who kept throwing anxious or half-amused glances back to me, as Tate lectured him on the subject of a filthy puddle on the edge of the trees we were approaching. It was a shell hole, about fifteen yards off. I could make out the black shine of the water, and I didn't like the look of it. As Butler screwed down his brake, Tate was saying something to the effect: 'I mean to have a sample of that water.'

'Why, sir?' said Dawson. 'In ten minutes you can have a glass of ale in the mess.'

But I knew what Tate was about. His plan was to fit all the engines with a hose and a lifting injector to take on water from the shell holes. That way, the Boche would be *helping* us by putting down shells near the tracks – a notion that appealed no end to Tate. On the other hand, the two-foot lines were never likely to extend far enough for the engines to run low on the water put into them at Burton Dump. And muck floating about in a boiler caused more trouble than it was worth. Tate was muttering something about 'a simple filter to stop priming' – it was all Greek to Dawson. Oliver Butler, standing over his brake, was eyeing me. I believed he was thinking of different water – Naburn Lock – and it was then that I had my idea of writing to the wife to ask about the late history of that spot, and whether the name Butler was involved in any way.

Tate jumped down from the wagon. He called out, 'Does any man have a billy?'

Tinsley leant into me and said, 'There's one in the locker.'

I said, 'Don't bloody encourage him,' but too late: Tinsley was repeating the information out loud. Tinsley opened the locker and handed over the can. As Tate made towards the shell hole, I switched my gaze to the twins who were sitting cross-legged on the wagon. 'Fine style . . . Fine Style,' I heard, and having lit their cigarettes, they both turned to look at Tate, as though expecting to be entertained. They, at least, seemed to have put Naburn Lock from their minds. Tate was standing by the edge of the pool, contemplating the water. He hadn't yet bent down to take the sample when the whistling started. At that point Tate did crouch down – not for fear of the shell, but to collect water – and so there was one thing going up and one thing going down. I knew after the count of three that the shell would be close, and if I'd been stone deaf, then Alfred Tinsley's eyes – he was frozen in the act of sweeping the footplate – would have told me as much. I had my hands over my ears when the thing came down. The night became day for an instant, and I saw Tate dive into the water, at the sight of which Tinsley leant away from the engine and spewed, for only the top half of Tate had dived. His legs had been slow off the mark, had remained behind, and for a moment they had remained standing. The shell had been shrapnel, not high explosive, and the last of the bullets were now raining down into the black water. I turned my head towards the wagon. I was listening to my own breathing, and it seemed a bloody cheek, disrespectful to Tate, that it should be carrying on, even if the breaths were coming too fast. Oliver Butler was crouched behind his brake wheel; Dawson had simply turned about so that he now sat facing away from what he'd just seen. But the twins continued to stare at the spot where Tate's legs had toppled.

'He's 'appened an accident,' I heard one of them say.

'*Proper* job,' said the other.

In the silence that followed the shell, I thought of all that brain . . . all those schemes at the bottom of that black water. My next thought was: there's no commanding officer here, and it was as though every man had the same thought, for all started talking at once. Oliver Butler was calling out to me, 'Open her up, we're getting out of here.' Dawson was pacing next to the wagon, saying over and over, 'Takes the fucking cake, that does . . . It takes the fucking *biscuit* . . .' The twins were muttering fast to each other, pointing towards where Tate had been and saying, 'He's there and there. *That's* him, and *that's* him.'

I passed Tinsley a bit of rag that hung on the fire door handle – this to wipe his face. But he'd recovered quickly, and was apologising by now, moving over to his brake and making ready to unscrew it.

I said, 'Hold on, we're not going back without Tate.'

I couldn't say that it was any great feeling for the bloke that made me want to fish his top half out of the water. It was more the thought that it would not be manly to skulk back to Burton Dump without him. It would not be officer-like either. I was the driver of the engine, and the driver of the engine is the captain of the ship. I'd been a free agent for a while there at the regulator, and I'd got back my taste for independent action.

There was a tarpaulin on the wagon. I scrambled over the coal bunker, and dropped down next to it.

'Come on,' I said to Dawson, 'we're going to get him.'

'It's the shock, you know,' he said. 'You're in bloody shock.'

But he was following behind – with hurricane lamp in hand – as I struck out to the shell hole. Dawson could talk about shock. He was gabbling away nineteen to the dozen. 'His legs ought to be round here somewhere,' he said, as we closed on the pond. 'I mean they can't have gone far – not on their own. Christ, they've come apart. There's *one*. Or is that somebody else's fucking leg? I think that's another over there.'

'That leg's definitely his,' I said, indicating the first one. 'We'll come back later for it. Bring that light over here, will you?'

He did so, but needn't have bothered. The water wasn't deep, and the upper half of Tate was on the edge of it.

'How much do you suppose his bloody parents spent on his education?' said Dawson.

'Never mind about that now,' I said.

'Are you fucking *kidding* or what?'

I said, 'If we stretch out the tarp, we just pull him onto it with one heave. You take one arm, I'll get the other.'

We pulled him up, and I saw that without his cap he had a bald spot. I found myself thinking: well, at least *that* won't get any bigger. We heaved. Dawson looked away, but I looked on. I thought: there's no point looking away. Your imagination only makes up for what you don't see. Tate was normal, if soaked, down to the third button of his tunic. After that . . . well, I had an idea of an untucked shirt. I did close my eyes then, in spite of all, for I knew there'd been more to it than an untucked shirt, and as we laid him on the tarp, I heard from the wagon a fascinated sort of voice – it was one of the twins – saying, 'See his leavings, our kid', and at that *I* nearly chucked. I caught up the lamp that Dawson had set down near the tarp.

It illuminated the two legs in the rutted mud. There were only about two yards between the legs but I thought: never before have they been so far apart. Dawson picked up one with his eyes closed and head tilted to the side. I did the other, trying not to look, and also trying to stop my brain gauging the weight of it, but the part of my brain that gauged weight was paying no attention to the part that told it not to. (The leg was much lighter than I would have thought.)

The tarp, folded on the wagon with the various parts of Tate underneath it, looked much the same as the tarp folded on the wagon with nothing inside it, and when we rolled back into Burton Dump, a crowd of Royal Engineers closed around us, some holding lamps. They were all dead keen, all from the Tate mould, and excited to see that we'd got rid of our shells, and brought the engine home.

One of the lamp-lit faces belonged to another Captain. I knew his name: Muir; a quiet sort of chap, and evidently a professor, or something of the sort, at Oxford or Cambridge.

'How was the running?' he said. (He didn't seem to have noticed the absence of Tate.) 'I know Jerry was making himself rather troublesome . . . Glad to see you all back in one – '

'Sir,' I said, just to check him, stop him saying the word that was coming.

On the wagon, Dawson was lighting a Woodbine and shaking his head at me at the same time.

That first ride out had been on a Monday. We didn't go out again that week, so the batteries continued to get all their shells by MT alone. Leo Tate was buried on the Tuesday on the edge of the Dump just beyond the locomotive lifting gantry, under something that looked more like a tree than most of the trees in the vicinity. He was buried in the middle of the night – all important operations took place at night – and every man attended. The good thing, I supposed, was that he had no wife or children. There was talk of Burton Dump becoming 'Tate Dump', but this was not thought respectful. A dump was a dump, after all.

Anyhow, the thing he'd started continued to grow. More shells came in every midnight, and sandbags, barbed wire, trench posts and other fixings, not to mention food for the forward areas, so that a whole wall of Maconochie tins began to be built in the yard. The place was guarded day and night by what seemed like a whole troop of sentries, and sky watchers were posted around the clock looking out for enemy planes and balloons; also, the first stages of the tracks leading forward were kept covered by tarpaulins and other camouflage. Two more Baldwins came in on low loaders from Albert, and Tinsley and me were put to fettling them and doing nightly shunting turns about the Yard so as to run them in and check for faults. Other crews would be drafted in shortly, but for the present we had all the driving turns to ourselves.

On the Tuesday, I was waiting for the night's work to begin while drinking tea in the engine men's mess (which was lit by flickering candle stubs, and contained an avalanche of unclaimed boots) when Oliver Butler walked in. He'd evidently been searching me out, for he came straight up to me, and handed me a copy of the *Yorkshire Evening Press*, back numbers of which he would have sent out to him. At first, I thought he meant me to look at the news of the Somme campaign ('Slight Progress'), then – though it seemed unlikely – the usual advertisement for Bile Beans, which started with the words 'When Life Was Simpler, Life Was Longer' (how it got from that to Bile Beans I didn't know, never heaving read it right through), but in fact he meant a small item in the section 'Yesterday In York'.

'Third one down,' he said.

The heading read 'Sad Discovery in Woods': 'The body of a woman was discovered hanging by the neck from a tree in

Knavesmire Woods early yesterday morning. The finder was Mr Geoffrey Parker, keeper of the woods. He called in the police, who later reported that the body had been identified as that of Mrs Jane Harvey of 4, South Bank Road, York, by her husband, Frederick Harvey. Mrs Harvey was known to have been in a depressed condition ever since the death of her son by a previous marriage. William Harvey died late last year while on manoeuvres with the 17th Northumberland Fusiliers (the N.E.R. Battalion) on the Yorkshire Coast. An inquest is to be held.'

That meant an inquest into Jane Harvey's death, not William's.

I handed the paper back to Butler, who of course had been staring at me as I read it.

'Who was William's father then?' I asked him.

'Don't you know? Nor do I.'

It was as though he thought I knew but wouldn't say, and therefore he would do likewise.

'Bit of a boost for those who say it was suicide,' he said, pocketing the *Press*.

'How do you make that out?'

'Depression, suicide,' he said. 'It obviously runs in the family.'

'Only it runs *backwards*,' I said.

Butler shrugged and quit the mess, just as Tinsley walked in, saying, very bright-eyed, that he'd heard some decent Welsh coal was to be sent to us. I cut him off, telling him the news about Harvey's mother, and he fell silent. He kicked his heels for a while, then walked out. It went to his credit in a way that, ever since the death of Harvey, he'd never tried to take back his earlier remarks about him; there was none of that stuff like, 'He had his faults, but he was a capital fellow, really.' Tinsley stuck to his guns. He hadn't liked Harvey, and that was all about it. The one who seemed most upset over Harvey was Oamer, and you could be guaranteed to silence him for a good couple of minutes at any mention of the boy.

On the Wednesday night, the materiel train from Albert brought, in addition to the usual goods, Captain Quinn and Oamer himself. In addition to his duties in the running office, he would remain our section commander, and would be billeted with us in the little hut we occupied among those circling the Yard, ours being painted with the word 'DETACHMENT'.

In the small hours of Thursday, while shunting shells with Tinsley, I watched Oamer and Quinn as they moved back and forth about the Dump, sometimes separately, sometimes together, the greatcoats pulled up against the rain as they met the RE blokes they'd be working with, and generally got their bearings. Quinn wore his left arm in a black sling. A bit of a conversation between him and another officer floated over to me in the quiet moment.

'It's funny how not being shelled or shot at or gassed for a month can really buck you up,' Quinn said, 'It makes all the difference in the world. But now I come here, and I learn about poor old Tate . . . It really is too awful for words. I will be writing a very long letter to his father. Of course, I haven't got the foggiest idea what I'll be saying, but I feel I ought . . .'

An hour or so later, when I was sitting on the buffer beam of the Baldwin and smoking a Woodbine, with Tinsley eating his snap close by, Oamer came over to us.

'Interesting sort of engine,' he said.

'It shrunk in the wash, Corporal.' I said. 'How's your finger?'

'Well, it's not there,' said Oamer, and he showed us that he wore a leather sheath over the stump, 'although my brain doesn't seem to have got the message quite yet.'

'If it had been your trigger finger they'd have sent you home,' said Tinsley.

'Speaking of that,' said Oamer, 'I'm in a position to tell you that Sergeant Major Blake here, who's one of the very few men in the Royal Engineers to take any interest in army matters, will be holding a kit inspection tomorrow at nine o'clock sharp.'

'I was hoping to be asleep then,' I said, and I gave Oamer the news of Tinsley's mother. He kept silence for a minute, and I saw Tinsley watching him carefully as he did it. Oamer muttered something that I believed to be from Shakespeare – something about how you could never say the worst thing had happened, because then something *worse* would come along. Recovering himself, he said, 'Sergeant Major Blake is very keen on rifles, and he prefers clean ones to dirty ones. He will be expecting yours to come up gleaming, Jim.'

'How's that?'

'You're in line for a stripe,' he said, and young Tinsley was good enough to exclaim, 'About time!'

'In fact, two stripes. You're to be made up to corporal.'

I didn't mind letting on that I was delighted about it, and I immediately thought of the letter I would write to the wife.

'But what about Thackeray?' I said. 'I had the idea he wanted every man in the section kept back because of what happened.'

'Right then,' said Oamer, 'I'll put you in the picture. Can we get under your roof?'

He gestured at the half canopy over the footplate of the Baldwin. We climbed up, and Tinsley opened the fire door so we could have the benefit. Oamer took out his pipe from his tunic pocket, and began to fill it. (That was the real reason he'd wanted a roof over his head.)

'Now *I'm* to become a sergeant,' said Oamer.

'Holy smoke,' said Tinsley, who was poking the fire with one of the long irons, 'the brakes really are coming off.'

And as we both shook Oamer's hand – it was all a bit of a kerfuffle in that combined space – I wondered whether the kid might be feeling a bit left out.

'Thackeray did want promotions stopped,' said Oamer. 'You're right about that. He still has the section in his sights, and he means to question the lot of us again. Well, you know that . . .'

'I saw him in Albert,' said Tinsley.

'It's about the closest you'll see him to the front line,' said Oamer. 'Anyway, Captain Quinn has had his fill of him.' Oamer, having got his pipe going, pitched the match into the fire. 'You see, Thackeray's not a gentleman.'

'I think I'd worked that out,' I said.

'Captain Quinn sees no reason why deserving men should be denied promotions on his account. His line is: if Thackeray wants to bring a charge, he should get on and do it. Otherwise, he's invited Thackeray to stop meddling in a platoon commander's business. They've spoken on the telephone about it. I believe Captain Quinn was quite snappy.'

'I don't see him snapping,' I said.

'He does it very slowly,' said Oamer, 'and in a mannerly way.'

After a little more chat, he jumped down from the footplate, then looked back.

'How far forward do you go in this thing?'

'All the way,' I said. 'Pozières.'

'They're pushing on beyond there now,' said Oamer . . . which meant I might not have long to enjoy my promotion.

As Oamer walked off into the gloom, it struck me that I might have been promoted just to spite Thackeray, but I didn't care. I *wanted* him spited, and as a corporal I would be set fair for sergeant – then perhaps a field commission of the sort I'd heard were being given out pretty often, in the crazy way that things were going on.

'I like Oamer,' said Tinsley.

'Aye,' I said, nodding. 'He's a decent sort.'

Oamer was wrong about my promotion. The timing of it, I mean. Not ten minutes after he'd left us, I was called into the office of the adjutant at Burton Dump and handed a letter. 'From your battalion commander', I was told, and inside it were two stripes. The letter was short but friendly as could be, and it was not from Colonel Butterfield, who'd had a down on me for not joining the military police, but a Lieutenant Colonel Mountford, who'd replaced Butterfield some weeks before. I had been commended by both my section commander (Oamer) and my platoon commander (Quinn), and it was anticipated with confidence that I would keep up the good name of the battalion in my present posting. As I read it, Quinn himself, in soaking greatcoat, came into the little office. Close to, he did look a bit worn out, partly, I supposed, owing to the death of his friend. It was decent of him to have been battling on my behalf even while hospitalised. I saluted him, and then he shook my hand, saying, 'You ought to have a very small certificate. It hardly matters if you don't, but . . .'

I looked inside the envelope and there it was.

'Good-o,' he said.

Another salute, then he was gone.

I walked back to the detachment hut, which was empty all except for Oliver Butler. He lay on his cot with his hands behind his head. I supposed he was entitled to a bit of a relax. In the absence of regular trips forward, Butler had been working – and training – with the signals section at Burton Dump, and it was anticipated that he might man one of the forward control points when full operations began. He'd taken to the work, and it kept him off my back.

He half nodded at me when I walked in, and as I hunted up a spare hurricane lamp, and box of matches in the metal cabinets kept along one wall, he said: 'Keep it down, will you?' Well, it was the usual combination of not-quite friendliness and hostility. He was like a boxer. He would always give you the left and right in quick succession. He adjusted the position of his head somewhat. It was important to keep his hair from being disarranged.

I at last found a lamp with paraffin in it. I carried it over to my bunk and lit it. I then walked over to my kit bag, took out what I needed and went back to my cot. The lamp cast a leaping white light.

'It's too bright,' said Butler.

'Too bad, mate,' I said. 'I've a job to do. It won't take a minute.'

'It's four o'clock in the bloody morning,' he said.

It might very well have been, but most of the blokes at the Dump were still hard at it, and I could hear the sound of a lathe from the direction of the workshop. Butler looked on as I removed my boots and tunic – and as I took the two stripes from the envelope. It's true that I was putting on swank. The sewing on of the stripes could have waited until morning.

The needle in my sewing pack came ready-threaded, so I set about the job directly. Butler kept silence as I worked, but I could tell that the rhythm of his breathing had changed. After revolving (I didn't doubt) any number of remarks, he finally came out with the following:

'If you got those for any special show of initiative or valour in the field then I have to say I must have missed it.'

It was my turn to revolve some responses of my own. In the meantime I worked on.

'A full corporal . . . You've finally won the day,' he said.

After a further interval of silence I heard a clatter from his bunk. I first thought he was too disgusted to remain in the hut with me, but he instead walked over and offered his hand.

'Anyhow,' he said, 'congratulations.'

I knew this could hardly be his last word on the matter. Nonetheless, after contemplating his extended hand for a while, I stood up and shook it.

'Thanks,' I said, as I sat back down, and he returned to his cot. 'I should think you'll be on the end of a promotion yourself before too long.'

'What would I be promoted for?' he said.

'I don't know,' I said. 'Probably the sheer charm of your personality.'

He gave me a grin – genuine enough.

'I thought Thackeray had blocked all promotions for our little lot,' he said after a while, 'pending the results of his bloody everlasting investigation. But then again you're a copper.'

'Scholes was a copper,' I said, 'and Thackeray came down pretty hard on *him*.' I eyed Butler for a while, as I tended to do when the subject of Scholes came up. He didn't flinch.

'But that poor bugger was only a constable . . . and you're Oamer's favourite into the bargain. He's back, I know. I saw you chatting with him just now. I suppose he brought your stripes with him.'

'Not quite, mate,' I said, and I gave him the whole tale I'd had from Oamer about how Quinn had decided to take a stand against Thackeray.

After weighing this for a little while, during which interval I thought I heard bootsteps on the hard mud outside the door of the hut, Butler said, 'So now you have your stripes, and your engine to drive. You do a good job of it, don't get me wrong. You should see your face when you're up there at the regulator – like a bloody kid bowling a hoop. You're as bad as Tinsley.'

I had nearly finished sewing on the first stripe. I was wide awake – it was ridiculous, the galvanising effect of promotion – and I had in mind that I would irritate Butler further by writing to the wife when I'd done, rather than turning in.

'You know, mate,' said Butler, 'I don't quite get what Oamer sees in you.' After a pause he added, 'With Harvey it was obvious enough.'

'Oh yes?' I said, and I wondered whether he'd have the brass neck to come out and say it. It seemed that he did.

'Fusilier Harvey was what you might call a bonny little lad. Oamer being that way inclined . . . Well, the bloke's a bloody invert, there's no mystery about that.'

The stripe was pretty well fixed by now.

'Now here's a theory,' said Butler. 'A little hazard of mine. I only let on about it so that you might see how others could be thinking.' He stretched out once again on his cot before continuing: 'It's in Oamer's interest to keep in with all of us. Say he believes you saw some funny business between him and young Harvey. Perhaps he wants to buy your silence . . . and thinks a couple of stripes might do it.'

'Stow it,' I said, 'or I'll come over there and lay one on you.'

I cut the thread with my teeth and at that moment Oamer himself walked in, making directly over to the stove for a warm. Appearing to be his usual amiable self, he said to Butler, 'It'll be the first time you've been threatened by a chap doing embroidery, I'll bet. What are you rowing about?'

Butler, who'd fished one of his *Presses* out from under his cot and was pretending to read it, said, 'Sorry about the row . . . Corporal Stringer getting over-heated about nothing at all.'

Oamer was stowing his boots neatly under one of the unclaimed cots. Was he going to sew on his own new stripe? Rather, he took up his pipe. Every night before turning in he would clean it out before putting the ash and dead baccy into a twist of brown paper. He used a special penknife, which was made of silver plate and more like a piece of jewellery than a tool. I watched him get ready for his kip. How much had he heard of Butler's 'little hazard'? And was this theory just a product of Butler's sick imagination? The fact was that none of us knew Oamer, and for him to have quartered with William Harvey in the barn . . . that *had* been something out of the common.

Presently, the other blokes came in. Dawson had a letter in his hand from his old man. Dawson's old man – a widower, apparently – lived in a spot called Forest Gate in London. He hadn't communicated with his son for years, and it was a 'miracle' that the letter had found Dawson, who wasn't sure it was a miracle he liked. There were some choice phrases in the letter, which he read out. It started, 'Dear Son, So the war scare turned out not to be a scare after all . . .' and ended with a request for ten shillings to be sent 'sooner rather than later', so we all had a bit of a laugh at it, even Oliver Butler. Alfred Tinsley brewed cocoa, which had become a nightly routine; the racket from the lathe in the workshop gradually died down, and every man slept.

There was no bugle at Burton Dump. That was all part of the RE blokes' relaxed way of going on. When the man next to you woke up, and lit his first fag, or groaned out his first curse of the day, then you woke up yourself. It being a nocturnal place, the canteen served breakfast until getting on for tea time. But this day – a fine, bright one (which didn't suit the Dump at all) – the blokes of our section took it early, before returning to the hut for the kit inspection.

Every man sat on his bunk while working away with the cloth and the little bottle of oil kept in the stocks of the rifles. All save Oamer, whose rifle was kept in perfect nick at all times. He was using an old, spotted handkerchief to apply white paste to the buttons of his tunic, an operation he performed regularly. Harvey had told me the stuff he used was toothpaste, but I could not see a brand name on the tin he took it from, just as I could not have put a name to the white powder with which he dusted his feet most mornings, or the special pomade he put on his ginger hair. With his tunic off, he looked – no other word for it, really – fat. And his plump forearms – visible because the sleeves of his undershirt were rolled up – were a striking orange colour, on account of freckles and red hair.

I recall the twins lighting up before setting about the cleaning. My view of them was obscured by the stove, but I heard the scrape of the match and the quiet, repeated 'Fine style'. Alfred Tinsley was saying that this would be just the day for polishing up the Baldwin. The weather would let you see the shine on it. He then started in on how we were all to be given liberty passes to the town of Albert for the next night, which was a Saturday. Oliver Butler was stowing the cloth back in the stock of his weapon as he said, 'Perhaps we'll run into friend Thackeray. We might give him some new data.'

At this I recall the smooth way in which Oamer, who seldom said or did anything sharply, moved his tunic to one side, reached for his rifle and placed it across his knees.

'My own idea, for what it's worth,' said Butler, 'is that it's all a sight more complicated than we think. I mean, a person might be done in by someone who hates him, or by someone who has the opposite sort of attitude.'

Oamer reached down towards his webbing, which he had placed on the floor next to his kit bag.

Butler said, 'You do hear of things going on between blokes that get both parties involved shot . . .'

Oamer removed from the webbing one of the clips of ammunition that he had in there, and I knew then that he *had* heard Butler's slander of the night before.

Oamer loaded the clip into the magazine of his rifle, shot the bolt, and raised the sight to eye level, as though testing it. But he was pointing the thing at Oliver Butler.

Silence in the room.

Roy Butler, brightest of the twins looked at me, and for the first time addressed me.

'What's biting *him*?' he said at which Oamer called out, 'Silence in the ranks!' I could see his finger on the trigger, starting to squeeze. Oliver Butler couldn't hide either the sight or the sound of his rapid breathing.

'Oamer,' I said, as the bang came, and then there was ringing in my ears, the sound of Dawson saying 'Fuck, fuck, fuck,' the rapid rattling of the bolt of Oamer's rifle, as he ejected the remaining bullets – and every man in the billet looking at the dead, half-exploded rat lying by the boots of Oliver Butler.

On the Friday afternoon, I wrote a long letter to the wife, mentioning my promotion, and asking her to tell Harry I was at last making progress with *The Count of Monte Cristo*, which was true in that I'd given it to Oamer to read for me, or at any rate to read again, since he'd read it before, along with most other books in the English bloody language. I also asked the wife if she would mind taking a walk along the river to Naburn, to ask whether anything out of the common had happened in the vicinity of the Lock in recent times, since it was my opinion – self-centred though it might sound – that Oliver Butler's performance in the hut had been laid on for my benefit. Or rather, that he had meant to throw me off; distract me from the question of the Lock, which signified strongly in his life, as he well knew that I had discovered. In the letter I told the wife – more or less – why I wanted the data, only to recall, at the moment of finishing it, that I would have to give it in to Oamer, who would give it to Captain Quinn, who would read it over before despatch, just in case I had talked out of turn about our tactics or position. I hadn't wanted to tear up the letter, which had taken me the best part of an hour to write, and ran to eight pages, so I'd stowed it in my tunic pocket thinking I might remove certain pages and substitute others a bit more indirect.

On Friday night, a vast quantity of six- and eight-inch shells arrived, and it was our job to lug them over to the pallets in the Yard. When I knocked off, walking back exhausted to the detachment hut, I saw the full moon in the dark, dirty sky and for a second took it for an observation balloon. The big fear at the Dump was that we would come 'under observation'. With all those shells in the Yard, we were no safer at the Dump than on the runs forward.

These were meant to begin, in a regular way, on the Monday. Meanwhile, a Saturday night outing to Albert was on the cards, and the whole of the Dump was in holiday mood on the Saturday morning. The rain had held off once again, and in the afternoon, a football match was played in the space between the yard and the dead trees. Tinsley and I watched it as we moved the three Baldwins up to the coaling stages and water tanks in preparation for the Monday. It struck me that we were the senior crew – top link, you might say – at the Dump. The other crews would just be scratch parties of Royal Engineers, railway hobbyists, I supposed, who'd picked up driving and firing along the way. The plan was that more footplate men would be brought over from our battalion in due course, but it did seem as though the RE blokes could turn their hands to anything.

Well, maybe not football. This they played to a lower standard even than the teams of the York Railway Institute. We watched a goal scored after a defender had fallen over and the goalie had done likewise.

'Wonder players from the Empire!' Tinsley called out.

He was up on the high coaling stage, pitching the stuff into the bunker of the first Baldwin. The engines had running numbers: one, two and three. Well, anything else would have been unnecessarily complicated. Tinsley and I had painted the numbers on ourselves.

It was a pleasant sort of going on. Some birdsong from the broken woods . . . floating smoke from a couple of braziers . . . billies of hot sweet tea on the go; and silence for once from the direction of the front. We alternated between working on the engines, watching the football, and watching a bloke at the top of a ladder who was painting a sign on the roof of a new hut. He'd painted a big 'B' and then gone off somewhere.

Tinsley enquired, 'What are we going to do in Albert, Jim?' from which it appeared I would be going around the town with him. Well, he was a nice enough kid. But I would try to get Dawson along as well.

I said, 'I should imagine we'll be getting outside a fair bit of wine.'

'I fancy going dancing,' said Tinsley, and it was odd to hear that from somebody clarted in coal. 'Tom Shaw doesn't drink,' he ran on, 'but he's a great hand at dancing.'

'That's probably why,' I said.

'He won a gold cup at the Assembly Rooms.'

'Who's his partner?'

'He can have any partner he wants.'

I gave a yank on the rope that sent the water cascading through the canvas hose and into the tanks of the Baldwin. I said, 'There are certain women in Albert who organise dances, but the dancing isn't the point.'

Tinsley left off shovelling for a minute, saying, 'How do you mean?'

I thought: You bloody know what I mean. Tinsley was a kid who would take advantage of his youth – hide behind it. Just then, Oamer walked up. He called out over the sound of rushing water, 'Hot baths at half after three! Train time's at five!'

'Hot baths?' I said. 'Where?'

He indicated the new hut, and I saw the bloke up his ladder again, starting on an 'A'.

It was a great thing to have a bathhouse, but there was only one bath in it. We queued up naked outside, having handed our uniforms to an orderly. He carried them around to a sort of annex to the bathhouse – connected by hot pipes – where he steam cleaned them and (as we would later discover) covered them over with insect powder, taking care to fill the pockets with the stuff. When I got inside the bathhouse, I saw that the orderly in there presided over not only the bath, but also a boiler, and a network of pipes running from the boiler on which hung a quantity of towels. Oamer, quite naked, was helping the orderly sort out the towels, while periodically turning to usher the next man into the bath. As far as his body went, I noticed that the orange tint continued all the way down. Oliver Butler, who was standing two ahead of me in the queue, turned and, indicating Oamer, muttered, 'I believe we're under observation, mates' – and he'd kept his towel around his middle accordingly. He'd taken care to whisper, I noticed. He might knock Oamer behind his back, but he'd given up doing so to his face.

Andy Butler was in the bath and Roy, next in line, was taunting him, saying:

'And no widdlin' in the watter – I knew you of old!'

Dawson, directly in front of me, turned about, pulling a face.

'With luck,' I said, 'the bath wallah's going to change the water in a minute. He does that regularly – I'd say about every tenth man gets fresh.'

Roy, in jesting with his brother, had moved a little side on to us. His wedding tackle . . . it was quite a sight.

'I've never noticed that before,' said Dawson. '. . . Can't see how I missed it.'

Then *Andy* Butler stood up in the bath.

'Good Christ,' said Dawson. 'And they say lightning doesn't strike twice.'

Maybe Oliver Butler had not inherited that particular family . . . heirloom, so to speak. Maybe *that* was the true reason for the towel about his waist. Anyhow, I knew by his expression that he didn't like us talking about his brothers in that way.

When I was towelling down after my own bath (the water was just hot enough to make you wish you'd a bit longer than the regulation minute sitting in it), I glanced over at young Alfred Tinsley lying back in the water. He called out to me, 'What more could the quality want?'

'Oi,' said the bath orderly, 'out!'

Directly he climbed out, Oamer – still fussing about in the altogether – walked up to the lad and pressed a hot towel on him.

Albert Again

Coming into Albert for the second time, the town seemed to have recovered itself somewhat from its earlier state. But it was more likely that I was over my first shock of seeing it.

I had learnt in my months at the front that a house was not necessarily upright, and that it could count itself lucky if it had no holes at all in its roof. In any row of five houses in the streets around the railway station, as many as four might be upright, but there'd always be one letting the side down. You noticed the beauty of the ones that survived. The top floor was always a front-on triangle, with fancy, stepped brickwork. They were tall and thin, four or five storeys high, and most of the life was lived in the basement, which was partly, as I supposed, because almost any house at Albert might fall down at any time. I mean to say . . . they'd been through a *lot*.

Now that the Boche had been pushed back, the town – like Burton Dump – was out of ordinary artillery range, but still within reach of the big guns. The result was that if you went into Albert not knowing the French word for 'basement', you soon found it out: 'sous-sol'. Take any given shop or business premises. The front might say 'Boulangerie', 'Pâtisserie' or 'Notaire', but there'd be a hand-painted sign in addition pointing down and indicating 'sous-sol'. The whole town had gone underground.

The other words that any Tommy would pick up quickly were 'vin' and 'bière'. I was walking through the town with

Dawson and young Tinsley when Tinsley said, 'I prefer wine to beer. The *idea* of it, I mean, since I've never really drunk it. See here . . .' He pointed to a fancy written panel outside one of the upright houses. It gave the prices of the drinks sold within. 'A bottle of wine', said Tinsley, 'is generally one franc and twenty whatsnames . . .'

'Centimes,' I said.

'. . . And you get goodness knows how many glasses in a bottle, whereas *one* glass of beer is a franc – and there's a lot more wallop in a glass of wine than there is in a glass of beer.'

'Spoken like a connoisseur,' said Dawson, who was mooching along behind, hands in pockets. In the washroom, directly after the bath, he'd covered his face in a lather and set about it with a razor. It seemed he'd finally had enough of his not-quite moustache, but when he'd wiped away the soap, it was just as before.

Dawson seemed to be looking for something, and I wondered whether it was the same thing I believed Tinsley to be looking for, namely a place signified by a red light burning low. On the train coming in from Burton Dump, I'd decided – on looking at all the brilliantined hair, the shaving nicks on the chins, and the soap suds hardened into white crusts about the backs of the necks – that such a place was the true goal of every man in the carriage, even the twins.

Of course, most of the blokes in the carriage were not married. I *was*, and so the question of my own intentions came with complications. Whenever I thought of the red light, and how it might look, and where it might be, I thought of the wife. Best thing would be to have a drink, and see what happened. That's what I intended to do, anyhow, but we couldn't seem to find the right spot.

We came out into the main square, where the half-wrecked cathedral stood. On the top of the spire, the Virgin Mary, tilted a few degrees below the horizontal, held the baby Jesus.

'Famous is that,' said Tinsley. 'They have postcards with it on.'

'Having a lovely time on the Western Front,' I said.

'It's known as the Albert Memorial,' said Dawson, and when he saw Tinsley's expression – half believing it and half not – he had to laugh.

We found a basement estaminet just off the Square that looked all right – not red lamps but green ones, which, together with dark blue, none-too-clean tablecloths, gave an underwater look to the place. It seemed to draw quiet types. A couple of privates talked in low voices in one corner; a couple of officers did likewise in another. As we descended the stone steps, a tired-looking woman said, 'English menu' in a strong French accent and held up a little blackboard. She looked at us, waiting. The odd thing was that it was all written in French, except for the odd word that stood out in capitals like 'ENGLISH SHIPS' which, odds on, was 'English Chips', since it went next to 'Oeufs au plat'.

'Bonsoir, madame,' I said, and the woman nodded back. She wanted us to get on with the ordering.

'What *is* oeufs au plat?' asked Alfred Tinsley.

'Eggs on a plate,' I said.

'Where else would they be?'

'*Fried* eggs. So in English it's egg and chips.'

'I'll have that,' he said, and we all asked for it.

The woman made no move, but nodded. She was still holding up the little blackboard, still looking worn out.

'For dreenk,' she said.

The menu said 'Notre Vins', then came 'Vin Blanc 1ff'. Below that was written 'Cidre', and no price.

Tinsley said to me, 'Ask her if she has Vin Supérieur.'

He'd set his heart on this, having seen signs about the town announcing that it was only ten or maybe twenty centimes dearer than the ordinary stuff. I asked the question as best I could, and I could not make out the answer.

We sat down at the table next to the officers. They were only junior officers – one pip and two pips. Two pips was out of the Quinn mould. He was saying, 'That's final to my mind . . . But then again . . .'

We started in on the wine, which came in a bottle without a label, and without a cork – a dodge that most French barkeepers seemed to think they could get away with. I took a sip, while Alfred Tinsley drank off his glass in one go. He sat back, and said, 'My eye! Is that what wine's meant to taste like?'

'No,' I said.

Dawson passed me a Woodbine, before offering one to Tinsley.

'Go on then,' said the lad, and he set about trying to enjoy a cigarette for the second time in his life.

Dawson re-filled Tinsley's glass, and the kid knocked half of that back straightaway as well. After taking a draw on the fag, he eyed it as though there was something wrong with it. But it was just the same as all other Woodbines.

'I think a cigar might be more my style,' he said.

He seemed determined to go all-out this evening – and in all directions. Then he said, 'Why does Oliver Butler say all that stuff about Oamer? Making out that he's, you know, funny? A sort of nancy, I suppose is what he's saying. He's so keen to throw blame for what happened that I'm beginning to think he might have done for Harvey himself – him or his loony brothers.'

Watching Tinsley, I was wondering again about the torn number of the *Railway Magazine*. It was the only thing about him that I couldn't explain. Tinsley drained his glass, and this time took the liberty of re-filling it himself. 'Oamer's brainy,' he ran on, 'that's the only thing different about him. Did you see him coming up on the train? He was reading the fattest book I've ever clapped eyes on.'

'*The Count of Monte Cristo*,' I said.

Taking another belt of wine, Dawson said, 'I've got a book called *The World's Best Books*. It's awfully good. I'd read about half of it but then the war started.'

Dawson looked up and said, 'It's not the same as reading half of the world's best *books*, you know.'

Re-filling my own glass – Dawson, who'd seemed miles away, had barely touched his – I said, 'I'd stick to the *Railway Magazine* if I were you. But Alfred . . . How did one of yours end up getting burnt in the stove at Spurn?'

'Eh?' said Tinsley, setting down his glass, 'How do you mean?'

I thought: *If he's lying, he's doing it pretty well.*

The English Ships came, and Tinsley got stuck in, but Dawson was still in his daze.

'Look alive,' Tinsley said, and Dawson started eating.

The grub seemed to revive him, and when we'd finished eating, Dawson was all for quitting that particular basement, and finding another with a bit more life to it. So we paid the bill, and walked up into the dark street.

This one offered no other estaminet, I was sure – just the tall houses, looking tense, waiting for another shell to come flying in. But there was no indication of the battle going in the east, save the occasional rumble of what sounded like thunder, and a faint discoloration on the sky. I looked along the road, and a little old man had appeared there. The males of Albert generally *were* little old men, or blokes otherwise crocked – they'd have been in the French army otherwise. But this bloke *was* in uniform, even though he carried a very un-military carpet bag.

We stood near the street corner, and Dawson and Tinsley were after drifting *around* that corner. Tinsley was prattling about cigars: 'The time for a cigar is after dinner,' he said, 'and we've had dinner so it's time for a cigar.'

Well, he was already canned. Dawson was jingling the

change in his pockets while puffing on a fag. His cap was tipped right back, and a line of insect powder showed luminous in the crease of his tunic.

'Just want to take a peek around the corner, Jim,' he said.

He sloped off, and the little old man was coming up fast. He wore a uniform at least a size too big for him, and of a washed-out, greyish colour. It featured a black brassard with lettering on it, but he wasn't a military policeman. As he approached the white light of the lamp, he spoke, and it was a hard Yorkshire voice.

'Who's that man, bringing the King's uniform into contempt?'

It was the bloody Chief.

'It's Dawson,' I replied, being in a state of shock, 'the bloke you had a run-in with . . .'

'Might have bloody known.'

'Chief,' I fairly gasped, 'what . . .?'

I meant 'What are you doing here?' 'Where've you just come from?' 'What's this queer sort of uniform you're wearing?' and 'Why have you bloody *shrunk*?' Shaking his hand, I read the lettering on the brassard – read it out loud in my amazement: 'VTC'. Was it some part of the army? But the Chief was sixty-five. He couldn't be with the colours. He couldn't be at the front either, but he damn near was.

'Volunteer Training Corps,' said the Chief, and he looked sidelong, embarrassed. As he moved his small, scarred, gingery head, his cap seemed to stay still, being too big for him.

'But . . . what's in the bag, sir?'

'Don't "sir" me. I'm not an officer, am I?'

He indicated the three stripes on his arm. I smiled at him, and it was the first time ever that I'd been amused by the Chief without also being nervous.

'You've just the two,' he said, indicating my own stripes. 'Your missus'll be up in arms about that, I suppose. She'll be storming the bloody War Office.'

The Chief was trying to address me after his old fashion, but he wasn't quite up to it. Then I recalled that he ought to have *known* that the business on Spurn had held back my promotion.

'Didn't you get my letter, Chief?'

'*What* bloody letter?'

Behind me, Alfred Tinsley was returning from around the corner.

'Just had the nod from Dawson, Jim,' he said. 'He's found a likely place down there. Will you come along now or shall we see you later?'

This was a pretty half-hearted sort of invitation. Were the pair of them fleeing the Chief? Then again, it would be obvious to anyone that the Chief and I had a lot to talk about and so might be better left to ourselves.

I said to Tinsley, 'Right-o, we'll see you shortly.'

The Chief was eyeing me. 'The army's given you a pair of shoulders at last.'

'Well,' I said, 'I know how to stand now.'

'I wouldn't go that far, lad,' said the Chief. 'Look, for Christ's sake, let's get a belt of booze.'

So I indicated the estaminet I'd just come out of.

When we came to the bottom of the stairs, the woman didn't hold up the little blackboard for the benefit of the Chief. She could immediately see that here was a man who didn't really eat, but lived on smoke and alcohol. I asked her for a bottle of white wine, and took the Chief over to the table I'd quit ten minutes before. The bar was a brighter, bluer place now, with a few more Tommies in, and a stream of chatter and clinking glass.

'How long have you been out here?' I asked the Chief, pouring wine.

'Getting on for a fortnight,' he said, taking a box of cigars from his tunic pocket.

'And before that you were in York?'
'Aye,' he said, 'worse luck.'
Again this sounded a wrong note. The *old* Chief didn't go in for that self-pitying tone. I thought again of the letter I'd written him – the one I'd given to Oamer for posting at Romescamps. Had Oamer deliberately kept it back? He certainly wouldn't have forgotten to deliver it. Then again letters from the front very often went astray, as did letters sent to the Chief. Any communication without the immediacy of a bullet could take its chances as far as he was concerned. I'd seen him start the fire in the police office with unopened correspondence.
'The Volunteer Training Corps,' I said, taking a pull on the wine (which showed no advance on the earlier bottle). 'I think I've vaguely heard of it.'
'Aye,' said the Chief, lighting his cigar, and pushing the box over to me. 'Well don't strain yourself trying to remember. We're a sort of home defence militia,' he continued, blowing smoke. 'We stand about in the middle of York looking out for Zeppelins . . . Investigate reports of German spies.'
'Why aren't you an officer?' I said.
'*Officer*,' he said, with contempt.
The Chief was working class by birth. That's why he'd lit his own cigar before passing the box over to me. He was a fist fighter of old (hence the state of his nose), but not by Queensberry Rules. He'd risen within the police but that didn't signify socially. He could be a chief inspector whilst remaining true to himself, whereas he would have to have become a different man altogether if he'd been a commissioned army officer. Consequently, he'd stopped at sergeant major in the York and Lancaster regiment – out in the boiling desert with General Gordon and all those other red-coated lunatics. After his thirty years with the colours, he'd been in the Reserves for as long as possible, but now he was reduced to balloon-spotting in this funny rig-out.

At least he was still on the big cigars, though. Lighting up my own Marcella, I asked again, 'What's in the bag, Chief?'

'Cigarettes,' he growled, and I knew the explanation for this, and the whole question of what he was doing in Albert, would have to wait.

'Look here,' he said. 'The Somme battle – your lot were in on the start. What sort of show is it?'

'Well, I've seen some pretty warm times,' I said, blowing smoke, and feeling like a fraud.

Whereas being in the war had killed many men, I could see that *not* being in it was killing the Chief. With him, everything was upside-down. Most patriotic men resented those of their fellows who didn't fight. The Chief resented those that did. Accordingly I was torn as I spoke to him. I didn't want to make myself out a hero. Then again, I could see him glazing over as I told him our mudlarking exploits – the trench digging and fixing. He was hungry for details of being under fire; he seemed fascinated by ordnance – all the gauges of shell I'd dodged. And then there was his obsession of old: machine guns.

'You've felt the bullet go close?' he said. 'The little wind?'

I nodded and, seeing that the Chief looked quite defeated at missing out on this experience, I added, 'Only once or twice, mind.'

I reserved the full story of William Harvey for our second bottle. In the meantime I gave the Chief tales of a fusilier-sapper's life. When I told him about Burton Dump and the lines going forward that would be brought into regular use from Monday onwards, he couldn't help but grinning.

'It was railways that started this show; looks like they'll finish it as well.'

'How did they start it?'

'The Huns had to be sure they could defend to the east while attacking to the west. See – '

I thought he was going to show me the disposition of the German armies using wine glasses and cigars, so I cut in:

'But what are you up to, Chief? I mean, why are you out here?'

Since he couldn't put me off any longer, he explained fast, as though the business was just too daft for words. The Chief, who had practically run the York railwaymen's shooting leagues, had got up a 'shooting party' – him and some of his superannuated mates in the Volunteer Training Corps. They'd given demonstrations of marksmanship or failing that (since not all had retained A1 vision as the Chief had) general gun-craft. At first they'd toured the army camps in and around York. Now they were visiting some of the rest camps in France.

'The troops hate to be out-shot by an old cunt like me,' said the Chief. 'It spurs them on. If they do beat us, we give 'em cigarettes by way of a prize. We have army fags gratis from one of the York quartermasters, but . . .'

He was holding up the empty bottle, frowning at it.

I called for another.

'. . . But what we get from the quarter bloke', he ran on, 'is that powdery army stuff. Boy tobacco . . . So I lay out myself for decent fags from time to time . . .'

'I've taken up regular smoking,' I said.

'Yeah?' said the Chief. 'Well, you need a hobby.' He was reaching into the bag, saying, 'I got this lot from a little market they have here – '

I said, 'Are they Woodbines, by any chance?'

'What do you want?' said the Chief, 'Jam on it?' He put a hundred fags on the table in front of me, the packets marked 'Virginians Select'.

'For me?' I said.

The Chief nodded.

'I'm obliged to you. Now what's going on at York station?'

The Chief pulled a face: 'Half the porters are bloody women.'

The wife had told me that in one of her letters – leaving out the 'bloody'.

'How do they get on?'

The Chief shrugged: 'They're not equal to the heavier luggage.'

'What else? The government's taken over the railways, hasn't it?'

The Chief nodded.

'We have a bloke from London in the Station Master's office. All excursions suspended. All breakfast, lunch and dining cars suspended.'

'I suppose the only blokes left are the real crocks.'

'Apart from the express drivers,' said the Chief.

I thought about asking whether he'd heard of Tinsley's hero, Tom Shaw.

Instead, I started in on telling the Chief about the death of Scholes, but he'd heard the news already. I asked him about Scholes's old pal, Flower, who'd gone off to the Military Mounted Police.

'In hospital,' said the Chief.

'Shot?' I said.

'Not bloody likely,' said the Chief.

'Well then what?' I said.

'What do you think?' said the Chief. 'Kicked by a bloody horse.'

'Serious?'

'It is for him,' he said, with some satisfaction.

I then asked what – or whether – he'd heard about the death of William Harvey, since he'd obviously not had my letter about it. He had done: read of it in the *North Eastern Railway Journal*. He knew the circumstances had been considered suspicious, although the magazine had left out that bit. I gave him the story of the investigation, and the hard time of it we'd all had from Sergeant Major Thackeray.

'So you were all in the shit?' he said.

'Still are,' I said. 'Charges might be brought at any minute.'

'Any theories, lad?'

Of the many things I could have said, I asked him about Oamer – the character of the man.

The Chief said, 'He was a popular bloke in the booking office.'

'But what do *you* make of him?'

'Well, he's queer of course.'

'He's a good soldier,' I said.

'General Gordon was queer,' said the Chief. 'It's said Kitchener is.'

'But would Oamer be the sort to go off, you know, adventuring with much younger blokes?'

The Chief drained his glass, poured himself another one, drank it, kept silence for a good half minute. (He'd regained some of his old style now that we were talking of an investigation.) At length, he said, 'I know the bloke he lives with. He's Deputy Manager of the Yorkshire General Bank in Parliament Street . . . Name's Archibald . . . summat or other. They have a place on Scarcroft Road – big house. You're meant to think it's two flats, but that's just a tale. This Archibald . . . He's not a *young* bloke.'

'But you've not answered my question,' I said, and from the flashing glare he gave me, I thought the Chief was going to lay me out. *This* was the man I knew!

'I've no bloody notion,' he said.

The bar was filling up with soldiers. Once again, the Chief was looking a bit lost. He see could the other blokes eyeing his odd uniform and wondering about it. I watched him light up another of his Marcellas, and it looked a very lonely endeavour, as he puffed and blew to get it going. It was as though he was trying to make up for his age, his scrawniness and the funny uniform, by the lighting of a big cigar. When he'd got it going, he stood up, showing no sign of unsteadiness from the wine.

'I'm off,' he said. 'Lorry's waiting in the Square. I'm putting up with some King's Own Yorkshires a couple of miles west. Tomorrow it's back to Blighty.'

'How's the police office going on?' I asked, also standing.

'Just me and Wright at present,' said the Chief, as I set about stuffing the cigarettes into my pockets. 'Any bad lad coming onto York station has a free hand just at present.'

'Now that I don't believe,' I said.

Back in the street, under a lonely lamp, we heard a few distant crumps from the front.

'I did get forward a couple of weeks ago,' said the Chief, blowing smoke. '. . . But it was a quiet sector,' he added glumly.

'You look in fine fettle, Chief,' I said.

Still in this gloomy phase, the Chief said, 'Bloody shame about young Harvey. He was a good kid.'

'Was he?' I said, and I looked the question at the Chief.

'He would aggravate some of the blokes in the shooting leagues,' the Chief admitted. 'He was from an army family. His old man had been in the colours . . . won a medal out in Africa. The lad thought nothing of railways, you see – looked down on the oily blokes.'

I nodded. My own impression was confirmed. There had without question been grounds for a fight between Tinsley and Harvey on Spurn. As a battalion we were meant to be the-railway-in-the-army, but here was a case of the railway *against* the army.

'Did you hear about his mother?'

The Chief nodded.

'She married twice didn't she?' I said. 'And it was the first husband that was William's father?'

'That's it,' said the Chief.

'And he was the one who won the medal?'

'You wouldn't catch the second one in the bloody colours. He's spent his whole life behind – or in front of – the bar in the Station Hotel.'

I had the dawning sense of having been a fool about something.

'I thought that bloke, the barman, was William's father.'

The Chief was scowling at me.

'Who was his real father? I asked. 'What did he do when he left the army?'

'John Read?' said the Chief. 'He went in the Reserves for a while. For a job, he did nothing . . . No, that's wrong, he'd been a carriage cleaner for a while . . . But could never find his way . . . Went a bit loony. The kid carried the second husband's name.'

John Read . . . I knew the name.

'Whoever did it,' said the Chief, 'you'll bring him in.'

It was about the first compliment I'd had from him, and it wasn't right.

'You might look a bit gormless at times,' the Chief ran on, 'but you keep your eyes skinned.'

. . . But I was still thinking of John Read.

On the half-illuminated street corner, the Chief and I nodded at each other, shook hands, clapped each other on the back. About the only thing we didn't do, in the awkwardness of our parting, was salute. The Chief turned about and walked away. I remained standing, watching his retreating figure, breathing deeply the cordite air of Albert and trying to work out how drunk I was. I tilted my face up, and a thousand stars swung into view, like a packet of stars that had been spilt. That had happened a little too quickly. I was on the way all right. Three blokes were approaching along the street, but on the other side. Glancing down, I saw that I held two remaining packets of the Virginians Select. I made to stuff them into my top pockets when I discovered the letter I'd written to the wife. I called to the Chief, who turned slowly.

'Will you take a letter back home for me?' I said, going up to him with envelope held out.

He spat hard.

'Might as well,' he said. 'I *look* like a bloody postman.' He peered at the address. 'Why didn't you put it through the army post?'

I grinned. 'The contents are confidential,' I said.

'You dirty bugger,' said the Chief, and I looked over the road to see Oliver Butler and his brothers. Butler was eyeing me. He'd seen the Chief, and the handover of the letter. He turned and called to his brothers like a man calling to his dogs, and they moved rapidly away. The Chief did not seem to have clocked them. He was moving away more slowly in the opposite direction, and I watched him go, thinking: if you're in a lull at pushing seventy, you stay in a lull. Would he ever be back to commanding me at York station? The police office would never be the same, nothing ever would be. It annoyed me to think that the men who'd drawn up the notice announcing the formation of the battalion had not let on about that.

I turned into the street that Dawson and Tinsley had gone down. It was full of buried jollity, light leaking up from the basements, and the muffled sound of dozens of Tommies enjoying themselves. I came to a sign propped against railings. The moment I saw it, I said out loud to myself: 'Oh Christ.'

It read, 'COME IN FOR JOHN SMITH'S YORKSHIRE BITTER'. I read it over again, looking for some fault in the wording, some indication it wasn't true, but the buggers had even spelt 'Yorkshire' correctly. I descended the steps, and pushed open the door. That Dawson would be in there was a surety. No doubt this was the place he'd been looking for all along. Someone must have tipped him the wink.

I expected to find him roaring, but when I caught sight of him – which I did immediately on entering – he was sitting at a table talking in a normal fashion. Tinsley was beside him, smiling, and looking very composed, all considered. But then Dawson had only a glass of *wine* in front of him. Perhaps he had missed seeing the sign. No . . . I couldn't credit that.

Dawson was addressing a couple of RE blokes that I recognised from Burton Dump. Tinsley, seeing me come in, waved across the bar. This place was altogether more business-like than the other, and more fun too. The tablecloths were black and white squares, and the place was ram-packed with uniformed men. Was there a piano? I can't now recall, but there was an undercurrent of musicality, a lot of shouting, a great heat rising from somewhere. Dotted about the bar were other examples of the owners' good English: a sign reading 'BOILED EGGS', a second announcing 'BREAKFAST AVAILABLE ALL DAY', a third: 'THE PROPRIETOR AND STAFF WELCOME OUR VALOROUS BRITISH ALLIES'. Well, the writer was just showing off with that last one.

I pushed my way over to the Dawson table, where Tinsley pushed a wine glass over to *me*, and slopped in some red stuff from a bottle in a basket. The kid was looking very chipper.

'How are you going on, son?' I said.

'I feel a lot better since I was sick,' he said.

'What time was that?'

'Eight twenty-five,' he said. He was always exact as to time – it was the engine man in him. 'Bernie here gave me a cigarette and that did me a power of good.'

Tinsley evidently had a weak stomach, but recovered fast. Had he chucked up on Spurn? Not to my *knowledge*. The drink had just made him a bit more forward, and a bit more lively too. He'd joined in my scuffle with Dawson after all.

One of the RE blokes was saying to Dawson, 'But you're a Londoner – how did you end up in York?'

Dawson took a belt of wine. He was popeyed, but in a jolly sort of way. He said, 'The fact of the matter is that I just got on a train in London . . .'

'King's Cross,' Tinsley put in. He had to fix a place by naming the railway station.

'. . . And you had a ticket for York,' said the RE bloke.

'I had a ticket for nowhere,' said Dawson. 'I mean,' he added slowly, '*that I had no ticket at all.* And that's why I got off at York.'

'Eh?' I said.

'Oh, I missed that bit out,' said Dawson. 'The ticket inspector got on at York – '

'That would be old Jackson,' said Tinsley with a grin.

' – So *I* got off,' said Dawson.

'And you've been here ever since,' I said. 'I mean *there.* I mean . . . no . . . '

I must have put away a good deal more than I'd thought – that was always the danger of encountering the Chief anywhere near licensed premises. I was instantly sobered, however, by the loud French-accented cry that came from the man at the bar, 'Mister Dawson, we have found the barrel of the John Smith's beer!'

The RE man was saying to Dawson, 'Hold on a minute, how did you get through the ticket barrier?'

But Dawson was making fast for the bar. He came back a moment later with an enamel jug full of the stuff.

'Apparently, they found the barrel in the cellar,' he said. 'It's odd that, because I mean, we're *in* the cellar.'

He offered the beer around, and we all drank it from our wine glasses. Dawson did not talk as we did this. The talking fell to others. I watched him go back to the bar for another jugful after a matter of only a few minutes, and he did not offer this second one around. His face was changing as he drank, giving him the grubby, peeved look of the faces on the criminal record cards in the police office. The talk was going on merrily around me. A bloke was saying, 'He was fucking kippered at

High Wood. Boche flame-thrower. Below the fucking belt is that.'

John Read . . . that had been the name of the bloke I'd charged with indecent exposure. He'd been the last man I'd arrested before enlisting, and he was William Harvey's real father. What had become of him? Being drunk, it was hard for me to round up all the facts. They'd keep wandering away. He might well have gone to court and been lagged. He might have been sent down for six months. The Company solicitors would have handled the prosecution. They had all the witness statements . . . and if Harvey's father had been gaoled on this charge, would young Harvey have known of it; and would he know I'd been the arresting officer? If so, it would give him a reason to hate me. But he *hadn't* hated me, or if he had, he'd kept the fact well hidden. If he did know, he'd have a motive against me, whereas what Thackeray needed to find was a motive the other way about. Even so, this could be seen as the cause of needle between me and Harvey.

The man who'd talked about the flame-thrower was laughing – and laughing too loud – as I tried to get hold of the important questions: did Company Sergeant Major Thackeray know of my connection with Harvey's true father? Next question: would he be likely to find out? And what would he make of the fact that I hadn't told him? Well, I hadn't told him because I hadn't known. But he wouldn't believe that.

I found myself eyeing Dawson. He seemed to meet my gaze, saying, 'You fucking rotter.'

I thought: Here we go, another barney, and this time I won't be palling up with him afterwards.

'Fucking treacherous fucking copper . . .' Dawson was saying, 'Fucking *monkey*.'

And at that word I was let off. I might be a copper, but I was certainly not a monkey. I turned and there was Thackeray himself. He was with another military policeman. They were the only two blokes not holding glasses. The second bloke had a smaller moustache – not as good as Thackeray's, but Thackeray was being big about it, smiling at him. There were about twenty standing blokes between us and him. He did not appear to have heard Dawson's remarks – not yet – although the bar had gone a bit quiet. The barkeeper, seemingly panicked out of his good English, said 'English police here! End of beer and wine!' (Bars closed early in the garrison towns. Perhaps it was 'time'.) This caused uncertainty in the bar and another moment of silence, but Thackeray seemed to be indicating to the barkeeper that he was quite all right to keep on serving. I assumed he thought that blokes at the *front* were entitled to a bit of a drink-up occasionally. The stream of chatter started up again, and it might have been enough to keep Thackeray from hearing as, Dawson, standing, called out, 'The enemy's *that* way, in case you've forgotten.'

That was twenty-one days' field punishment right there – if not five years in a military prison – but Thackeray did not react. I began pulling Dawson towards the door (with Tinsley in tow), going a roundabout way, so as to avoid Thackeray and friend. When we were about halfway to the door Thackeray, who I really believed had not yet spotted us, laughed at something his mate said, at which Dawson yelled out, 'Can it, you warphead!'

Thackeray stopped laughing He began turning his head our way as I fairly threw Dawson at the half-open door of the bar. We tumbled out onto the steps.

'Did he clock us?' said Tinsley. 'If he clocked us, he'll *never* leave off.'

'John Smith's bitter . . .' I said, as we made our shambling way along the half-illuminated street that led to the railway station.

'Where?' said Dawson.

'You should lay off it,' I said, and he made no reply.

The railway station was packed with blokes. It too was half shrouded in darkness, but how can you keep a railway station secret? As we got there, two long dark trains came in. One was going to the war and one was going away. We climbed onto the one going *to*.

Aveluy Railhead and Points East: Early September 1916

'I'll just give her a breath of steam.'

Tinsley, shovelling coal, looked up at me and grinned. It had been the right thing to say.

Then – since I'd caught a bit of a chill – I pressed my right nostril and blew snot from my left down onto the footplate, at which his grin faded.

'I've just swept that,' he said.

'It's a bloody footplate,' I said, 'it's not carpeted.'

The light was fading over the Dump as I eased back the regulator. We would be the first train to go out. We had six carriages on – and Oliver Butler as chief brakesman. He stood on the rear of the back wagon, controlling its brake, and it would be his job to tell Dawson when to apply the brake on his own wagon, which was the third. It was to be hoped that these two brakes and those on the engine would do the job. Two other trains were all ready in the sidings to come onto the main 'Up' – the line that led to the front, where the 'hate' was building up nicely. The sky over there glowed green and red, colours that periodically shook.

Tinsley and I had both had a tot of rum. We'd taken it in the running office, where the lines going forward were all mapped out on a blackboard. Oamer had drawn thick lines (with the side of the chalk) for the lines already put down, and thin lines (with the end of the chalk) for the extensions and branches that would be laid shortly by the Butler twins, amongst others of the tough, silent, platelaying breed. Control points on the line – both existing and planned – were also marked. These took, or would take (since only one was actually operative at that moment) the form of one or more blokes in a dug-out. They would be equipped with a telephone and a lamp for indicating to the engine crews whether they could proceed.

We were stuck with this Somme offensive, which was a very bloody and slow one. Some of the New Army Battalions had been half wiped out, and word was that the whole of the town of Accrington was draped in black, for the Accrington Pals had had a particularly hard time of it at the start of the show.

The business in hand for us was the endless bloody scrap over the village of Pozières, or what was left of it. The narrow-gauge railway now went a little further towards that shattered village – about level with the latest line of reserve trenches, but there was also a new feature: a branch off to the right, which is to say to the east, for the supply of batteries targeting German strongholds at spots like Bazentin le Petit, Delville Wood, Ginchy, Combles. It was hoped to capture these places and make of them a new front.

We would be running along the new branch, and delivering our goods to two gun positions served by it. As we rolled away, I noticed that about half the blokes at the Dump, some holding lamps, had turned out to see us go off. They were watching the fruits of their labour, namely the start of the regular runs. Riding with us on the footplate was Captain Muir, the quiet sort who'd been dead wrong about us all coming back in one piece from the last run. He kept making notes in a little book that he pulled periodically from his pocket.

By shutting off steam, and opening the sand valves, I avoided wheelslip on the greasy rails as we climbed the incline to the first of the trees, and he made a note of *that* – or, more likely, of something altogether different, since I did not believe he was familiar with engine driving techniques.

I looked at Tinsley, who was shovelling coal.

'Little and often with the coal and water,' he said – this for the benefit of Muir, by way of explanation, because in moving to the firehole Tinsley would keep requiring the officer to step aside. 'Little and often . . . That's Tom Shaw's motto,' he said to me, as he closed the firehole door. I frowned at the kid, and he hesitated for only a fraction of time before cottoning on and *opening* the firehole door. That was one way to keep our production of smoke to the minimum – draw in cold air so as to discharge the products of combustion.

We were in good nick, keeping the pressure nicely: little simmer of steam from the safety valve. I leant out to see . . . Yes, grey ghost in attendance at the chimney top. We'd finally found a good place for our billy-can full of tea (wedged behind the lubricator pipes), and we had the grenade in our locker for blowing the whole fucking lot up at short notice.

On the debit side of the equation, it was pissing down; and if a shell landed on us or within ten feet then we were goners, not to mention – in view of the volatile load we carried – any other poor bugger within quarter of a mile. I put the odds against that happening at no higher than twenty-to-one, and I kept asking myself whether this meant that, after twenty trips, we'd definitely cop it? Captain Muir, the Oxford or Cambridge man, would know.

Moving further under the cover of our mean cab roof, and closer to the fire, I took out my Woodbines, offering them about. No takers, and in fact Muir made another note. What was he writing? 'Driver smokes Woodbines.' Not for long, I wouldn't be doing. This was my last packet; I'd have to start on the Virginians Select that the Chief had given me. Had the Virginians Select been selected by Virginians? It was a nicety that had occupied me ever since I'd clapped eyes on the packets.

A shell landed – first of the night.

It did not leave my ears singing, so it couldn't have been very near, but I could not see *where* it was, since we were enclosed by the broken trees, which would appear to repeatedly walk forwards so as to commit suicide – being in such a terrible state to begin with – on the track before us, but always stopped short or over-stepped the rails at the last moment. Blowing smoke, I looked over the coal bunker. Both Oliver Butler and Dawson were staring back my way. I could not quite make out the expression on Butler's face (being on the last wagon, he was too far off), but I didn't doubt it was a sour one. He at any rate had apparently not discovered that I'd once nicked Harvey's natural father, for if he had known, he'd have brought it up. Dawson put up his hand to acknowledge me. He also had a Woodbine on the go of course. Didn't see *him* on Virginians Select. Bernie Dawson and his sort were just made for Woodbines. Why, the cigarette practically smoked *him*. There was something easy-going about the Woodbine man, and that was Dawson's nature all right, except when he was on the John Smith's bitter. He'd said nothing further to me about our close shave in Albert with Sergeant Major Thackeray, and this was just as I'd expected. It wasn't shame that made him clam up; in fact, if you tried to bring the matter up, he'd just give you a polite smile and a faint look of puzzlement as if you'd been the one behaving badly, and so were being rather 'off' in recollecting the matter. Or perhaps he just didn't remember. He had clean forgotten about the cut to my knuckle sustained in the Hope and Anchor, or so I assumed.

Tinsley was shovelling coal again, but as he swung the little shovel towards the firehole, the engine jolted and he did a missed shot.

'Oh heck,' he said, and he was down on his knees picking up the lumps and chucking them in by hand.

'Keen,' observed Muir, who'd stepped over to my side to get out of Tinsley's way.

I nodded. 'He lives to write himself down "passed fireman".'

'And what will he do then?' enquired Muir, who obviously didn't know much about footplate life.

'Then he'll fire engines,' I said, 'for a little while . . .'

'Oh yes?'

'Well, twenty years. After that, he'll drive them.'

Tinsley had just regained his feet when the engine gave another lurch that nearly over-toppled us all, not to mention the engine itself. The twins had walked the track the day before, looking for faults, but both engine and wagons were shaking about like buggery. I moved the reverser back a notch to quieten things down a bit.

'That good old whirring,' Tinsley said, nodding to himself, 'that *beat*.'

We emerged from the remains of Aveluy Wood and began to climb. The shell noise was fairly continuous now, but nothing had so far come near. The rain had found the right angle for soaking us, and the track was slimy into the bargain. I put down more sand as we came by the crater-pond where Captain Leo Tate had died. The water remained uncollected, looking black and evil; in fact the quantity was growing. The different rumble came as we went over the Ancre on the girder bridge, and Captain Muir leant out, doing his best to see the bridge and the water below. He made another note.

We passed what Tate had called the Old Station; next came Holgate Villa. Men were moving about beyond it. What lot were they?

A new feature came up now: a passing loop. I could just make it out in the dark. In time there'd be a control point there. The twins had been part of the gang that had put that in – made a decent job of it, too, since we didn't jar on the points. We came into the next lot of trees, and were descending now, so the bloody things seemed to be coming up too fast. I turned and indicated to Oliver Butler that he might screw down his brake a little. Dawson saw my hand signal too, and he would do the same. We were now surrounded by the sound of German shells and our own gun batteries blazing away. There was a point with the noise of battle where you stopped trying to pretend there'd ever been any such thing as silence, and this was it. I wanted a cigarette but didn't have any left. The second bridge came up, and the gate in the ditch: Naburn Lock. I turned again at this, and eyed Butler. He returned my stare for a short space of time, then swivelled away.

We rocked on, going over new track now. Presently, Tinsley indicated the manned control point coming up. I went over to his side, and saw a white lamp, and the outline of a man holding it. As we approached, the man became a nervous corporal of the Royal Engineers. I went back over to my side, and saw where the branch curved away into a region of shell holes, spike-like trees, ditches and, by the looks of it, exploding shells. But what did the white light mean? It ought to have been green or red. I knocked off the regulator, and we cruised up to the corporal with the lamp. Tinsley gave me a quick nod, since pre-judgement of a stopping point was one of the great skills of engine driving, and I'd hit the spot exactly.

I leant out, and the corporal came up to me, lamp in hand. I bent down, and he craned up; our heads were separated by not more than a yard's distance, but still I had to roar, 'What's that mean?' while pointing down at the lamp.

'Oh,' he said, looking down himself. 'Filter's fallen out.'

For an RE man, he was a gormless bugger.

'What filter?' I bawled, 'Green or red?'

'Oh,' he said, 'green.'

'Safe along there, is it?'

He sort of shrugged, saying, 'Gunners are still at it,' and that was just the trouble: the Germans evidently had a fix on the gun positions along the branch, but as long as our guns were being fired, shells were needed. By shouting directly into

Tinsley's ear, I got over that he was to jump down and check the setting of the points for the branch, since I did not trust this clot holding the light.

Three minutes later we were rolling along the branch at five miles an hour, with a barrage coming down around us. Three had come down within thirty yards, and I had started to shake. I tried to hide this by moving about, touching the controls of the engine, even if they did not need to be worked. Muir was stock still, gripping the engine brake and not taking notes. Tinsley was talking to himself, and he seemed to be repeating over and over the virtues of his hero, Tom Shaw, although I could only make out snatches, as he moved between the coal bunker and the fire-hole door: 'An incandescent fire of medium thickness,' I heard him say. 'Dampers shut, firehole door open otherwise blow off.' Ahead of us, frightened-looking men of the Royal Artillery were coming out of the trees, and some of those trees were on fire. At the sight of the blokes, I pulled up. The gormless corporal had obviously had enough about him to alert them, by field telephone, to our arrival. Oliver Butler was down, and talking to them. It was his job to liaise as regards unloading the shells. Dawson walked up to the footplate, and stood on the step.

'What's this place?' he said.

'It's a *position*,' I said. 'The first of two.'

'Are you planning on stopping here for long?'

Another shell came, drowning him out.

The conclusion of Butler's conference with the gunners was that we would all have to help cart the shells to the gun position off in the trees. That suited me. The faster we could get unloaded the faster we could clear out. We formed a chain with the artillery blokes – about twenty in it, all told, including Muir. I took up my own position some way into the trees, and could see one of the Howitzers we were feeding, and the gang of blokes around it. The gun was like a dangerous animal – a giant dinosaur-bird that couldn't take wing, but kept trying.

Every time it spat out another shell the blokes span away from it with blocked ears, and the wheels of the bloody thing leapt a foot in the air.

The first gun position accounted for nearly half our load of shells. An artillery bloke handed Oliver Butler a chit that I knew to be a proof of receipt. At that moment I heard the whistle of a 5.9. We all crouched low and it came down on the other side of our train, nearer the front than the back. Another came down half a minute later in the same position; then a third. It seemed to me the Germans had us under observation; or anyhow that they'd got a fix on the gun position we'd just delivered to, but were persistently aiming a little long. Then again, if they hit shells on the three wagons that remained loaded we'd all go up, train crew and gun position both.

'Are we to let the Germans blow our engine up?' Tinsley yelled.

'The question isn't the engine,' I yelled back, and another fucking shell came. '. . . It's the ammo coupled up behind it.'

'*I* think it's the engine,' said Tinsley.

I said, 'Well, there's no point hanging about here. We either go and get it back or we leg it.'

'I vote leg it,' said Dawson.

'No,' said Tinsley, 'we get it.'

I turned round and made a gesture indicating that Dawson, Oliver Butler and Muir should get clear. They might think of alerting the gunners as well.

'Rendezvous at the control point, Stringer,' said Muir, which meant we would be retreating to the junction, abandoning the second delivery. Muir seemed only too keen to get away, and I couldn't help thinking that our own Captain Quinn probably wouldn't have backed off in such a hurry.

I looked at Tinsley and he looked at me; we began to approach the simmering engine at a steady pace. It was important somehow that I did not trip on a root or snap a burnt branch, and I had a fancy that Tinsley was looking at the business in the same way: we were *stealing* the engine back. Another shell came down on the far side of it, and that was a little further off than the previous, but then came another that was *closer*, and I had the idea – although it seemed impossible – that the Baldwin had rocked on its rails.

'Twenty tons,' I shouted at Tinsley, 'and it bloody tilted.'

'Five tons of *coal* 'n' all,' he said.

We were within ten feet of the engine. If the pair of us cop it now, I thought, I will never see my children again; Tinsley will never graduate to the footplate; the wife will never get her kitchen garden . . . and I will never read *The Count of Monte Cristo*. But I wasn't going to do that anyway.

We got to the engine, and climbed up. The pressure was fine; the fire was fine. A shell came. Tinsley screwed off the brake, and I pulled the reverser. Another fucking shell – couldn't these fucking Krauts leave off for a single moment?

'I'll just give her a breath of steam!' I practically screamed at Tinsley, and we started to roll. He was dead white. I recall that he was nervously running his filthy hand over the few pimples he had about his chin. He was the age for pimples. He wasn't shaking, however, whereas I had once again started to shake. As we rolled under the rain of shells, I tried to tell myself that the difference was down to Tinsley's not having as much to lose – no wife and no children to leave behind – but there was no reason why a lad shouldn't have more pluck than a man of thirty-three.

I had come to the end of my courage; I was in sore need of a Woodbine, but I'd smoked my last. There was just one chance left . . . I put my hand inside my soaking greatcoat, and felt my tunic pocket. Well, I was on bloody velvet: a whole packet of the Virginians Select! I'd forgotten I'd had them there in reserve. I had no match, but Tinsley would have one. Who ever heard of a fireman without a match? He saw my hand as

I took the light, and he said, 'Cold!' so as to provide me with an excuse for shaking. I thought: he's up to the mark, this kid.

We'd rolled back to the control point, but the shells were still falling, and the half-witted corporal was nowhere to be seen. He'd taken refuge in his dugout. Dawson and Butler were waiting. Butler held a hurricane lamp; I could see by it that he had a strange expression on his face; I couldn't make it out. Behind him, Muir was shouting into the dugout. I believe he was saying that we would have to return to Burton with our half load, and that the half-witted corporal ought to telephone through to the gun position expecting a delivery, and tell them it was no go. If the next Baldwin had already set off from Burton Dump, we would have to work out a crossover at the passing loop.

I then heard Butler's shout: 'Good work Stringer! Bit of all right that!'

That was him all over. He knew that the odd word of praise counted for more than if he'd come out with them all the time. It was a kind of power that he exercised.

As we rolled, he climbed onto a wagon, as did Dawson; Muir got up onto the footplate once again. He congratulated Tinsley and me, and I thought it only fair to say, 'You've the boy to thank really.'

Tinsley's determination to reclaim the train had probably saved the life of every man in the vicinity, for the shells were continuing to fall where the train had been, and I was sure that one or more had landed square on the line over there. As we trundled backwards, we did seem to be leaving the worst of it behind, and I gradually stopped shaking. Of course, the kid had seen me, so I'd have to take care about talking down to him in future.

We came to Naburn Lock, and I opened her up a bit as we started reversing along the gentle ascent to the New Station, then the passing loop. As Holgate Villa was drawing slowly forwards on my right, I drew Tinsley's attention to rather low water in the gauge. I then looked backwards, and saw Dawson at his brake, smoking and looking sidelong, and Oliver Butler on his brake behind. I turned back forwards. Tinsley was working the injector as another shell came, and we both ducked at the sound of its whistling flight, knowing the cab walls and the cab roof would give some protection either from the blast if it was high explosive, or from the bullets and pieces of shell casing if it turned out to be shrapnel. All the shells that had come near so far that night had been H.E., but this was shrapnel. I knew by the spattering sound – like a harder rain – of the metal fragments on the wagons and shells behind. I turned around, and I saw – too fast – the white face of Oliver Butler. There was nothing – by which I mean there was *nobody* – between me and him. Dawson was down, stretched flat on the shell boxes of his wagon. I didn't even knock the regulator off, but began scrambling over the coal bunker to get back to that wagon. At the same time, Butler was coming forward from the back of the train. He got there before me, and he removed Dawson's tin hat, and put his head close to Dawson's, as though listening for breath. But when I got up to the two of them, I knew there would be none. I stood, balancing on the wagon and looking down at Dawson's face, which Oliver Butler had turned slightly to the side. The shrapnel had blown in from the left, coming under the tin hat, and taking that side of the head away. Most of the funny moustache remained, which he would now never either grow to a proper length, or shave off entirely.

The next evening, Fusilier Dawson, not being an officer, was buried a decent distance away from Tate in the little graveyard behind the lifting gantry.

There were not above a dozen greatcoated mourners, standing in steady rain, including Oamer, Oliver Butler, the twins (who had dug the grave), Tinsley and myself, and work – including engine movements – still carried on at the dump so that the engineer who doubled as chaplain had to shout 'In the midst of life we are in death . . .' and I thought: We are certainly in the midst of *shunting*.

I noticed that the chaplain-priest had marked his place in the prayer book with a used match, and I didn't think he'd have done that if it had been an officer he was burying. He retained the match in his hand while reading the service, and I had a powerful urge to knock it away.

As the twins set about filling in the grave, Oliver Butler came towards me, meaning to speak (I thought), but turned away at the last.

That same night, three more Baldwins came to the Burton Dump on the materiel train, together with a couple of dozen new wagons and many more track lengths for carrying forward and making new lines.

It was the start of a flood of equipment.

A lifting gantry and a new lathe came; more telephone lines led into Oamer's running office, and all the time the shells piled up in the yard. The weather worsened, dissolving the mud of the Dump, so that the shacks began to tilt at weird angles, and along with the rain came cold. The blokes moved slowly between the huts, and salutes – never a big feature of the place – went by the board as they passed each other, huddled in greatcoats and oilskins or, failing that, lengths of tarpaulin. I would see Captain Quinn wandering about, usually in company with Muir, and saying things like, 'This incessant rain *is* unfortunate.'

One night the materiel train brought in a 9.2-inch rail-mounted gun – a thing about the size of a house. The twins came out of the detachment hut to look at it ('Oh mother!') and I saw Quinn going up to the Royal Marine blokes who'd accompanied it in, and asking, 'What are you planning on doing with that thing?' Well, they *had* thought of firing it – and from Burton Dump. Quinn was having none of that. It would betray our position in an instant. But it took him two days of office work before he could get shot of the thing.

By the middle of September, the new Fourth Army front had been established on the above-mentioned line from Bezentin Le Petit to Combles. The push was then on for spots like Courcelette and Flers to the east, with British, Canadian and French Divisions all being involved. Our job was to keep the shells rolling forwards, but we'd sometimes collect wounded men from the dressing stations by the lines, and bring them back lying on the wagons where the shells had been. They would then be taken from the Dump by field ambulance and driven to the British hospital west of Albert.

Sightings of the tanks – the land ships – that were involved in this push became the big novelty of our runs. These, like us, were part of the new face of warfare, but we saw endless numbers of crocked ones, lying on their sides, or upside down like cockroaches unable to right themselves, and we knew that many had become tombs for the men inside. Then again, two of the Baldwins had been blown off the tracks by shellfire. One had been righted, and one lay belly-up in a ditch near the village (as was) of Longueval. One driver and one fireman had copped it, and they went into the graveyard.

Tinsley and I remained a team, and a good one, but he would occasionally question my instructions. He told me the death of Bernie Dawson had 'knocked him flat', but it didn't affect his concentration on the footplate. As he fired the engine, Tinsley would mutter his little rules of thumb – 'Keep a good depth of coal inside the door' and, especially 'Little and often with the coal and water', and I would look on, smoking my Virginians Select with one hand on the regulator, and saying nothing.

A few days after Dawson's death, we lost Oliver Butler as

a guard, various other blokes being substituted according to availability. He – Butler – would henceforth be in various forward areas, working on the field telephones in the control points, his telephony badge gained at Hull finally coming into its own. He was now practically a Royal Engineer himself, and this he considered a step up.

It was, I believe, four days after Dawson's death that Oliver Butler came up to me in the canteen at the Dump, which was also the bar. It was a better place to sit than the engine men's mess. The time was about two o'clock in the morning, and I'd just returned from a run. Like the other half dozen blokes in the place, I wore my greatcoat. A sign behind the makeshift bar read, 'Cheap Sauvignon', but I was on beer.

Butler carried a hurricane lamp over to my corner and sat down over opposite.

'Going on all right?' he said.

'Well, I'm still here.'

Butler was fishing as usual. 'Poor old Dawson, eh?' he was saying, as I looked about the room. The RE types had put up pictures around the walls – pictures of things like bridges and dockyards that had taken their fancy. With the common-run of Tommy, it would have been half-dressed women, but the REs were different. 'He was a good fellow too,' Butler was saying. 'Happy-go-lucky. You need blokes like that around – they're a regular tonic if you've an anxious nature yourself.' He kept silence for a moment, before adding, 'You and I have anxious natures, Jim, and who can blame us?'

I took out my packet of Virginians Select, offered Butler one, which he declined, and lit my own.

Butler said, 'As he was pegging out on the wagon, Dawson confided something in me, and now I'm going to confide it in you. You're the trusted man of the detachment, and I'm looking to you for advice, all right?'

As I blew smoke, I had an inkling of what was coming, even though I could scarcely believe it.

'He – Dawson – said he got up in the middle of the night for another go at the Smith's – you know the night I'm speaking of. He went through to the hall, and there was young Harvey, being his usual uppish self. He said to Dawson, "No man in his Majesty's army should put away as much beer as you do", or something like – and they were the last words the kid ever spoke. Dawson laid him out, dragged him over to the sea wall, put him in the water. You don't believe me, Jim.'

I eyed him.

'Of course it might be that Dawson only said what he did to get some other bloke off the hook. What do you reckon, Jim? Now . . . what ought I to do? Shall I let on to Thackeray? I believe he's been making enquiries in York – by telephone, of course.'

'How do you know that?'

'Oh . . . Quinn's up in arms about it,' he said, which was no answer.

'I can see from the way you're looking at me that you think I'm shooting you a line. I suppose it goes to your credit that you won't think ill of a friend . . . So I'll leave you to it,' he said, indicating my cigarette and beer.

He stood, and quit the room without another word, and there was a kind of dignity in the way he did it, I had to admit.

The next night, Oamer rode up with me and Tinsley. He wanted to look over some of the new control points. The line now pushed on a further four miles east beyond Pozières, running towards the above-mentioned village of Flers (which was officially captured but still fought over). On its way there, the line skirted the north edge of High Wood, and a short spur ran into the trees for the gun positions secreted there. It was the control at the start of the spur that Oamer was particularly interested in.

Old Station, Holgate Villa, New Station, Naburn Lock . . . The name posts rolled by clearly in the strong moonlight. After that, the York names stopped. Nobody had had the heart to carry on with the game after what had happened to Tate. We were under only moderate shellfire at the start, and that some distance off, but after the halt for Pozières (where we got rid of most of the shells) some big stuff – six- and eight-inch – did come near, and it rocked the engine.

'That a regular occurrence?' Oamer enquired as we rolled on.

'You're wondering why we're still alive,' I said.

'I'm only glad you are, fusilier,' he replied. 'I'm only glad you are.'

When we came to High Wood, Oamer consulted a document – his plan of the control points – and I stopped the engine where he indicated. To our left side was a dark field of frozen mud with a couple of concrete fortifications; on our right side, stricken trees and men moving about within them – moving either too fast or too slow, and seemingly without reference to orders being shouted by unseen voices.

'Where's your control?' I asked Oamer.

'Here or hereabouts,' he said, and he climbed down from the footplate, and entered the woods. 'No telephone line as yet,' he called back, 'so I can't follow the trail.'

I could see some disturbance in the burnt branches when Oamer disappeared from view – a cold wind blowing. Shells came in – heavy stuff by the sound of it, but far off. The wind blew again: a machine-like, whining noise.

. . . Silence in the woods for a space . . .

I looked up at the moon. Most of it was there. It was the reason that I could see too much. I was not sure that I liked the moon. It would reveal what was meant to be hidden. I stepped down from the footplate holding our hurricane lamp and my rifle. I went into the trees. Tinsley stayed on the footplate, rifle in hand. A moment later, he called, from behind my back, 'Look out, Jim!' Then came the fast rattling of a machine gun – the Boche taking advantage of the moonlight. No bullet had hit Oamer though. He was striding back through the trees towards me, coming from my left.

'Wait,' he called, and he'd seen some movement in the woods.

I shouted, 'We're under observation,' only, that last word being so long, I didn't get it all out. Another machine-gun rattle came; a longer one now – well, there was a lot of moonlight. Oamer was down. I ran towards him through the trees with Tinsley following.

I touched Oamer's shoulder; he rolled over, smiled up at me, and I thought: here comes a piece of philosophy – his last one. But instead of speaking, Oamer was moving his hand – his good hand, the one with a full complement of fingers – reaching under his greatcoat. I could not see blood as yet, but I knew that when he withdrew his hand, it *would* be bloodied. When his hand emerged, however, it was as white and smooth as before, and it held a book: *The Count of Monte Cristo*. I knew the thing by its dark cover, and by its enormous size. Lying there on the hard mud, with his head resting comfortably on a black tree root, and the shells coming down quite close by, and the cold wind stirring the trees, Oamer passed it up to me with a look of wonderment on his face. A bullet nestled in the book; it had drilled a hole nearly, but not quite, right the way through. A twist of smoke and a smell of burning rose from its paper nest.

'Good-o!' I said.

Tinsley and I helped Oamer up, just as though he'd fainted in, say, Betty's Tea Rooms, St Helen's Square, York, which I could quite imagine him frequenting, and where I *had* once seen a man faint.

'Thank God it's so densely plotted,' he said.

I looked at Tinsley, whose face was white, and it did occur

to me that, just as either Oliver Butler or Oamer might have loosed off the bullet that did for Scholes on the first day of the Somme battle, so Tinsley – the sound of his own shot being drowned out by the machine-gun rattle – might have fired on Oamer from the footplate of the Baldwin.

Mainly Amiens: Late September 1916

Dearest Jim,

What joy to have your letter, and to read that you are a now a non-commissioned officer. I told Lillian, who told Peter, who asks, 'Does this mean that you will be sitting in the saloon bar of the Old Grey Mare from now on?'

(Is that a joke, Jim?)

Other messages while I am at it. Sylvia says that, when the bombs come, you are to 'make yourself small'; also 'What are duckboards?' and 'Do you like figs?' (I don't know why this last, and she is asleep now, so I can't ask her.) Harry asks, 'How are you getting on with the "Count of Monte Cristo", and are you up to the release from prison of . . . Somebody or other. Jim, you are going to have to read this book and send him a separate letter all about it. If anything could raise you further in his estimation, which I rather doubt, then that would do it. Harry is really very proud of you for driving engines at the front, and for my part, I can't see why there isn't a 'Boy's Own Paper' story especially devoted to your work! Quite honestly, I also see no earthly reason why you shouldn't be a commissioned officer before long, now that you have got a foot on the ladder. I believe that more and more men from the ranks are being commissioned all the time, and it seems this can happen quite suddenly, and to the unlikeliest of people, if the evidence of our soldiers' buffet at the station is anything to go by. I am thinking here of a certain Major Plumptree (I assure you, that is his name) who has been making a nuisance of himself in the buffet these past weeks. Don't worry by the way, Jim, I have been to Naburn on your strange mission, and I will come to that presently, but meanwhile I simply must set down some of the choicest inanities of the man Plumptree.

He belongs to one of the York regiments, or so he says, but all he ever seems to do is come into the buffet to drink tea, eat cakes and make very forward remarks to the girls before going into what we call the retiring room (this is another carriage that we added since my last letter to you, Jim) in order to sleep and, I may say, to snore. He says that he will never speak of the horrors he has seen on the Western Front – possibly, I suspect, because he only ever saw them from a very great distance. He quite monopolises the tea rooms, and he has an opinion on everything. As I told you last time, there are now many women working on the station, as ticket checkers, cleaners, clerks and so on. One of them, Edith Wilkinson, who works on the ticket gate, came in for a word with me the other day, and Plumptree asked her, 'Why are you in uniform?'

'I'm a ticket checker,' she replied.

Plumptree exclaimed, 'But you're a woman!' and at that I could not keep quiet.

'There are no flies on you, are there?' I said, and he told me he would be making a complaint about me.

What happened about this complaint I've no notion, but he was back the next day, and as Mary (one of the servers) mopped up the tea and cake that he'd spilt, he said he was willing to tolerate the idea of women working on the station (as if anybody had asked him) on the grounds that three women could do the work of very nearly two men if 'trained to the hilt'.

Do you have any vacancies for spare Majors out where you are, Jim? You could ask your officer commanding to write to him care of the buffet.

Well then, to Naburn, and my enquiries on your behalf.

Of course it is barely a mile from our house, but I went from the middle of town, after a morning of work. It was a rather rainy day . . .

And I couldn't help but smile, for that word 'rainy' was just then spotted with a drop of the stuff, as I sat reading beyond the half-broken platform canopy of the station of Albert. Beside me sat Alfred Tinsley. We were waiting for a connection for Amiens, liberty passes in our pockets. At the start of the rain, we moved under a less broken part of the canopy, and sat down on a luggage barrow, where he resumed his reading of the *Railway Magazine* with the same keenness as that with which I returned to the wife's letter, thinking how lovely it was to hear from her, and wondering why she'd had to go round the houses quite so much before getting to the nub of the matter. But then Naburn evidently *wasn't* the nub of the matter in her life. I read on.

It was a rather rainy day and I was the only passenger on Black Leonard's pleasure steamer. I'd never heard him speak before, and in fact, he hardly does speak, but his few utterances are always extremely gentlemanly. As we came out of the town, and sailed through Thorpe (do you 'sail' when it's a steamboat?) our village looked perfectly lovely, Jim, with the canopy of yellow and orange leaves over the water, and the afternoon lamps glowing in the Archbishop's Palace. As we went past there, Black Leonard said, 'I *like* today.' Just that: three words. Nothing more until our arrival at Naburn, when I held out a shilling for him, and he said, 'Free ride.' I said, 'But I am not a soldier.' He said, 'You qualify under a different heading', and I *would* write that he was wasted on that boat of his, had not my trip been so very enjoyable.

I set all this down, Jim, to make you feel better about having sent me on such an exhausting and mysterious mission. However, it was all downhill from then on.

The landing stage at Naburn is some way from the lock, and my boots were soaked through by the time I got there. There was nobody at the lock, not even a lock-keeper as far as I could see, and no boats going through. The tea place, Martindale's, was closed, and the door glass was cracked. It was a world of water: the falling rain . . . the rushing of the water through the weir beyond the lock . . . the soaking fields. Well, I felt a perfect fool standing there, and it seemed to me that the question you wanted put – 'Has anything notable happened at the lock in recent times?' – was very likely to be answered in the negative. I then recalled the little reading room in the village, and the fire that burns there. I might go there, have a warm, and enquire. I was about to set off when I saw a trap approaching along the road that runs over the fields from the village to the lock. The man driving it was a glazier, come to replace the window of Martindale's. He told me his name was Harry Robson, and that he lived in Naburn, so I asked *him* whether anything notable had recently happened at the lock, and I got a very funny look for my trouble, but he did speak up eventually, while taking a mallet and chisel to the broken glass.

'You mean Matthew Waddington,' he said.

'Do I?' I said. 'Who's Matthew Waddington?'

'Cattle drover,' he said, and I did wish he'd stop bashing away at the glass, and just address me directly for a minute.

'And what was his association with the lock?'

'He was found dead in it, if you call that an association.'

Well, I questioned him closely (isn't that what you policeman say?), and it appeared that the body of Matthew Waddington had not been found inside the lock, but floating up against the outside of the lock gates at the town end – upriver, in other words – and this in the middle of July, 1914. Matthew Waddington was, according to Harry Robson, 'an old beer eater' – a heavy drinker. He then started in on a long description of him, for it seemed that Waddington was well known in the village. It was difficult to make out what Robson was saying, because he would keep hacking away as he spoke. At first, I thought he was speaking unflatteringly of Waddington, but this was not the case: the man was often 'beered up' but kept himself to himself. 'He had his cottage and his garden, and that was him, nicely suited.' He was a big fellow, 'Built like a . . . ' (Well, I can't write it down.) And something that would interest you, Jim: he had once worked at the cattle dock at York station. He might have been 'in bother' with the police once or twice as a younger man, but there'd been nothing of that recently.

When he'd finished telling me this, Harry Robson said he'd drive me back to Thorpe, since he was heading that way, but I would have to wait for him to finish the window. Well, he was intolerably slow at his work, so after a while I thanked him, and set off to walk through the rain. The next day, I went to the Library and found the report from the 'Press'. I copied it out for you, and there will be an extra charge for this, Jim.

Appearing on Monday 22nd July, 1914, under the heading 'Naburn Lock Mystery', it ran, 'The body of Matthew Waddington, aged 50, a cattle drover of Oak Field Lane, Naburn, was recovered from the River Ouse at Naburn Lock yesterday evening by P.C. Hartas and P.S. Hill. It appears that Sidney Stewart Taylor, a retired pharmacist, was going home along the river when he saw an object floating in the water. He informed David Brown, a lamplighter, and the two gave information to the police, who discovered the body of the deceased in the water. An inquest is to be held.'

The inquest was held a week later, and I did not copy out the report. It was too long, Jim, but there wasn't much to it for all that. Sidney Stewart Taylor and David Brown gave evidence. They seemed from it to be very respectable – as you would say, 'above suspicion'. A doctor gave evidence that Matthew Waddington had been dead, and in the water, not above a week. He was found to have suffered a blow to the forehead, whether from a fall or a blow could not be stated, and his liver was in a very poor condition. He was known to have had a weakness for alcohol. An open verdict was returned.

So there you have it, Jim: nothing else notable had occurred at the lock as far as I can tell, and this is one more death among all the other thousands. I mentioned it to Lillian, and she <u>had</u> heard of the matter from Peter, who knows the Naburn gravedigger. (He mixes in all the best circles, does Peter.) She said the police force in Naburn – that is, Hartas and Hill – were sure Matthew Waddington had been murdered. I think this will not surprise you, but quite honestly I do not want to know any more.

I pray for you every day in St Andrew's Church, and I know you will laugh, but after all you are, as you always point out at the start of your letters, 'still living'. (Jim, there is no need to point that out: if you were not living you would not be writing.)

I will close now. Write again soon, and do keep small.

With all my love,
Lydia.

PS: In your last letter, you said that some leave might be in the offing. When, Jim?

Half an hour later, I returned the letter to my greatcoat pocket after reading it over for the third time, at which moment the engine gave a whistle, a sure sign that we were a long way behind the lines.

We were approaching the town of Amiens in a very old French 'Nord' carriage which boasted open seating – that is to say, no compartments. In spite of the brass 'Défense de Fumer' signs on the backs of the seats, I personally had a Virginians Select on the go, and the signs were ignored by most of the thirty or so blokes riding up. The majority were Burton Dump men, equipped with the same liberty pass as rested in my pocket, and among them was Oliver Butler. I looked up to see him facing my way about five rows along. I couldn't see his brothers about, though. Amiens was a civilised place, not suited to their rough-house ways, and perhaps Oliver had told them as much.

Alfred Tinsley sat opposite to me. We knew Amiens by the approach of a great cathedral spire. Famous for its cathedral, was Amiens – its cathedral and its station, which was now closing around us.

The place was normal, as before: civilian services running to time, gorgeous-coloured advertising posters. The station dining rooms, located on our arrival platform, seemed all fitted out in gold, and there was a white-coated bloke sitting inside, folding napkins. Some military wagons and troop carriages *were* to be seen, but these were in far-off sidings. I pointed out a British 2-8-0 to Tinsley, and he said, 'Well, there are heaps of those round here', and didn't seem particularly interested.

The ticket collector looked long and hard at our passes, but finished off his inspection with a respectful nod.

'That's the Frenchers all over for you,' I said to Tinsley as we strolled through the ticket gate. '. . . Like to keep you guessing.'

Coming out from under the station glass, we saw that Amiens was enclosed in a thin white mist of the sort you only seem to get in the afternoons. It was like the half-formed idea of snow, and the place was freezing. Still, they had the tables set out in front of the cafés, and there were people sitting at them too – usually greatcoated soldiers with pretty, muffled-up women. I saw a man smoking, and then passing the cigarette to the woman. I'd never seen that done in Britain. Women seemed to be a speciality of Amiens – beautiful ones, I mean and we saw some real peaches.

'They've got everything here,' said Tinsley, 'women, proper buildings that stand up, tablecloths on the tables.'

We came upon the cathedral, and the size came as a shock – every part of it trying to be higher than the other part. The Germans had been in Amiens at the start of the war. How come they hadn't wrecked it?

'This is Gothic,' I said to Tinsley when we were inside. 'Like York Minster . . . I think.'

It *was* like York Minster, only more so. Tinsley put some change into a box marked, 'For the Poor of Amiens' – rewarding the town for being normal. Watching him wandering about in there, I thought of the bullet that had landed in *The Count of Monte Cristo*. I had taken it to one of the Royal Artillery blokes at the Dump, and without saying where I'd found it, I'd asked whether he thought it came from a British or a German weapon. He said it was too misshapen to say, but most likely

German. As regards the book itself, I'd asked Oamer if I might keep it, and he'd agreed, saying, 'It's not going to save my life again, is it?' I would now be able to give it back to Harry with the best possible excuse for not having read it, and I decided that as far as the lad was concerned, it might as well have saved *my* life as Oamer's.

Behind the cathedral was an area of narrow canals running between ancient-looking houses connected by wooden bridges. It was a beautiful spot, but I looked into the waters of the canals expecting to see dead men floating there, and when I looked into the sky it appeared to be unnaturally empty and silent as though something had lately been taken away. As we drifted about, the light fell, and the buildings became distinct by virtue of the different colours of light showing from them. About half of them turned out to be pubs or restaurants, and this quarter was evidently a big draw for the Tommies. We had three or four glasses of beer apiece, then went into a little restaurant and ordered what turned out to be a quarter of a chicken apiece with herbs and fried potato – and gravy. There was no gravy at Burton Dump, never had been and never would be. The owner of the place came up to us and asked 'Bon?'

'*Très* bon,' I said, but that only encouraged the bloke to say something else in French that I didn't get, but that I fancied might be, 'Thank you for fighting the war – I hope you win it.'

'You know, I could live in France,' said Tinsley, as we were fishing out our francs to pay the bill.

'You are doing,' I said.

'After the war, I mean,' he said, and I was struck by his confidence in using that expression.

'If you lived in France you couldn't be a train driver in York,' I said.

'I know,' said Tinsley, 'that's the trouble.'

He must have been a bit squiffed because he started in about how the locomotives were more exciting over here, the carriages wider-bodied, the stations bigger. They had bigger ideas about everything in France. Only he couldn't live without tea, and they didn't run to that. When we left the restaurant, the owner said, 'Bonne journée.'

'That means "Have a good journey",' said Tinsley. 'It's the politeness of the French for you.'

After our supper there was a bit more drifting, but it struck me that, while Tinsley's body might be wandering aimlessly in the maze of little houses and canals, his mind was not.

'What are you after?' I said.

'Oh,' he said, and he coloured up. 'Something Bernie Dawson told me about ages ago.'

'A pub?' I said.

'Not exactly a pub,' said Tinsley.

'I think you want to be over that way,' I said, indicating a quarter where the lights in the windows burned lower and redder. He'd missed his chance in Albert, so here was another opportunity.

'Fancy coming with me?' Tinsley enquired, looking in the direction indicated, and not at me. 'I think you should.'

Towards the end of one particular cobbled street, the only people on view were women, mostly sitting on the first-floor windowsills, and looking at the blokes walking past – the uniformed ones especially. Tinsley stopped, and eyed one back, going crimson in the process. I was sure it would have been the longest he'd ever looked directly at a woman – about three seconds. It was enough though, and she jumped down off the window ledge, indicating that he should follow her into the house.

'I might just go in here for a glass of beer,' Tinsley said, turning to me.

'*Afterwards*,' I said, '*wash* it.'

'What?' he said, with a strange sort of grin, 'the beer glass?'

The woman had left the door half open, disclosing an ordinary sort of living room of a good size with two soldiers – sergeants – sitting in it, smoking cigars, having either just finished their business there, or smoking in anticipation of it. I removed my cap, and watched from the doorway as a woman – an older version of the one who'd been on the windowsill – came into this room from a smaller one to the rear, and spoke to Tinsley. She used some word like 'assignation'. Wasn't her friend a pretty lady? An assignation was possible for seven francs, so Tinsley fished about in his pockets for a while, before announcing to the woman, 'I've only got five.' She didn't understand, or pretended not to. Tinsley turned and looked at me, his face redder than I would have thought it possible to be, and I handed him two francs.

'Thanks, old man,' he said, 'I'll pay you back,' and he added in an under-breath. 'You know, I'm more shaky than I was on the first day of the Somme battle . . .'

But he hadn't been shaky at all before that show, as far as I could see.

'Per favore,' he said, turning and handing over the coin to the woman.

'That's Italian,' I said from behind him. 'You're in France.'

But it made no difference. While the two sergeants smoked on, he was being escorted into the rear room.

'I'll see you in the goat bar!' I called out. (This was an estaminet with a painting of a goat over the door. We'd walked past it a couple of times.)

I was fishing for cigarettes prior to quitting the house when the madame returned with another woman, about of an age with the one of the windowsill, and a first-class belter it had to be admitted, being small, dark, and dancerish, with an amused expression.

The madame stood her in front of me, and told me the name of the girl was Françoise, so I put out my hand, and we *shook* hands, at which Françoise laughed a little, but only a little. (I looked sidelong at the sergeants to see if they thought this a funny going-on, but they just continued with their own talk.) Françoise eyed me steadily as the madame gave an account of all the points in favour of her. This was done mainly in French, but sometimes an English expression would break in, such as, 'You will like her', at which I thought: *I already do*. I believe the idea was that I would interrupt this speech, pay over the money and go off with Françoise, but seeing I was making no move, the madame came to halt with the question:

'Oui ou non?'

This was a clever stroke. Even I could understand the enquiry, and to say 'Non' would surely appear rude to Françoise . . . Only I kept thinking of the wife going all that way to Naburn in the rain for me, and I knew I would have to get out of it. I wished I knew the words for 'I'm sorry but I have another appointment', and I was trying to think of something along those lines when Françoise took a step towards me, put her hand delicately on the back of my head and, standing on tip-toe, whispered something into my ear. It sounded like the greatest secret ever told – in French. They both stood back and watched me, and then a brainwave came to me in the form of a single word. I recollected it from the time of the battalion's arrival in France: the word that Captain Quinn would be ever-likely to say if he were French.

'Malheureusement . . .' I said.

Well, it did the job in an instant. Françoise fairly spun away from me and sat down with the two smoking sergeants, who she seemed to know of old. I made the remainder of my excuses to thin air, turned and quit the establishment. Ten minutes later, in the countrified-looking estaminet with the goat painted over the door, I was wondering whether I might in all conscience have gone with Françoise, only with the request: 'Par main'. It was rather annoying that the phrase had only come to me at that moment.

There was a tap on my shoulder; I turned about, and there was Tinsley, still looking rather flushed.

'Did you wash it?' I said.

'Leave off, Jim,' he said. '. . . She was very nice. Will you stand me a beer, old man?'

I wondered if he'd be 'old manning' me forever, now that he'd lost his ring.

'She was very polite,' he ran on, as I called for the drink.

'Well that's something,' I said.

'At the end she said "termine" or "terminez", or something.'

'Right,' I said, nodding.

'Is that a good thing or a bad thing that she said that?'

'Well, it depends which one it was.'

Tinsley blew out his cheeks.

'Anyhow,' he said, as I passed him his beer, 'I'm a man about town now.'

'*What* town?'

'I mean . . . man of the world.'

'Get that down you,' I said, indicating the beer, 'it's nearly train time.'

We rode back towards Albert in what might have been the very same carriage we'd come out in. As before, Tinsley sat over opposite me, and he had to crane around, while I looked directly forward, at the retreating dark spire of the Amiens cathedral. Our afternoon out had been the next best thing to an afternoon of home leave, of which there still seemed no prospect. Also as before, almost every man in the carriage smoked. Not Oliver Butler, however. He was facing me, and of course eyeing me too, from halfway along the carriage. It was as though he had read the letter I had in my pocket, but he could not have done. I'd guarded it closely since its arrival. The wife had unearthed the one kind of event at Naburn Lock that could have caused the sort of reaction to any mention of the place that I'd seen from Butler, namely a death. For a surety, he knew what had happened to this Matthew Waddington, and it was odds on that either he'd done for the bloke himself, or the twins had. The twins were favourite, of course, the pair of them being cracked, but I doubted they could do anything without their brother knowing. The next question was whether or how this connected to the death of William Harvey. Had Harvey known anything of the Naburn business, and threatened to speak out about it?

And then had *Scholes* known what Harvey had known? And had Oliver Butler put a bullet into him on that account?

Alfred Tinsley was leaning towards me. He had something to say, but he wasn't saying it. The carriage was lit by low gas, giving just enough of a blue-ish light for me to see that the smoke over the men's heads was mainly old; that it was stale smoke from past-cigarettes, signifying that most of the occupants were now asleep.

'Jim,' he said.

'What?'

'Why did you give up the footplate?'

I recalled, for Tinsley's benefit, the hot summer's evening when I'd run that engine into the shed wall at Sowerby Bridge. I'd done it while employed as a fireman (well, passed cleaner anyhow) on the Lancashire and Yorkshire railway. I told Tinsley of the two hours of questions from the Shed Super that had followed, explaining to Tinsley, as I had explained to the Super, that my mate had told me the brake had been 'warmed', but that it had *not* been, with the consequence that the steam sent into it on my first application of the brake immediately condensed, and the thing did not work.

'Did the Super not take the point?' said Tinsley.

'He did seem to,' I said, 'but then I got the chop.'

Tinsley sat back, looking appalled. Oliver Butler, I noticed, was not asleep. But at least he was looking out of the window

– at the dark French countryside, which was going past at the rate of about twelve miles an hour – and not eyeballing me.

Tinsley now leant forward again, then turned sideways . . . so that he too was looking out of the window, and I believed that in that instant he'd changed his mind about something. We began to run over some points, and since we were going so slowly, a great and prolonged clattering was set up.

'Tom Shaw would go nuts,' Tinsley said, looking at me once again.

'Why?'

'At this crawl.'

'Traffic's heavy to the front,' I said. 'The driver's kept back by signals, you know that.'

The rattling did not let up. Presently, I asked, 'Why does he not enlist, do you suppose? Your man Shaw, I mean?'

'Somebody's got to drive the expresses,' said Tinsley. 'The government directs all the railways now . . .'

'I know.'

'I don't believe they'd *let* him go.'

I doubted that, but kept silence.

'He's not a coward, Jim,' Tinsley said, leaning forward again, in a confidential tone. 'He's not afraid of crossing the top brass. I've known him pull some pretty bold strokes.' As he spoke, we were leaving the points behind, coming back to a clear length of line. 'Why, he's capable of anything, is Tom Shaw.'

A match was struck somewhere along the carriage, and I said, 'I suppose he doesn't smoke, does he?'

'Oh, he has the odd one,' said Tinsley, and I was beginning to think once again that Tom Shaw did not exist. Yes, I had seen a photograph, but that might have been of anyone. I took one of my own cigarettes, and offered the pack to Tinsley. He took one, for perhaps the third time in his life, and we were back on another lot of points, clattering as before.

'Even Tom Shaw has to obey signals,' I said.

'Signals, yes,' said Tinsley. 'But he'll pay no mind to the running office. If he wants to get in somewhere ten minutes ahead of time, he'll just do it.'

'He ought to join up,' I said.

'Oh, I expect he will in *time*,' said Tinsley, giving a queer sort of smile, and I wondered: Does that mean that Tinsley will start *speaking* of him as an enlisted man, Shaw being a product of his imagination? Or was the smile meant to signify that he was letting go of a myth that had supported him? Then again, Tinsley didn't seem the fantastical sort.

We were once more clear of the points, gaining speed a little. Tinsley leant forwards again, closer than before. He blew smoke to the left, so it didn't go in my face, and said:

'I did for Harvey, Jim.'

I eyed him for a while, then shifted my gaze to Oliver Butler sitting beyond. He seemed half asleep. Tinsley and I sat on the right hand of the carriage; there was nobody on the seats immediately to our left.

'I thought you knew,' he said, '. . . when you asked me about the magazine.'

I gave a single shake of the head.

'I got up at about one in the morning – '

'To be sick?'

Tinsley frowned, as though offended by the notion.

'I got up to go to the jakes,' he said, looking again at the slow unwinding of shadows beyond the window. 'I'd shipped a lot of beer of course, but it was . . . more than a piss that I needed. I went over to my kit bag to get some paper, Jim. All the bags were up on the little stage, you recall, up with the rifles . . . and when I opened the bag up, I was looking for my *Railway Magazine*.'

'Hold on,' I said, 'you were never going to use that for – '

'Not on your life, Jim. I was hunting for some newspaper

that I kept specially, but I knew the magazine – it was the November 1915 number – had been on the top of the bag, because that's where I'd put it – on the top so's not to get crushed. Only it wasn't there. So I was half looking for the newspaper, and half fretting about the magazine, thinking perhaps I'd put it by my bed after all, or left it at the farm . . .'

I nodded. 'Go on.'

'Just then, Harvey walked in, and he'd been about for a while, because he had a glass of ale in his hand that he'd taken from one of the barrels. He wasn't the same with anyone his own age as he was with the older blokes, you know. He'd put on swank about his dad who'd got a medal in Africa. He hated the railways, Jim. They'd made a slave of his old man. His dad was nothing, you see, just a casual somewhere in the Company . . .'

(At this I wondered whether he too had mixed up the two 'fathers' of Harvey, not that it made any difference.)

'Harvey was only on the railways for the uniform – for the blooming gold braid, shouldn't be surprised. He'd always meant to enlist as soon as he was of age, and then the formation of the battalion was announced, and he came in. Only of course, he wasn't up to it, and that made him angry. At least, he was angry with me, Jim.'

The kid was white, but he seemed to have mastered himself pretty well.

'Harvey was giving me a bit of a slanging, saying I didn't have the looks of a soldier, calling me a railway nut, but I paid him no mind. He'd turned up the lamp on the table, and he was looking at the notice Oamer had left there, so he could see we had our marching orders, that we were going out, and I think it knocked him, Jim, because he *knew* he wasn't up to it. Anyhow, he took another pint, and downed it fast.'

'In a different glass?'

Tinsley shrugged. 'Think so.'

The two glasses on the table.

Tinsley blew smoke as though he wanted to get the stuff away from himself as fast as possible.

'I admit, Jim, I might have said something along those lines . . .'

'Along what lines?'

'Something like, "Well, now we'll see who's up to snuff, and who gets the horrors at the sight of a bayonet".'

'It was *exactly* that, wasn't it?' I said.

'It was, Jim. Those words exactly, and of course I'd take them back if I could, but there's no help for it, is there?'

I kept silence, because there wasn't. However, I still could not credit the idea of Alfred Tinsley as a killer.

'He said, "Well, you can forget about your railway hobby now." Then he walked out, collecting up his rifle.'

'Out into the storm?'

'Just so. I called after him, "What do you mean by that, you pill?" But he was having none of it. Just marched out, slanging me. Well, I went after him. I mean, who wouldn't, Jim? And since he'd taken his rifle, I took mine, just to put the frighteners on him. I didn't know what it would come to – bit of shouting, I suppose. Well, I came out into the rain and I could hardly see a thing, but I finally made him out walking on the sea wall, the abutment – '

'Revetment,' I cut in.

'I walked towards him, and he had his rifle pointing at me. I said, "We'll have this out, but drop the bloody gun, will you?" He said, "I've a mind to shoot you down." I said "You wouldn't bloody dare", and he said, "I've burnt your fucking magazine. It's in the fucking stove." So he'd taken it from my kit bag, and he'd put it in the stove – the November number. I could have shot him just then, but I didn't. I was holding my rifle by the muzzle. I swung it, Jim, and crowned him with the butt. I hit him in the region of his left eye, and he would have had a shiner in the morning, but it was nothing worse than that, only . . .'

'Go on.'

'He fell onto the bloody . . .'

'The mooring post . . . the bollard.'

'. . . The upright for tying the ships, that's it. Cracked the other side of his head against that, then just . . . rolled into the water. Just went in . . . haversack, rifle 'n' all.'

Tinsley sniffed and crushed out the stub of the cigarette with his boot, saying, 'Thanks, Jim, for that. I'm obliged to you . . . Once he'd gone, he'd really gone, I mean completely. I stood on that sea wall; I looked down, and there was no trace of him, and the sea was still going wild – hungry for more, sort of thing. Well, I can't swim. I admit it, Jim, I turned away.'

He sat back, then immediately came forwards again.

'I didn't murder him did I?'

I shook my head. It was manslaughter, more like, and Tinsley would be able to claim self-defence. He certainly hadn't shot at Oamer, either, because why would he do that, and then spill the beans to me?

'I'm not liable?' said Tinsley.

I gave no reaction. My thoughts were racing in a circus.

'There were no witnesses,' said Tinsley.

That was true enough.

'Why tell me?' I said, but I knew really. After our adventures in the Baldwin, and our times in Albert and Amiens, I'd graduated to being a person he could confide in.

'I didn't tell you at first,' he said. 'Well, you're a copper.' He sat back, adding, 'I told Dawson.'

My thoughts whirled faster. In that case, Oliver Butler had *not* been lying about Dawson's confession. Dawson had done it to get Tinsley off the hook. It had been amazingly white of him – might have earned him a place in heaven. If so, I hoped they had a good supply of John Smith's laid on.

The train was beginning to slow.

'Anyone else but Thackeray,' Tinsley was saying, 'and I'd have let on about it all, but he gives me the willies. I know I should have spoken up when I saw what he was putting Scholes through, but . . . I *am* in queer aren't I, Jim?'

I said, 'Do you want me to speak to Quinn, get it all straightened out?'

'I do,' he said, 'but just not yet. I mean to set it all to rights, but I want to do it myself . . . Did I say that his cap had come off? He'd fallen in with his rifle and his haversack, and they were washed away. But his cap was still there, sitting on the sea wall near where he went in. By some miracle the wind hadn't taken it, and no wave had reached it. I picked it up.'

'Did Scholes see you? He said he saw something.'

'He may have done. There might have been somebody moving about near the jakes when I was at the sea wall.'

'What about the bike?'

'Tripped over it, Jim. I was coming back from the sea wall, in an awful state, as you can imagine, and I went clattering into the blamed thing, which he'd left lying about between the wall and the hut. I cut my head in the fall, Jim, and it bled a little under the hair. I took my own cap off to check the damage; I set it down, and the wind had it away. Well, of course, I had another cap – I still had Harvey's. I put it on; it fitted perfectly, and just for that reason, I decided to pass it off as my own. I wasn't thinking straight, as you can see.

Later, back in bed, I made up my mind that I *would* tell everything, but then Quinn came in holding my own cap, and he was mad for once, and I couldn't bring myself to explain about it all. I was sure someone would work it all out. Apart from anything else, I suddenly had this very bright cap badge – because you know how Tinsley would go at it with the polish. And I left his glass on the table – well, his two glasses, you're right about that. I always meant to tell the truth, but in the right way . . . and in all the questioning, I just couldn't see my way to doing it. I will tell it to Quinn, I promise you. Meantime, you won't split on me, will you Jim?'

I shook my head.

'I won't split,' I said.

The blokes in the carriage were beginning to wake, and to stand. We were now coming in to Albert, clashing over a mass of points. The man in the seat directly behind Tinsley stood, and the greatcoat he was putting on looked quite normal, but when I raised my eyes to his head, I saw something amiss. The head was too small; he turned about, and his eyes were wrong as well – it was Roy Butler, the cleverer of the twins. For once, Andy was not at his side, and for that reason I had not heard Roy: he'd had nobody to speak to. It was an extraordinary thing to see him acting independently, but then I recalled that he had once – when Oamer had levelled the rifle at his brother – gone so far as to address me without prompting. Oliver Butler had clearly known of his brother's presence, but they had travelled separately within the carriage, and my only hope was that this was in order that Roy Butler could sleep. If he hadn't slept, then it was likely he would have heard Tinsley. This in turn meant that if Tinsley didn't tell his tale to Thackeray in very short order then someone else would do it for him, and I could see Roy Butler speaking to his brother at that moment, and looking our way as he did so. I did not believe he had slept.

The mercy was that Tinsley, reaching into the luggage rack for his haversack, had no idea of this.

Towards Le Sars: Early October 1916

The target of the Fourth Army was now the German Transloy Line, which ran in a roughly south-easterly direction from Le Sars to Le Transloy. It would be attacked from the captured villages standing directly west of it, including Courcelette and Flers. As already stated, the two-foot track had extended almost to Flers at the close of September.

At the start of October, the platelayers at Burton – the Butler twins among them – extended the line *into* Flers itself with a succession of girder bridges to cross abandoned British trenches. And a branch was built aiming from there towards Le Sars, the better to pound that end of the Transloy Line. Oliver Butler had been detailed by Oamer to man the control at Flers, which was a dangerous spot, being very forward, and to work on the telephonic communications in that area.

On the day after our trip to Amiens, Tinsley and I coupled the Baldwin up to six flat wagons loaded with shells, all intended for gun positions along the Flers–Le Sars branch. We waited until dusk, then took our rum. (If you did it the other way about, the rum died in you, and you might as well not have had it.)

'I'll just give her a breath of steam,' I said.

The rain had turned to sleet and there was no moon as we rolled through the first woods, past the pool where Tate had died, over the makeshift Ancre Bridge. I knew this evening that they were not just a series of mileposts – they amounted to more than that, and I believed that Tinsley thought so, too. As we ran over the girder bridge – at which point we began to come under shelling – I heard him mutter 'Little and often' while he was swinging the shovel. He was not much inclined to speak, and I wondered whether he'd regretted his confession (if that was quite the word) of the night before. At Naburn Lock, the sign announcing the name was still nailed to the post. Oliver Butler would have passed it often, sometimes on foot and alone, but he had never taken down the sign, in spite of his dangerous connection (for I was sure that one existed) with that place, and with Matthew Waddington who had come to grief there.

After an interval of crossing old British trenches by girder bridges, we came to a bombsite, Flers, and I saw a green light wavering into view. A man held it, and he had stepped out of – and also up *from* – the floor of a broken house. It was Oliver Butler, and his control point was in the basement of that place; telephone cables ran into it. When I rolled the Baldwin up to him, we nodded to each other. He had not, as far as I knew, yet ratted on either Dawson (after Dawson's own 'confession' before dying) or on Tinsley after his loose talk on the train. It struck me that he had now found his place in the world: he had his telephone lines, and a whole Somme village of his own – a little empire of ruins; and he had his lamp, and he was giving us the green, letting us know it was safe to go along the branch to Le Sars. Tinsley was saying as much as he put coal on at my side: 'We've got the green, Jim, let's go.'

The shelling had lessened somewhat in the previous minutes, even though we were hard up against the front line, and things were quiet at first along the new branch. It ran over a field of hard mud in which a number of enterprises had come to grief. To our left was a small copse, but all the trees were burnt. A house had once been built there, but only one wall remained. On the other side of our line, someone had tried to tow a gun carriage through the field, but it now lay on its side, and two soldiers had walked in the field but they now lay dead, side by side like a married couple in bed, just a few feet from the railway line. It slowly came to me (for the field was dark) that one enterprise was being carried on in that very moment. In the copse to our left, two men were moving about. I could tell by the shape of their tin hats that they were Tommies . . . and they were breaking the burnt trees, destroying them further, as though not content with the work the shells had done. Puzzling over this, I put a cigarette in my mouth, and I heard the whistle of an approaching shell. As I lit the cigarette I heard – owing to the surprising slowness of the speed of sound – the bang of that same shell being fired. I thought for the moment that *everything* was slow, but was proved wrong a moment later when there came a great, fast crash and a shout from Tinsley; the line was holed directly in front of us, and I had no sooner made a grab for the brake than we were into the hole, and going over.

. . . Only now the infectious slowness had returned, and as the Baldwin toppled, we were able to walk out of it, so to speak, stepping off the wheels as it finally crashed into the mud. The wagons were dragged over a second later, the shells toppled off, and our two brakesmen leapt clear. Tinsley and I watched the still-spinning wheels of the Baldwin, illuminated by the flickering Verey lights of the front.

'I never thought that would happen,' said Tinsley, after a while.

'I did,' I said.

A shell came down in the field somewhere behind us.

'We can right it with a jack,' he said.

But we weren't carrying a jack.

Tinsley was closing his eyes against what was now soft snow.

'About what you said, last night,' I said to him, but another shell was racing up and up directly above us, and his face wore a questioning look. There came a great light, but no explosion.

I held my breath waiting for the explosion, but instead there was only the light, and the full scale of the disaster stood revealed: our fallen engine, the fallen wagons, the spilled shells; our brakesmen looking on. The shell had evidently got stuck in the sky – it was a light shell rocket, and the white flame swung beneath a small parachute. Beyond it the white clouds raced against the blackness of the heavens, like many pages being rapidly turned. I saw the spirals made by the falling snow, and I saw again my friend Tinsley – the whiteness of his face, a few pimples there, but also the beginnings of a manly handsomeness. I saw the Tommies in the distant trees, and knew what they were about – wood fatigue; the collection of fuel. They were like figures from an older world. I thought of Christmas, and Good King Wenceslas walking with his servant. The hanging light had not stopped the Tommies about their wood-gathering, but I felt wiser than them in that moment, and I knew that it *should* have stopped them. As they pulled the branches down, the sound of sharp cracks came echoing towards me. I looked to the other side of the line, and saw the two dead soldiers. The light showed me that they were Germans. Stepping over the track, I moved towards where they lay. There was a rifle there, and even though I held my own rifle, I picked it up. I could not say what I was about. I was perhaps tidying up the field, being in a daze, the train having turned over.

The shock of all this was increasing and not decreasing. I turned and faced Tinsley, and said something, but I could not make myself heard over the cracking of the wood from the copse, which was in fact the firing of bullets. The words formed in my head: *We are under sniper observation,* and Tinsley immediately proved the fact by falling over. He fell both down and away, and something went from him as he fell. The light in the sky then went out, and I saw the flame fall. I saw where it lay in the field – a small, ordinary fire. I had a mental image of a log burning on a fire, and I heard the unnatural squealing of the sap coming from the wood, which became by degrees a whistling.

The shell was on me, and in me – into my leg. I was lying flat under the increasing snow, with the two rifles about me. I turned one way and our brakesmen were coming running. From another direction came an artillery man, shouting:

'What the hell's going on? We told the Control to hold you back.'

I saw behind them a figure with a lamp, moving more slowly, and looking half concerned: Oliver Butler, 'the Control', who had been told to keep us back. But I was melting into the ground where I lay. I thought: I have one more chance to make a movement before the pain becomes intolerable, but I discovered that I was wrong about that.

PART THREE

Blighty Again

Ilkley Again

When I was half awake, but still under the gas, I looked through a gap in the curtains and saw, in the dawn light, Ilkley Moor, a good deal higher than it had been before, and moving towards this house, and towards me, closing in. It then came to me that this was a great bank of cloud, with a ragged top, but I was still not quite thinking straight, because it seemed very clear that this bank of cloud was called the Western Front, and so the Western Front was coming to Ilkley.

I shifted my position a little, and saw on the bedside table, alongside my pocket book, which was stuffed with letters of recent date from the Chief, a packet of cigarettes. But a smoke was just then out of the question. I knew that I had surfaced, so to speak, only briefly from my long sleep. But at the sight of the carton, I recollected the matter that had plagued me ever since I had come to 'Ardenlea', namely the lighting of a cigarette – heard, not seen – at a late stage on the journey back to Albert from Amiens, with Alfred Tinsley sitting before me, and the train crashing over points.

The uppermost parts of cloud were now breaking away from the Western Front, looking first like sea waves, and then floating clear. I was aware of a bad pain in my leg, but it was remote, more like a pain I might be reading about rather than actually suffering. It was time to go back to sleep.

On waking, or rather not quite waking, I saw there was only the Moor beyond the window – the Moor at its normal height, under a sky that threatened snow. The wife came into the room, and it was comical to watch her trying to make an entrance so quietly. She sat down on the visitor's chair, and I could tell that she did not quite know what to do, so she rose up, and kissed me, then sat down again, looking slightly embarrassed. I liked the grey-blue of her dress, the darkness of her eyes, but it seemed best to contemplate them from a half-sleeping state. This was like a sort of deal made between myself and my bad leg. If I did not provoke it, then it did not provoke me.

The wife looked restless. She had more energy than was required for almost any situation in which she might find herself, and I was sure she must have had enough of this gloomy house and its silent, shaking men. She was eyeing me closely. Perhaps she thought I was shamming, not really asleep and so, just in case, she began to speak:

'I have just spoken with Hawks, the surgeon, Jim, and he assured me that the operation had been a complete success.'

She looked at me uncertainly for a while. She didn't know whether to carry on with her speech or not, but in the event she did so.

'I told him, "That's what you said that time", and he replied, "Your husband was very unlucky in what happened to him in the previous operation." I said, "He certainly was."'

At this, the wife bit her lip, or not exactly that, but somehow gave me the idea by her expression that she regretted saying that to Hawks, and also regretted telling me that she had said it. She carried on:

'He's right this time though, Jim. I know he is.'

Another pause, then she said, 'Well, I think I will go for crumpets at Betty's Tea Rooms today! I've been meaning to do that ever since I came here!'

But it was forced jollity, and the next moment, she was almost in tears as she said, 'There is a man called Thackeray coming to see you, I am not allowed to be here when he does.

But Hawks will be with you,' and she stood up in a flurry, with a rustling of her skirt, adding, '. . . because Hawks is an officer, and there must be an officer present for what the man Thackeray has to say.'

She turned to the door very noisily and was gone.

It might have been an hour later, or five hours later, that Thackeray was standing at the foot of my bed. Hawks was at the side of it, in the visitor's chair. I recall, as though by way of preparation, Thackeray talking to Hawks, saying, 'There are some good men in here', by which I supposed he did not include the men from the New Armies. He explained to Hawks that the task he was about to perform might have been given over to another military policeman, only he – Thackeray – had had to escort an important German prisoner from France to the York Castle, where he was to be held from the duration of the war. So he was killing two birds with one stone. At this, he turned to face me, stood to attention, and started with the killing.

He asked me some quick questions, machine-like. The one he liked best, I could tell, was: 'Why did you take hold of a German rifle after your train crashed at Flers?'I believe he enjoyed greatly both the question and my answer: 'I've no clear notion.' He then told me my name and my rank. I had thought he was already standing to attention, but he went up straighter still in order to say that he was charging me with the murder of Fusilier William Harvey . . . and he gave the date and the place, the place being Spurn Head. He asked if I understood and I heard myself saying yes. Thackeray looked at Hawks, and Hawks nodded on my behalf, but Thackeray wasn't done yet, and he started all over again. He was now charging me with the murder of Fusilier Alfred Tinsley. Once more, he gave a date, and the place: Flers, France. He had instructed a member of the regimental police of my own battalion to guard me during my convalescence. I was to obey without hesitation his orders, and the instructions of the staff of 'Ardenlea'. Presently, I would be visited by my counsel, a man supplied from the Army Legal Corps. I would, when fit enough, be removed to the military wing of Armley Gaol in Leeds, to await court martial. Thackeray then walked around to the side of the bed with a tremendous squeaking of boots that seemed to cause some pain to Hawks, handed me the charge sheet, and was gone.

Hawks remained behind, and removed the bandage from my leg. I saw the patch of iodine, and the bristling cat gut, like barbed wire, and I did not much care for the sight, so I distracted myself with talking in – no doubt – a dazed sort of way. I told Hawks that Thackeray had found a motive for me vis-à-vis the boy Harvey. I had arrested his father on York station. The prosecution had not been proceeded with, since Read – the father – had fallen severely ill before the matter could come to the police court. But word of the arrest had spread, and the disgrace stood. It was Thackeray's belief that Harvey had come to know of it. It was also Thackeray's belief, I explained to Hawks, that on the stormy night in Spurn, when I had been up late in the building called the Hope and Anchor, Harvey had picked a fight with me over this, and that we had come to blows on the sea wall. He – Thackeray – had found it telling that I had at no stage volunteered the information about my arrest of William Harvey's natural father. Furthermore, I had admitted to having cut my knuckle on Spurn. I had said I had done this before the arrival of Harvey on the peninsula, and this Thackeray did not believe.

As to the second charge, this all rested – I explained to Hawks, as he re-bandaged my leg – on the fact of Tinsley having been shot and killed by a bullet from a German Mauser rifle. I had been discovered lying wounded from a shell with such a rifle close at hand. Inspection of the magazine showed that one bullet had been fired. An artillery man called Dobson – the one who had told me, as I lay wounded, that 'the

Control' (Oliver Butler) had been instructed to hold the train back – had testified to having seen me point the rifle towards Tinsley, although he would not swear that I had *fired* at Tinsley. The evidence for this second charge was stronger than that for the first, but the two were connected, in that my motive for killing Tinsley was taken to be that he knew – and had let *on* that he knew – that I had done for Harvey on Spurn. He had, on the afternoon of his final day, asked Quinn how he might get into touch with Thackeray, and Thackeray believed that I had known of this.

Hawks had no doubt been told most of this already by Thackeray, and so he said nothing in response. He might have wondered how I'd got such a good idea of the case against me at this early stage. Well, I had pieced together the picture using the pointers given by the questions of Thackeray, my own guess-work, and from my correspondence with the Chief. Thackeray had quizzed the Chief about my arrest of the indecent Read. He – Thackeray – had told the Chief that charges were likely, and the Chief had evidently replied that, if brought, they would certainly be defeated, which reply would very likely have done my case more harm than good, diplomacy not being one of the Chief's points.

My 'guard' was a Corporal Brewster, the one I'd thought might have been called Baxter of the two regimental police who'd politely questioned our section after the death of Harvey. He arrived with the snow, and slipped on the doorstep of 'Ardenlea' after ringing the bell. He began shamefaced, and so he continued. He had not been in France, but had been kept back as part of a something called the 'Hull Dock Garrison'. Accordingly, most of the blokes in the house wouldn't give him the time of day. They'd all heard of the charges against me, but it did not seem as though I was under a cloud. Inasmuch as the charges were believed – and I had no idea how far they were, since a gentlemanly reserve applied to discussion of them . . . Well, bad things happened on the front. All men who'd been 'through it' knew that, and quick judgements were to be resisted.

Brewster was rather stooped for a military policeman, as though perpetually ducking the shellfire that he'd never been subjected to. Having been cold-shouldered by all the blokes in the house, he came up to my room, and told me that he personally had nothing against me, and that I might move freely about the house on my crutches, and he would see his way clear to letting me roam the grounds once my leg had got a bit better.

For four days, I lay in bed. I wrote to the Chief saying I'd been charged, and he told me to expect a visit from himself at some point in the near future. On my first night downstairs, I sat in the library with my crutches by the side of my armchair and a packet of Virginians Select on my lap. There were a dozen of us in there, and we were watching a fellow from Leeds – name of Ross (although whether that was his first name or his last, I wasn't sure) – who was an amateur magician, and who performed tricks with cigarettes. This was a species of war work. He toured the hospitals and convalescent homes entertaining the men. He had lost an eye at Mons, and so could not be accused of slacking, and he began by giving an account of how this happened. He then started in on his tricks. All of his audience smoked, so he was well away. He would take a man's Woodbine, and put it into a packet of, say, Churchman's, then hold out the packet, and the Woodbine would rise up. After he'd done this a couple of times, I noticed my guard, Brewster, watching from the doorway and grinning in his shamefaced way.

Ross would offer a cigarette from his own packet; he would then turn this packet around, and it would have become a box of matches. He performed a couple of other tricks, just as good, and he was going on very well indeed until he tried a bit of business with Anderson, who was very badly shellshocked. Well, Anderson could remove the cigarette from the packet as instructed; he was able to inspect it carefully, as also instructed, but the returning of the cigarette to the packet . . . that was quite beyond him owing to his shaking hand, and so the trick had to be abandoned. Ross seemed to lose heart after that, and he went off shortly afterwards.

Over the next two weeks I began to walk in the grounds, trying to master crutches along with all the other crocks, but my progress was evidently the fastest that Hawks had ever seen, and my target became the lower slopes of the snowy Moor, which lay directly beyond the gates of 'Ardenlea', and the white house up there, a place where folk would take spring water baths: it was called the White Wells, and seemed to have been assembled from the surplus snow all around.

The grounds of 'Ardenlea' received a fresh dusting most mornings, and a little ritual developed: Anderson and Birch (who was just as nervy as Anderson) would go out every morning and break the ice on the fish pond. They would always be watched by Major Dickinson, who was the most senior man in the place, and who propelled himself in a bath chair, being partly paralysed through shellshock – he didn't *believe* he could move his legs. Breaking the ice, and so giving the fish what Major Dickinson called – it was a queer expression in the circumstances – a 'dog's chance' of surviving was the highlight of the day for all three, and I had the idea that the job never took as long as they would have liked.

These three men would talk of a stranger who had been seen in the grounds lately. Dickinson (who was a bit nuts, shellshock aside) believed him to be after the fish, some of which were valuable, but the other two reported that he'd been seen looking up at the windows of the house. My own suspicion was that this man was looking for me. I knew he would not be friendly, and I wondered whether Brewster would find himself having to guard me from him. Brewster carried a gun, and the Chief in one of his letters had urged me to do likewise, for I'd told him of my expectation.

But I did not want to be guarded from my visitor, should he arrive, by the man Brewster, and I did not particularly want to shoot my visitor either. I wanted to talk to him, my aim being to confirm my suspicion about the cigarette lit on the train from Amiens. I wanted to draw him in, and then draw him out.

I began to encourage Brewster to walk with me in the frosted garden, and I would look up at the Moor, at the White Wells. 'I've no hope of getting up there,' I said. 'But I might get halfway.'

The fish pond trio were going past us at that point, and I believe it was to get points with them that Brewster said, 'Want to try? Don't mind me. I can keep cases on you from here, if I want.'

But he didn't want to, and the next day I got halfway to the White Wells on my own and, as far as I knew, unobserved from the house. Later that same day, the wife came, and then the man from the Army Legal Corps – my lawyer. This fellow's name was Roberts. It was his second visit, and he told me he thought he could prove that the rifle with which I'd supposedly shot Tinsley hadn't been fired for ages at the time of its discovery by my side.

The next morning, I offered to sign for Brewster the special bail undertaking that required me to keep to the house and grounds and that he had not got round to asking me to sign up to that point. He said, 'We might amend it to include the path up to the Wells, or shall we just take it as read?' He seemed as amiable as ever, but later on that morning, while walking past the office of the Matron, Oldfield, I heard him say to her, that if I made it up to the White Wells, it could be safely concluded that I was fit enough to go to gaol. Oldfield replied something to the effect she'd be glad to be shot of me.

That afternoon, I went all the way up to the White Wells in falling snow. The sky was the colour of . . . I would say the dirty white of a young swan – the colour of a signet – and it made a pleasant change to see something soft coming down from it. The white cottage that housed the Wells was closed, and the stone bench before it was covered in snow. I waited a while beside this bench, then returned to 'Ardenlea' when the cold began to hurt my new-set bone.

At four o'clock the next day, with darkness closing in, I cleared the snow off the bench, leant my crutches against it, lit a cigarette, and sat down. I surveyed the lights of Ilkley, which were somewhat subdued on account of the Zeppelin threat, giving the effect of many small points of gold under a purple sky. Presently, a man came across the Moor from my left, and sat down by me on the bench. It wasn't the man I'd expected – not quite.

'Some leave finally came through, then,' I said to Oliver Butler.

'Well, I'm not *deserting*, Jim,' he said, and he took in the view for a while, before saying, '. . . sailed home a week ago . . . and it's back to France tomorrow.'

I offered him a cigarette; he shook his head.

'Well, you got to him in the end,' he said. 'I knew you would. He was questioned . . . let me see . . . the day before yesterday by your governor, Weatherill.'

'That was on account of letters I've sent from here,' I said, indicating the low lights of 'Ardenlea'. 'I put Chief Inspector Weatherill in the picture.'

'You're proud of the fact, and that does you credit, Jim. You've a brass neck . . . amongst other things.'

'You gave us the green light against orders.'

'Those orders were more confused than you might think, Jim. Remember, this is the British Army.'

'It surprised me because it seemed to me at the time you

ought to have let the boy live. Roy had overheard the conversation – most of it – that I'd had with Tinsley on the train back from Amiens, so you would have known that the kid was about to come clean over what happened on Spurn. Thackeray would have called off his investigation, and that's what you'd been hoping for all along, given that the twins were always the likeliest suspects on the face of it. So you'd a reason to see Tinsley live; trouble was, you'd obviously been given a *better* reason to see him killed – him and me both, in fact. That's why you gave us the green light to go along the dangerous stretch at Flers. What could that reason be? I revolved it all the way back in the hospital train, thought of everything I knew about Tinsley. Well, it didn't amount to much. He was a railway nut . . . and then there was your friend.'

'Not my friend *really*, Jim.'

'Tinsley's hero, Tom Shaw, bicycled into the engine shed over muddy lanes, yet he always kept clean. He lived in a place that had a railway connection to York. Naburn fitted the bill in both cases. And he looked a nasty bastard from his picture.'

'You worked it all out from *that*?'

I shook my head.

'Going over that chat between me and Tinsley on the train from Amiens, one sentence rang out clear. "He's capable of anything, is Tom Shaw." The train wasn't going over points just then, you see, and it struck me – in recollection – that it *had* been going over points during every other part of our talk that touched on Shaw. So it seemed to me that Roy wouldn't have heard those parts – which were all to do with how, if Shaw wanted to arrive early at a station, he'd just go ahead and do it. Tinsley was making out that he was bloody-minded as an engine man, not saying he was a killer. But that would have been lost to Roy in the jangling of the points. He'd have heard Tinsley's account of the Spurn business – we'd run clear of the points by then – but all he would've picked up on the matter of Shaw was that Tinsley believed him capable of anything.'

In Ilkley, all the lights showing in the window of a mill went off in an instant. More snow was coming down.

'Somebody struck a match just after Tinsley said that. It was Roy, and he was lighting up because he was worried. It was the first time you or him had heard of the connection between Tinsley and Shaw. It had just always fallen out that you were elsewhere when Tinsley mentioned him. It might have struck you, when you were getting off the train, that we'd been keeping the connection secret from you, having found out about the killing of Matthew Waddington. I mean to say, you knew I'd been curious about Naburn Lock. You probably knew I'd looked into what had gone on there, having seen the way you and your brothers reacted to seeing one of the little Somme stops named after it. And in Albert you'd seen me in conference with the Chief.'

Oliver Butler gave a kind of snort, and moved position on the bench. 'So you *didn't* know?'

'Tinsley didn't know what Shaw had done, and nor did I – not then: not on the train back from Amiens. *I* wasn't sure that Shaw existed, and I didn't know for certain until I wrote to the Chief from here asking him to look up him.'

Butler was removing an item from his greatcoat pocket.

'You wanted to silence Tinsley and me,' I said, seeing that it was a revolver he held, 'because you thought we knew Tom Shaw had killed Matthew Waddington, about which you were wrong. But why would the matter be of any concern to you in the first place? Why would you fight Shaw's battles? It could only be that you were involved . . . I don't believe you personally had a hand in killing Waddington.'

'Good of you to say so, Jim.'

'Killing's not really your way of going on.'

'Well, we'll see about that.'

'You've got too much to lose.'

'That's debatable.'

'I'm thinking of your wife.'

'So am I, Jim.'

'So it must have been your brothers.'

Butler inspected the gun – a revolver; he set it on his lap.

'They'll be questioned in due course,' I said. 'The Chief said he might get Thackeray on the job, only it's a crime committed in civvy street. Shaw's already let on to the Chief that he knew Andy and Roy. Pair of head cases, he calls them – makes out they had it in for Shaw for some reason. He's starting to cough, no question. When the Chief puts the blocks on a fellow, that's generally the result. They'll swing at the end . . . all three.'

Some of this was true; some of it wasn't, as I believed Butler knew. I couldn't really claim the credit for what he came out with next . . .

'Matthew Waddington owed Shaw money,' said Butler, seeming to address one particular illuminated street corner in the town below. 'Waddington was a tough customer. Shaw's a little bloke, and he wanted back-up when he confronted him at the lock. He paid the boys a pound apiece . . . Well, it's a lot of money to them.'

'You pay those boys to do a job, they do it well. The Army found that out.'

'Saved *your* life on July 1st,' Butler put in.

'True enough,' I said. I'd forgotten about that – how the twins had saved my life by their digging.

'Waddington', Butler continued, 'said Shaw would have to wait a little while for his money. Shaw said he wouldn't wait. Waddington came at him, so Andy and Roy stepped in, just as I stepped in for you when Dawson came at you on Spurn.'

I'd forgotten about that as well.

'Anyhow,' I said. 'It ended in a killing. And you were involved because you knew of it.'

That, I was sure, was why he and his brothers had enlisted: put distance between themselves and Shaw. But the mystery was . . . why all the panic among the three Butlers over Naburn Lock? They could just have denied everything.

I asked Butler, 'Will you say all you've just told me in court?'

'Say all what, Jim? I've said nothing.'

Silence for a space. Ilkley, I decided, was just the right size of town. It had trams, but I did not believe they were necessary.

'You didn't shoot Scholes on July 1st, did you?'

He held the revolver in his right hand now, weighing it.

'Don't be silly, Jim.'

The bloke was emerging with a sight more credit than I'd have thought possible.

'Dawson told you he'd done it,' I said, '. . . took the blame. Why didn't you tell Thackeray?'

'Thought of it, Jim, but I didn't think I'd be believed. It'd only throw more suspicion my way.'

Silence for a space.

'I never knew which way Thackeray would jump. He was – is – bloody loony. He might be thinking of bringing the charge against *you*, for all you know.'

I eyed Butler. He wasn't putting on side. He didn't know.

'Thackeray's been here,' I said. 'I've been charged with the murders . . . Harvey and Tinsley.'

'*What?*'

Butler saw me as a man trying to charge a killer, not as a man being *charged* with killing.

'I'm on a sort of special bail,' I said. They'll cart me off to Armley nick in a few days.'

'How *many* days?'

I shrugged.

'I knew they'd found you near a German rifle,' said Butler, 'but . . . Why would you kill Tinsley? How do they make it out?'

I gave him the theory. 'I suppose I'll tell the court martial what really happened on Spurn, but I've no evidence, and Tinsley's not around to back me up, thanks to you and your fucking green light . . .'

'Don't talk rot, Jim.'

'And I don't suppose you're going to pitch in and help.'

'How?'

'By saying your brother overheard Tinsley's confession, of course, and told you of it directly.'

'Jim,' he lied, 'I know nothing of what was said on that bloody train. Anyhow,' he continued (which choice of word *proved* he was lying), 'you've put me right in it by going after Shaw. I don't owe *you* any favours. Quite the opposite, in fact.'

He stood up, turned and faced me, revolver in hand.

'I can see the difficulty you were in right from the start,' I said. 'You were involved in one bit of business – at Naburn – where a bloke's knocked about the head and put into water. You knew that investigation might be re-started at any minute. Then another comes up along the same lines . . . Somebody might see that the twins made a connection between them.'

Butler was eyeing me, and it was a direct look, not sidelong, as when Tinsley and I had rolled past him onto the dangerous stretch of line. He continued to hold the revolver in his right hand. The hand was gloved. His left hand, also gloved, he brought up to the revolver. He set back the hammer. As he did so, the finger of his glove became caught, nipped in the mechanism. With a look of irritation on his face that I was not meant to see, he pulled, and quite suddenly the left hand and glove came away from the gun, which he had continued to point at me all along. We were now back to square one. Well, not quite, because the hammer was now cocked. It was a single action gun, and we both awaited the single action – the pulling of the trigger, with Ilkley puffing away peacefully below us. I did not feel the cold in that moment, and nor I believe did Butler. Presently, he stepped forward and set the gun on the bench beside me.

As he walked away, I called after him, 'You've told the man Shaw where I'm to be found, I suppose?'

No reply.

I called louder, 'He's been here already, creeping about in the garden!' Again no reply. I reached for the gun, and carefully uncocked the hammer.

The gun – a service revolver – proved to be fully loaded. On returning to 'Ardenlea', I put it into the trunk in my room. The fact that Butler had left it for me meant he'd told Tom Shaw it was on my say-so that he was being questioned over the murder of Matthew Waddington; that I had found him out. It also meant that Butler had then *regretted* having told Shaw this and was charitably equipping me for what was to come . . . or that he wanted me to do the job of dealing with Shaw . . . or that, having meant to do for me himself, and having funked it, he couldn't stand the sight of the thing, or . . . I gave it up.

The end result anyhow was that he was leaving things in the balance, as he had at Flers. He would assist a man's fate, but he wouldn't *become* it.

The next day, I received a parcel, forwarded from Old Man Wright, the clerk in the police office at York station. Inside it was a letter from Mrs Tinsley, of Albemarle Road, York, and five years' worth of *Railway Magazines*. The numbers for 1911 to 1914 were bound in red cloth with gold lettering. The ones for 1915 came loose. November 1915 was in the envelope in which Mrs Tinsley had received it from the back numbers department of the *Railway Magazine* offices in London, and she explained that she'd sent off for it to make good the missing number. There was a good deal in the letter about what a tremendous chap I was, according to the letters Tinsley had sent home.

Tinsley had been only a kid but he'd had a philosophy of

life, which said that you ought not to try and avoid trouble, but should put yourself in its way – only then did you deserve whatever good things might occur in your life. It was a philosophy I admired, and it was for this reason that I left the revolver in the bottom of the trunk while continuing with my programme of walking the Moor.

Or it might be that I was suffering 'a depression' – a condition much talked of among the soldiers of 'Ardenlea'.

'Ardenlea',
Ilkley,
Yorkshire.
November 4th, 1916

Dearest Lillian,

I'm sorry not to have been back for the children last night. There has been another drama here, in the place where 'life passes in a pleasant dream' (you will remember).

I arrived at mid-afternoon yesterday, to be told by the Matron that Jim was out on the Moor – and this in the falling snow. I went straight out there myself. It was becoming rapidly dark, but I saw Jim progressing slowly on his crutches. He was halfway up towards the bathing place that sits on the lower Moor here. I then . . . I then saw what appeared to be a scene from a play or a film – a scene from one of the 'Westerns' that Jim takes me to at the Electric Palace, and the world of this drama was black and white, with small black figures against the snow, just as the world of the films or bioscopes is black and white.

I watched a small man I did not know (he was just a shadow to me, but I could see he was small, and very fit) making quickly towards a small man that I did know, namely Jim. The first man had his arm held out, as though pointing at Jim and accusing him . . . only it was a gun that he held, and I thought: this man means to shoot my husband, and I found myself thinking that this was extremely bad manners, and that I would on no account stand for it. I made a move in the direction of the man, and then I saw the flame as he fired the gun. With the stage melodramas, and in the Westerns, you hear the bang but you do not see this great leap of orange flame, and it shocked me so that I called out some wild words I cannot now recollect.

And yet it was as though my Jim did not know his part in the play or the film, for he remained upright, and it was the man with the gun who had fallen at the very moment of firing. It was then that I saw a third man on the Moor: Weatherill, the Chief Inspector. He had shot the man who had fired at Jim.

He – Jim's Chief – was making slowly towards Jim with his own gun carried loosely, while I ran pell-mell in the same direction, and some of the fitter men from the house came streaming up the hill after me, having heard the shot. The faster I moved, the slower the man Weatherill did, and I saw him come to a stop in the falling snow, and light a cigar.

The first small man – the stranger – had completely missed Jim, but had been terribly wounded by Weatherill's shot. He was carried into the house, and when I saw him in the light I realised that his coat was quite soaked in blood, so that when they took it off him, and lay it down on the floor of the hall, the blood continued to flow from it, just as it was flowing from the man himself.

Oldfield, the Matron, telephoned through to the hospital for an ambulance as Weatherill screamed questions at the man, who was obviously in agony. I saw on the floor a paper that had dropped from his coat. It was half covered in blood, but I could make out that it was a certificate from the railway company addressed to 'Thomas Shaw, Engine Driver'. In spite of the blood, I caught it up, and did not know whether to give it to the shot man, or to Weatherill, or to Jim. In the event, I gave it to Jim. It began, 'You are hereby informed that your services are required in connection with the working of the railway. You will not, therefore, at present be required to join the army . . .'

Jim and Weatherill then left with the man in the ambulance. Jim's guard here, Brewster (I have told you of him before), was quite happy to let Jim go, and it is clear that what this man Shaw has to say – if anything, for he seemed hardly capable of speech – could have an important bearing on Jim's case.

Not much else is clear, I'm afraid.

I will write to you again tomorrow, dear.

You will of course not mention a word of this to the children.

With love,
Lydia.

In the library of 'Ardenlea', a fellow was giving a Gramophone Concert for the benefit of the invalids. The fellow – whose name I do not recollect – had a lot of gramophone records and a lot of very strong opinions about them. First of all, he *liked* all his gramophone records – there wasn't a dud amongst them, evidently – and he was particularly keen on the symphonies among them. The symphony was the highest expression of the musical art. He had just given part of 'something new from Elgar', with whom he was on terms of the closest friendship, or so you would have thought from his talk. At the end of it, he lifted the needle and said, 'Well, that's woken you all up.' But it hadn't. The two men nearest the fire – two Marines, late of the Chief Mechanical Engineers' Office at York, who'd been shelled and badly burned in the same armoured car – were fast asleep, in spite of all the loud parts.

But then it was a very good and soothing fire that was burning in the library.

The symphony man was now taking out a record by Brahms. He blew the dust off all his records before playing them, even though there was quite obviously no speck of dust on them.

'Now Brahms, gentlemen,' he said, 'was German.'

'Poor show,' said Major Dickinson, but he did not wheel himself out of the library, which he very easily might have done. In fact, he and the record man nodded at each other, just as though this little exchange had gone perfectly to plan.

The man put the needle down on the record, and sat in the chair he had placed next to the gramophone. He bent his head as the music started, as he always did, out of respect to the composer, as I supposed. But I did not care for Brahms, who was even keener on the quiet-then-suddenly-loud business than Elgar. The man's music seemed to go with clattering of one of the nurses as she came in with the cocoa, and it reminded me that a library ought to be silent.

I lit another cigarette and removed myself mentally from the library . . .

. . . That morning, the wife had come into my room with her portmanteau in her hand, and an opened envelope tucked into the belt of her skirt, and I could see it was an army envelope. 'Sorry for opening this,' she said, being not in the least sorry.

She held the envelope over the counterpane of the bed, up-ended it, and three little cloth squares fell out directly. The letter floated down a moment later. Well, the pieces of cloth were diamond-shaped rather than square, and I showed the wife how they would fix onto a tunic sleeve.

'Captain Stringer,' she said, and she stood back, marvelling at me.

'A field commission,' I said, 'they're pretty rare.'

'As an officer,' said the wife, 'if you came into the soldiers' buffet at the station and had *cakes* with your tea on a Sunday afternoon, you'd have the silver service.'

'That's a big if,' I said.

Leaning suddenly forward, she said, 'What on earth did you do to deserve it?'

'Search me,' I said.

'It's all very well to be modest,' she said, 'but I don't think you should be saying things like "Search me". Not as a captain.'

In fact, I knew. This was the doing of Muir, the officer with the notebook. He had observed – and noted – my rescue of the train and its load of shells from the German bombardment. I'd saved a pretty big bang there. Or rather, Tinsley had, with my assistance.

The wife said, 'Today, Harry gives a talk on the book – in front of the whole school.'

'*The Count of Monte Cristo*? Will he talk about the book or the hole in the book?'

'Both. And about how it saved your life . . . which *he* believes it did, at any rate.'

My tale about the book had never really 'taken' with the wife.

She caught up her portmanteau. She was leaving 'Ardenlea' for good, and I would soon be doing likewise . . .

In the library, the nurse was continuing with her clattering, in that she was going around the room closing the curtains, and so concealing the total blackness beyond. In fact, it was probably snowing. The stuff had been coming down for days – fast and silent, a mysterious but generous offering. It was also snowing at the Burton Dump, Oamer had written to tell me, in a note that congratulated me on my commission. The push was now on for a spot called Beaumont Hamel, which was a little way to the north, requiring new branches from the existing 'main line'.

Brahms was not being very well received. One of the Marines – Howell – had set down his cocoa and gone over to the shelf where the bound volumes of *Punch* were kept. The record man took the hint, and said that by way of closing his programme of music he would give us a rest from crashing and banging (well, he didn't quite put it like that), and would play us 'one of the Nocturnes by Debussy'. This was not a symphony, which suited me, and Debussy was French, which suited Major Dickinson. Nocturne meant 'of the night' – my French was up to *that* much – and the record man explained that this particular piece was called by a word I can't recall that meant 'Clouds'.

Night was the thing, though. William Harvey had died at night, and we had run our trains at night. (The first day of the Somme battle had been conducted in broad daylight, but that to my mind had been a mad exception in every way.) I thought of the war and of death in general as taking place at night.

I figured the man Shaw, dying at midnight in a room full of policemen at the Ilkley hospital. (Word had spread fast among the coppers of Ilkley, and they'd all come for a look at a killer.) The last thing he would have seen, I calculated, was the thin shaving of moon that had moved into position above the one window in that place. After he'd died, the Chief had drawn the blind, and I had imagined the moon sailing on to another window, rather put out at this rudeness. Why the Chief had drawn the blind I couldn't have said. Out of respect for Shaw? Well, he had practically shouted the man to death with his questions. But the confession had been obtained.

There had been, as Oliver Butler had told me, a fight over money at Naburn Lock. (Well, the war itself was just the same thing when you came to think about it.) Shaw had tied the brothers in by paying them another pound – on top of the one they'd already earned – to sign two papers on which he'd set out what had happened. (They *could* sign their names, after a fashion, and I thought of the scrawl next to the hoops board in the Hope and Anchor.)

And this was why Oliver Butler had gone all out to cover up the story of Naburn Lock: it could not be denied.

I had then stepped in, and done a bit of shouting of my own, in order to secure the information I needed to put myself in the clear, and in due course I had got it. Shaw said that Oliver Butler had told him the true story of events on Spurn – the one overheard from Tinsley by Roy Butler on the train from Amiens – and he repeated this for the benefit of all the coppers. Of course, this had been of only incidental interest to Shaw and the Butlers. Their only concern was that Tinsley and I had apparently known that Shaw was a killer.

Shaw had come after me so as to remove a witness. It was a lost cause, as he admitted, since he had already been questioned by the Chief, and was in line to be charged. But he was a violent sort, and that was all about it. Towards the end, Shaw said that if we let him go, he'd enlist the next day, which took me right back to the deal the Chief had made with Bernie Dawson at the start of it all. But Shaw was going into delirium. His next idea was a better one: being a Catholic, he asked for a priest. But he pegged out before any of the Ilkley coppers could lay hands on one.

Over opposite me in the library, Howell had laid the volume of *Punch* aside. He was listening to the music: the Nocturne of Debussy. We all were. It called to mind the gradual spreading of night, and somehow the rumbling movement of machinery in that night. I pictured Burton Dump, and the materiel train from Acheux reversing without warning and with no proper illumination, having just been unloaded. Oliver Butler had evidently been crossing the tracks with a new sort of field telephone in his hand, studying the thing and not paying proper attention to his surroundings. The confession of Tom Shaw had put him right in it, but now he was right out of it – gone off into the night. What would happen to his brothers remained to be seen. Two days after learning of Oliver Butler's death, I had been informed by telegram that a – or possibly *the* – Deputy Judge Advocate General of the Army Legal Corps had authorised the dropping of the charges against me. Of course, I would have preferred to hear the words from Thackeray himself.

The record man was now blowing the dust off another record – a second Nocturne by Debussy. This – in site of being another night piece – was more cheerful, and as it began, the fellow asked us to imagine 'all the excitement of young people dancing at a fairground'.

I sat back in my chair and tried my best.

Historical note

The North Eastern Railway *did* raise its own battalion for the Great War, and it *was* called the 17th Northumberland Fusiliers. The men were known as the 'Newcastle Railway Pals' although there were plenty from York among their number. Much of the early training of the battalion was roughly as described. It went to France in early 1916, and my account of the role of the battalion on the first day of the Somme is quite closely based on fact.

Generally, the men were involved in trench construction and maintenance, and in building railways, mainly standard-gauge ones. Their involvement in the *operation* of railways seems to have been slight.

Narrow-gauge lines did play an important part in the bringing forward of munitions, and on both sides of the conflict. The first British lines were constructed (by the Royal Engineers) during the late phase of the Somme campaign. But Burton Dump is imaginary, and the narrow-gauge lines did not come into their own until the following year, with the construction of the extensive networks around Arras and Ypres.

It was observed in *The Railway Gazette* Special War Transportation Number of 21 September 1920 that the light railways of the Great War, and the men who built and operated them, had 'played no small part in civilisation's struggle'.